Thoroughbred Tales

An Anthology of Fiction from Thoroughbred Times

THOROUGHBRED TIMES BOOKS™
An imprint of BowTie Press®
Lexington, Kentucky

Thoroughbred Times Books™
An imprint of BowTie Press®

Library of Congress Cataloging-in-Publication Data

Thoroughbred tales : an anthology of fiction from Thoroughbred Times.
p. cm.
ISBN 978-1-933958-20-0
1. Thoroughbred horse—Fiction. 2. Horse racing—Fiction. 3. Race horses—Fiction.
4. Sports stories, American. I. Thoroughbred times.

PS648.H64T47 2007
813'.01083579--dc22

2007002823

Cover illustration by Tami Zigo
Illustrations: Yvonne Todd, viii; Kerry McCulley, 14; Tami Zigo, 54, 70, 84, 96, 110, 138, 150, 162, 180, 196, 212, 230, 246; Sandy Slater, 120; Lane Boldman, 260

Printed and bound in the United States.
10 9 8 7 6 5 4 3 2 1

Thoroughbred Times Books™
An imprint of BowTie Press®
Thoroughbred Times Company
2008 Mercer Rd.
Lexington, Kentucky 40511
www.thoroughbredtimes.com

Contents

The Hanging in the Foaling Barn *Susan Starr Richards* 1

The Legacy *Alan P. Henry* 15

The Saratoga Derby *K. M. Jones* 29

The Passing of the Torch *Avalyn Hunter* 55

Mr. Bo's Last Dance *Alan P. Henry* 71

Teaser *Scott Travis Hutchison* 85

Phoenix *Caroline Nesbitt* 97

Time Exposure *K. M. Jones* 111

The Painting *Alan P. Henry* 121

Tack Talk *Dennis M. Patterson* 139

The Foundation *Avalyn Hunter* 151

Third Jewel *Bill Melzer* 163

It Can Happen Here *Catherine Dupree* 181

The Murderer, the Pony,
and Miss Brown to You *Susan Starr Richards* 197

Arlen Gone *Kevin Harrington* 213

Ice Storm *Danny L. Talbot* 231

Root Doctor *Scott Travis Hutchison* 247

Huggable Tom *Howard P. Giordano* 261

Foreword

It sounded like fun, something out of the ordinary for racing: Why not hold a fiction contest?

As an art form, racing fiction had all but disappeared, save for the writing of a few distinguished authors like Dick Francis and William Murray. Fiction, at least short fiction, was as hard to find as a sure thing at 10-to-1.

And that struck us as an unfortunate omission for a sport with so many potentially intriguing stories. While the best-known aspect of racing takes place at the track, our sport is part of a very broad, rich tapestry that also includes foaling barns and auction rings, the backstretch, veterinary clinics, betting windows, and simple, everyday life, which together provide a mother lode of possibilities for the unfettered imagination. As the great sportswriter Red Smith once said, "There are more stories at a racetrack than anywhere else."

We felt if we could tap into this wellspring of material from the minds of racing people everywhere, we might just have something. So we inaugurated the THOROUGHBRED TIMES Fiction Contest in 1992, with the winners—normally the top three finishers—published in issues of our weekly magazine. We have renewed the competition every two years since.

From the beginning, the response from writers was better than we had dared hope. Given an opportunity to write about racing, hundreds of authors and would-be authors dashed to their keyboards to craft stories. The 1,000-plus submissions we received over the years ran the gamut of human—and sometimes equine—emotion, from the poignantly sad to the uplifting and joyous. We learned that a surprising number of people had a good racing story to tell, and that some very talented writers can produce multiple worthy tales.

Eighteen of the best stories that appeared in the TIMES's weekly pages between 1993 and 2006 are compiled here in a single collection, *Thoroughbred Tales*, a veritable best of the best of our biennial fiction contest. Five authors are represented by more than one short story.

Thoroughbred Tales is the product of 15 years of dedication on the part of the TIMES's staffers. Mary Simon has been a guiding light, reading almost every single entry ever submitted and helping oversee the judging process. Editors past and present, Amy Owens and Don Clippinger, also pulled long hours as they guided authors through the editing and production process, and talented staff artist Tami Zigo inked most of the eye-catching illustrations for the weekly, as well as the cover art for this book.

Ultimately, however, the lion's share of credit must go to the writers, those who poured their hearts into their stories and came up with magic. THOROUGHBRED TIMES is proud to have played a part in their creative process, and we are certain that these *Thoroughbred Tales* will delight readers and lovers of racing for years to come.

Mark Simon
Editor in Chief
THOROUGHBRED TIMES

Acknowledgements

Many individuals had important roles in producing this anthology of fiction, but most important were the authors who shared their creativity, writing skills, imagination, and sense of wonderment with readers of Thoroughbred Times over more than a decade and a half. Some are professional writers and some were newcomers to writing for public audiences, but they all possessed the rare talent of conjuring up a good yarn from an inner wellspring and telling that story well. Congratulations and thanks to all those writers who enriched the pages of Thoroughbred Times and this anthology.

Both the fiction contest—an innovation in the Thoroughbred industry—and this anthology were the creations of Mark Simon, founding editor of Thoroughbred Times and now its president and editor in chief. Several editors helped over the decades. Regular contributor Mary Fleming Simon nurtured both the contest and the stories themselves through formative years, and former Managing Editor Amy Owens contributed her flair for well-written fiction to the contests in 2003 and 2005.

Illustrations accompanied winning stories when they were published in Thoroughbred Times, and portions of those drawings introduce each of the stories. Many of the illustrations were created by staff artist Tami Zigo, who not only depicted crucial scenes from the stories but also captured the essence of the writers' whimsy through her drawings. Her own sense of whimsy is readily apparent from her cover artwork. Jeanette Vance, art director of Thoroughbred Times, took the fiction anthology concept and developed an attractive presentation that adds to the allure of the stories and makes them both approachable and easy to read. Chief copy editor Deanna Bowden went through each story meticulously to assure that the author's words and intentions were preserved.

Don Clippinger
Editorial Director
Thoroughbred Times

The Hanging in the Foaling Barn

by Susan Starr Richards

HERE IT WAS 3:30 in the morning. Between foaling mares and nursing sick foals, Luther hadn't slept more than three hours straight in the last two weeks. Tonight, at last, everything looked quiet, and he had gotten to bed with the prospect of being able to stay there all night for a change.

And then the night man called up to tell Luther he was going to hang himself in the foaling barn.

Luther sat there a minute, thinking something serious was happening—a mare was ready to go, a foal had a fever. "Tell you what, Maurice," he said at last. "If you want to die so damn much, why don't you just go in Brownie's stall and stand behind her and touch her once on the butt? You'd get your picture took in a hurry."

"Why, Luther—" intoned Maurice's vague, startled voice—"She might just hurt me."

Luther smiled sweetly at the telephone. "That's true. You probably wouldn't stand anywhere near the right spot, and she'd probably just kick you someplace internal, and you'd crawl out into the hallway and lay there all night turning blue, and I'd have to fight all the mares past you in the morning before I could even turn out."

Luther took a big breath. He thought about it. "All right," he said. "All right. Only for God's sake don't hang yourself in front of the foaling stall. Wiggy's been snorting and staring in there every evening, still looking for that dead meadowlark the cat left in the corner last week. She won't go in, and then she keeps looking in all the corners and snorting that way. And in the morning she runs over top of you trying to get out. She'll never relax enough to have that foal. And if she does, she'll probably think it's a dead meadowlark, she's so dumb.

"Not as dumb as you are, though, Maurice. You got to call up and want to kill yourself here in the middle of May. Couldn't you wait till June, at least, when foaling season's over?"

He slammed the phone down. Then sighed.

WHEN Luther had first known him, Maurice was leading apprentice at River Downs. He'd ridden a lot of winners for Luther over two summers there. Back in those days he had yellow hair like bright wheat straw, and those tall, slender girls that always love jockeys leaning all over him. A strut to go with it, and a flat back in the saddle. And a way of waiting on a horse most bug boys had no knowledge of, sitting still till it told him to move, and then only moving to disappear into it as it ran, till it was all one beast, man and horse, running together at the wire. Luther had believed Maurice had a chance to make it at the real races.

But even then he was drinking, and then the weight got to him. He was an exercise rider for a while, and then a groom, and then Luther lost track of him entirely. When at last he showed up working at a gas station in town, still talking horses all the time, Luther had given him the night job for old time's sake. He still drank, of course, but then most night men did. He didn't smoke, at least, so he wasn't likely to burn the barn down. And he claimed to have nightmares so bad that he never would sleep at night. It might even been true—in 11 years of foaling, he'd never missed a mare.

The only trouble was, toward the end of every foaling season, Maurice started considering suicide. Of course, that just made him normal. Everybody started thinking about killing themselves, or someone else, this time of the year. But Maurice would get into ways and means. One night he tried to drown himself by driving into the farm pond, but since it was only four feet deep, he'd only managed to drown his Chevrolet truck. Luther bought him an old car to replace it, and then the next spring he tried to ram the car into the big oak by the driveway. His aim wasn't too good, so he made several passes at it, and by the time he gave up, he'd taken out about a quarter of a mile of fairly new plank fencing and let the barren mares loose all over the farm.

But he'd never tried to kill himself in the foaling barn. Luther found himself not just irritated but indignant at this. The foaling barn was where the heavy-in-foal mares came swinging in every day with their huge bellies swaying rhythmically, and the new foals staggered up on their feet for the first time and tried to kick somebody right away. Everything there wanted to live so much, was so full of life. That was why you always felt so bad when sometimes they didn't make it. To try to kill yourself in the foaling barn, Luther believed, was sacrilegious.

Of course, he never thought for a minute that Maurice had any real intention of doing it. "But he's fool enough that he might just accidentally get it done," he said to himself.

He sighed again. His clothes were right there by the telephone, ready, waiting for some mare to call him up and say she was foaling, waiting for life to call him up, instead of some dummy saying he wanted to kill himself. "Hang on, Maurice," he said. Then laughed out loud, once.

A BRANCH came out and slapped at Luther's arm as he jerked the truck around the corner by the woods. Luther slapped back at it. The yearling colts came swirling up, blazing white-and-green-eyed in the headlights, racing the truck down the fence at a dead run, sliding on their butts like baseball players to stop in a scramble half an inch short of ramming through the gate for the second time this week. "That's right," he said. "You all keep trying to kill yourselves, too."

The lights were on in the barn hallway, a big, floating square of light with the dark trees outside touching the roof. Grids of shadows in the squared-off reaches above. The mares looked up, big-eyed, interested, some of them speaking to him, ever-hopeful of extra grain rations. The tack room was empty. He called. No answer. But he heard a little shifting noise up in the loft, like something afraid to move and afraid to sit still. Maurice was up there, all right. He was sitting in the hay bales. Luther could just make out the top of his hair, which didn't look like wheat straw any more—more like old grass hay, by now.

Luther went in the foaling stall to check on Wiggy. "She do any more digging?" he called up to Maurice.

Maurice didn't answer for a while. "Been real quiet," he said at last. "Don't worry," he added, in his sing-song, mournful voice. "You ain't going to need me tonight."

"What about that new baby? You see him pee yet?"

"I done wrote you a note about that."

There it was, on the clipboard by the door, written in Maurice's own edifying style: "The colts kidney acted."

"Be with you in a minute, Maurice," Luther said. "My kidney's about to act." He went into Twinkle's stall to pee. There she was, talking to her little sick baby, so happy to see it on its feet again and nursing on its own. Not a bit happier than he was, though, after getting the foal up every two hours for the last two days.

Luther calmed down some as he stood there, listening to the foal slurp its milk. All around him were the mares, munching slow and peaceful in their stalls, and some lying down and talking in their sleep to their new foals that hadn't been born yet, the way they do toward the end, having baby dreams. And here it all was in the middle of green fields stretching out in the dark, and the fireflies outside going on-off, on-off, and the air smelling like a grape popsicle the way it always did down by the woods this time of year.

And there was Maurice hiding up in the loft, wanting to kill himself. Talk about racehorses being crazy. At least if a horse killed itself, it was because it was trying to do something else, playing or fighting or just running.

Luther started climbing up the ladder, cursing silently as he maneuvered himself up over the top. He did not like heights—not even the 12-foot height of the loft.

A rag-tag rope made of a bunch of shanks tied together looped up to the central two-by-eight above the hallway. At the other end of it was Maurice, huddled up on a hay bale like some stray cat waiting to be kicked, holding a makeshift noose in his hands.

"Look at you," Luther said. "Forty-one years old. Still healthy, in spite of all the alcohol you've put in your system. Sitting up here on a hay bale wanting to hang yourself with a lead shank. Couldn't you just kindly wait awhile? We ain't always going to be alive, you know."

Maurice said in a pitiful voice, "I waited long enough. I'm just doing what I should've done a long time ago."

"That's the truth," Luther said. "At least you sure should've done it before 3:30 in the morning. How come you didn't want to hang yourself just after supper? I had about 20 minutes then. I could've worked you in."

Maurice was silent. The mares chewed, stopped, thought about it, chewed again. A foal whinnied in its sleep, jumped to its feet, and its mama spoke to it softly. Maurice glanced out into the middle of the space above the hallway, as if he saw something there.

Luther didn't like that look. It reminded him a little of Crazy Harry, a horse that saw things—spooks—and no matter how many times you told him, "There ain't nothing there," he wouldn't believe you. He was always so sure there was something just up ahead of him that was going to jump on him that he would almost get you to believing it. Harry would freeze, and snort, and arch his neck, and bug his eyes, and start looking both ways to decide which way to bolt, till you'd find yourself saying, "What the hell is it? Where is it? What's it going to do?" You just couldn't pay attention to Harry at all, or he'd convince you the world really looked like he thought it did. What you had to do, Luther reminded himself, was to give him something else to think about.

"Suppose you get it done," he said, nodding at the rope, settling himself on the bale opposite Maurice. "Then what? How do you know you won't come right back again? How would you like that?"

Maurice stared at him kind of cock-eyed, the way he did. "Come back as a ghost, you mean? Ghosts can't feel nothing."

"But you'd remember feeling things. How it feels to be hanging in the middle of the barn, for example, with your head ripped loose from your body." Maurice hunched up a little bit more on his bale. Luther sank back on his. It was beginning to feel soft already.

He tried to calculate what he could do that would get him back home and to sleep quickest. He could hit Maurice on the head and tie him up with the shanks and leave him here until morning. Or he could leave him alone and let him jump. But that rope probably wouldn't hold, and he'd wind up just breaking his leg, and then Luther would have to do something with him in the morning. And anyway, Luther was against things breaking their legs in his barn. Even humans. Even Maurice.

"If only they hadn't taken me off of He's No Angel," Maurice said.

"Hell. They took you off that horse 20 years ago. And they didn't even take you off. You only rode him the once, remember? When that other boy had days?"

Maurice nodded dreamily. "He win by 20. I never asked him for a thing. If I'd just stayed with him, I'd be riding in New York today."

Luther shut his eyes, feeling sleep right there behind his eyelids, dark and soft. "Yeah, and if things were different, I'd be breeder of the year. But I ain't planning to hang myself about it. What you need to do is to cool out a little. Life ain't all that serious to be worth killing yourself about."

Maurice was silent again for a while. Then, "You remember that time I win on Circus Cat?" he said.

Luther grinned, reluctantly. This was one Maurice could always get him in on. Circus Cat was one of Luther's all-time favorite horses—not the best he'd ever bred, but probably the bravest—a tiny little filly who ran against the older horses at marathon distances on the local tracks, sometimes 50 lengths out of it in the backstretch, always hopelessly beaten going into the turn, and more often than not on top at the wire. In the race Maurice was talking about, even the winner's circle photographer had been faked out—she was still second when he took the picture of them all running at the end. Luther himself had turned away, saying, "Not this time," sure she was second, till he heard the shout as they put her number up.

"You remember what that guy said about her afterward?"

They recited it together, as wondering and staccato as the trainer of the second horse had said it after the race, shaking his head in disbelief. "That-sucker-came-from-freaking-Tennessee!"

"She did, too," Maurice said. "I can still feel it."

Luther could still see it, himself—the filly still trailing the field clearly when she came out of the final turn, then burrowing into the pack until she was almost invisible, just an impression of speed, a bay shadow, slipping sketchily through all those great, big, solid horses that seemed twice her size, to emerge third as the two leaders ran for the win. Then disappearing again between those two, then suddenly there, diving like a demon for the wire. "She was a wonderful little filly," he said softly. "You suited her down to the ground, too, Maurice. I have to say that."

Maurice nodded. His eyes had dropped to the rope again. "She was the last winner I was ever on. You put me on. When nobody else would. You was always good to me, Luther. And I let you down. I let everybody down. But I'm going to make it all up to you now. You ain't never going to have to worry with me no more."

Luther leaned back against the bales, nodding. "Whatever you think, Maurice. I wouldn't want to tell a man his business. But all I want is to get back in the bed." He closed his eyes once, nodded, opened them again. He wasn't sure how long it had been. But Maurice had stood up, and he had the noose around his neck. He turned away vaguely toward the edge of the loft, holding his arms out from his sides, as if he might explode. The rope lifted up a little around his neck; he tugged at it daintily with one finger. But he didn't move. "Standing tied," Luther said to himself.

Maurice straightened his shoulders. "I'm going now," he said in a loud voice. "I want to go. It's now or never." Then he stood there, as if he were waiting for something to happen.

"Looks like never to me," Luther said.

Maurice glanced over at Luther. "Life don't make no sense," he said, in a cracked, inspired voice. Like he'd finally figured it out. "At least, my life don't. You think your life makes sense, Luther?"

Luther thought. "Not this part of it. Here I am sitting in a barn loft at four in the morning discussing life with a party who's ready to kill himself. What do you care?"

"That's right," Maurice said. He took a deep breath. He wiggled the rope around his neck, once, like straightening a necktie. Then he started walking toward the edge of the loft. He was taking baby steps, but he was heading that way.

Luther growled. He got up and took two big steps and caught up with him. "Give me that," he said, reaching out to snag the noose. Maurice walked faster. "No. Stop, I tell you."

He grabbed Maurice, turned him around. Maurice backed up. The rope pulled tight. Luther grabbed the rope. Maurice grabbed Luther. A slow waltz, Luther stepping forward, Maurice backward.

"Stop, now, what are you pulling on me for?" Luther said.

"I ain't pulling. You're pushing. I want to do it. Just let me go on and jump."

"You ain't jumping. You're hanging on to me. Give me this rope, I tell you."

They swung toward the edge of the loft together, their shadows huge, flapping against the light.

"Take that thing off your neck, now." Luther was breaking a sweat. "Here. Don't crowd me, you crazy booger. I ain't going to jump with you. This ain't no lover's leap." He was on the edge with his back to it, the space opening dizzily in the back of his head. They teetered forward together, and for a moment he was sure they were going over flat-out, heading for a great big double belly-whopper on the floor of the barn. Then they teetered back again.

Luther lunged forward, swung Maurice around with one big jerk of his arms. His heart was pounding wildly.

Now Maurice stood with his back to the opening. He still had a stranglehold on Luther. His eyes, close up, were blood-red, filling Luther's vision, like the eyes of a horse that had been in the stall too long and was fighting you to get out, banging on the walls, climbing all over you. Luther wrestled himself loose and stepped back.

But then it was as if all that red had gotten in his own eyes. He saw Maurice crouched before him, looking strange, black lines running all over his face like it was a cup about to crack. Talking in a funny, screechy voice, saying "Don't, Luther," or "No, Luther," or "Whoa, Luther" over and over again. Behind him was the great complex orderly opening above the hallway. Luther could feel the push coming all the way from his heels, could see Maurice rocketing off into the clean space behind him.

But then there was a big blow in Luther's middle, like he'd been kicked. And he was sitting on the floor, alone in the loft. And the rope was holding. It was swinging back and forth like a pendulum, while Luther watched it in disbelief, certain that Maurice had to be the weight at the other end of it, since nothing else could be, but trying hard to think of some other explanation.

The rope started swinging and started jiggling, twitching, like someone was fishing with it. There was an unfamiliar noise, coming with the twitches, grunts of effort it sounded like. The rope's motions got tighter and tighter, the grunts got louder and louder. His breath knocked out, sucking for air himself, Luther listened respectfully. Was it that much work—hanging?

Then the whole barn seemed to shift, get up and crawl a little under him. Maurice's hay-colored hair, sticking straight up, was reappearing over the strawy edge of the loft.

Now, when he had discussed the possibility of Maurice coming back from the dead with him a few minutes before, it had never occurred to Luther that he might really do it. The rope was still taut. It still held his weight, clearly, it still twitched and wiggled. But Maurice's hair was not down there at the end of it where it should have been. It was, somehow, bobbing or floating or flying back up toward the loft again, back toward Luther.

And there was Maurice's whole head, staring at Luther over the edge. It opened its mouth several times to speak, but there was just a gurgle. At last it said, in a surprised, interested voice, "This mare's foaling." There was a little whistling sound, and the head disappeared again.

Luther sat there staring. Maurice had just come back from the dead to tell him his mare was foaling. Then he said, "What?" He jumped up and ran over to the edge. There was Maurice, all of him, head and arms and legs, wrapped around the rope, grinning up at Luther, looking livelier than Luther had seen him in years.

"Hell, Maurice," Luther said. "You're going to have to do better than this. You ain't anywhere near dead." He grabbed hold of the rope and hauled Maurice in hand-over-hand, like a big fish, and they both scrambled back down the ladder.

And there was Wiggy, the silver birth-sack already sticking out of her like a great big light bulb, a front foot already visible in it. Luther walked in and looked at it. "Big foot," he said, looking at Maurice. "Real big foot."

And she was a little mare. They pulled, she pushed. She got up and she lay down. The head was hard. "Pull, Maurice," Luther said. "He just winked at me." The chest was harder. "Come on, baby," Luther said to Wiggy. "You're getting it." The hips were impossible, it seemed. "We've got to rock him," Luther said. They grabbed the forelegs of the foal and swung them in half-circles. "Like twisting the cork out of a bottle," Luther said, grinning at Maurice. "You ought to be good at this." The foal thrashed, throwing them around. "Hold on, boy," Maurice said. "You're about there." At last the mare gave a huge groan, and the whole thing came squirting out with a big rush.

Then there was all the navel-painting and cleaning up and rubbing on the colt and talking to him and getting him up to nurse, which took forever because he was so big. At last they sat at the end of the stall full of clean, new straw, one in each corner, while Wiggy took her ease at the other end, with her new colt beside her. Not yet gray or bay or brown, his soft, mysterious, undersea color, indefinable, silky, shining from within, his beautiful neck arched as he rested, nose on the ground. He had a great big, white star, just like his mama did.

Luther had seen that star in a lot of winner's circle pictures. Wiggy had been a good racemare, but she hadn't become the broodmare he had meant for her to be. She'd had some nice horses for him, though—the best he'd bred, in fact. And he still believed in her, unlike some of the mares he'd kept. And last year, because she'd foaled so late, he'd gotten her to a better horse than he'd ever dreamed of being able to breed to. It was more money than he'd wanted to spend. "But you've got to keep gambling," he said to himself, "to keep your mind limber."

Still, Luther had always been amazed by how much class his horses lost just in the process of growing up. When they were born they were all Derby or Oaks winners. As weanlings, they won major stakes. When they were yearlings, it was just minor stakes. And when they went off to the races, he just hoped for a good solid $7,500 claimer.

But that's the way it is with all of us, I guess, he thought. Look at Maurice—riding high at 17, then retiring early, as they say in the *Form*. Wanting to hang himself at 41. And here he himself was. He'd made a little splash early on, raised some nice horses, sold some high-priced yearlings. But the champions he'd known he was raising when he was young had somehow become just horses. He was still just a small breeder. He still mucked his own stalls and rubbed his own yearlings. And he still had his hand on every one of his horses, every day, and he knew by now that was what he did it for.

But he looked now at the foal in the straw before him, his quick breathing and perfect little head and the complex of bones that would round out into sweet, smooth horseflesh and carry him to his fate. And he saw that white star getting larger and larger, coming down the lane at him like the engine light on a fast freight train, while the others in the field rattled along, behind forever.

"He could be any kind," Maurice said, startling him, reading his thoughts. And then doing it again, speaking softly, kindly, almost laughing, "You was trying to kill me. Wasn't you?"

Luther grinned at Maurice. "For a minute there I thought I might have to," he said. "You can kill yourself all you want," he added, "but you ain't doing it in my foaling barn." He knew all that didn't make any sense. But Maurice nodded, as if he understood it perfectly. Luther rubbed his sore middle. "What did you hit me with, anyway?"

Maurice grinned back at him. "My head. I rammed you so hard I went over backward."

"That figures," Luther said, nodding. "I thought you was a goner. But you grabbed onto the rope, didn't you, when you went off? And then you climbed right back up it, like a bobcat on a leash." He shook his head. "I should've tied your hands back behind you, you know. Like they do in the cowboy movies. Do a job, do it right."

"Don't worry about it," Maurice said, quietly, drowsily, watching the foal. "It don't matter."

Luther groaned and pulled himself upright, ready at last to go home to bed. But he stood there a minute, listening to the meadowlarks outside singing their high, sweet songs, the sound reaching out to the edge of hearing and beyond, till it seemed to him, as he listened, that the whole world was just one great, big, green meadow starred with dandelions and full of racehorses, their long silhouettes sliding along fluid and silent, their reverent, long necks bowed to the earth. He glanced over at Maurice, wondering if he could understand that, too.

But Maurice was asleep, his face looking softer and younger in the coming light, delivered from his nightmares into morning dreams, as they had both been delivered back into their innocence by the neat, smooth, strapping, velvet fellow they had just helped into the world. His mama was up now and eating around him in a circle, her nose turned always to him as if she were tethered. Around them, in the foaling barn, all the other mares were standing quiet in their stalls, looking out the windows at the rising sun.

The Legacy

by Alan P. Henry

AS ALWAYS, the two met on the clubhouse side of the paddock 30 minutes before the first race. Doug, hyper as ever, saw Peter first, and rushed up behind him. "Today's the day we win it all back," he shouted, slapping Peter on the back. "Doubles, perfs, tris, the whole deal. Starting with a lock in the first. And I brought the wheelbarrow to haul it all home."

This, of course, was vintage Doug. A guy who never met a gimmick he didn't like. A guy who honestly believed, on each and every day he'd been to the track, that he was going nine for nine—longshots and all. Just like, as a corporate chemist for 35 years, he'd honestly believed that with the right combination of luck and timing, he'd bring in The Big One back at the lab.

"Oh, God," Peter wheeled and instinctively groused back. "You and that damned wheelbarrow again. That unused damned wheelbarrow, I might add."

And this was vintage Peter. Never a class advantage big enough, or a track bias pronounced enough to invest total faith, or more than $50, in. A total chalk player. Not unlike the way he approached his job as an actuary. Close to the vest. Low risk. Low expectation.

Peter's expectations for his partner's emotional and physical well being on this afternoon were low, too. Doug had called a week earlier—to break the awful news. The cancer, apparently, was fast-spreading and inoperable. He had a year to live, maybe.

But Doug was one of those rare guys who'd always refused to take bad news badly. "You just take it one day, one race at a time, and hope to stay in the game," he liked to say. And his unbridled expectation at having found a "can't lose" in the first left no doubt in Peter's mind that any conversation about cancer or the future was, for the moment at least, totally unacceptable.

"I'm talking about a win by the length of the grandstand," Doug gushed. "I mean, they're gonna need a search warrant to find the rest of the pack."

"Whatever you say, Doug," Peter grinned. "Just do me a favor. Before you donate all your money to someone else's wallet, put a sawbuck in your shoe so I don't get stuck with dinner. Again!"

The good-natured needling. The constant jawing. That's the way the back and forth banter had gone 37 years ago, when Doug Connor and Peter Garland met for a weekend at Oaklawn Park to pop a few brews, revisit Syracuse University sexploits, and indulge their nascent passion for the ponies. And that's pretty much the way it had continued once a year, every year since—through a combined three marriages, four kids, two family deaths, and half a dozen job relocations.

The tradition, sealed in a Hot Springs mineral bath the day following Ike's second inauguration, allowed for no excuses, no exceptions. One weekend a year, Doug and Peter left home and went racing together. Period.

On even years, Saratoga. On odd years, wherever the mood struck. Grand dames in full plumage, mostly: Keeneland, Churchill, Gulfstream, Santa Anita. But on occasion, bag ladies on their deathbed, too: Green Mountain, Narragansett, Bowie. "If they've served the sport well, then we should honor their passing," Doug had said the day he and Peter had helped bury Bowie.

For this, the odd year, the pair of 63-year-olds had chosen a January weekend at Gulfstream Park. Peter, now living in Phoenix, wanted to see his eldest son, Daniel, who'd recently moved to Fort Lauderdale. And besides, he killed Florida tracks. "Chalk runs truer under palm trees," he'd always insist.

Gulfstream was perfect with Doug, too. Widowed three years earlier, he'd just moved from Chicago to Boca Raton to be near the people and things he needed most: His son Alex, whose friendship and shared love of horse racing with Daniel immensely pleased both fathers; year-round Thoroughbred action, and the oncologists who were promising to keep him alive until the next Breeders' Cup.

"I think the paddock of a racetrack is my favorite place to be," said Doug, as he intently studied the horses being led into the saddling area for the first. "Look at them. Look how cocky they are. They all think they can win. They've all got hope."

Peter quickly figured out what that meant. Now was no time to grieve. Now, on a gloriously balmy South Florida afternoon, was the time, probably for the last time, to join with Doug in celebration of their friendship and the sport that had so magnificently bonded it together over so many years.

The ponies first. Cancer and its inexorable conclusion later. Not an unreasonable ordering of priorities, it seemed. To either man.

FOLLOWING CUSTOM, the pair purchased seats in a box at the sixteenth pole. Doug, ever the portly mish-mosh of clashing polyester stripes and plaids, focused immediately on the win pools, searching for the "smart money." Peter, a well-kept beanstalk of a man who never stopped shopping at Brooks Brothers, tended to the immediate housekeeping chores, carefully laying out the instruments of the trade. Binoculars. Heavily marked *Racing Forms*. "The Sheets." And a flask of Old Crow to erase the nastiest of what Doug liked to call "those woulda, coulda, shoulda moments."

Order achieved, the time was at hand, once again, to get even. If not for life, at least for a season of bets-gone-bad at their "home" tracks: Turf Paradise and Arlington Park.

Trouble is, Doug's lock, the shimmering chestnut filly Jan Belle, turned out to be a "walrus," and thus ran dead last. "Sap could have run faster," Doug snarled, in his typically abrupt post-race analysis.

The second brought no relief, either. "You can stick a fork in that pot roast. She's cooked," scoffed Doug, as Lovely Leslie, the front-running bearer of his cash and handicapping credibility, faded into the pack at the eighth pole.

Nor was the third the charm. A shipper from Detroit, taking a class hike into a "non-winners other than" off a 60-day layoff, nosed out his pick and paid $39 to win. "Take that donkey down," Doug shrieked, again tapping his ample supply of insults for horses that cost him money.

Peter, who rarely bet with Doug on the theory that the road to insolvency is paved with winners paying more than $20, had decided that today he was going to roll with Doug's picks. "How can I not, given the situation," he'd said to himself at the window before the first three races. Which meant that 86 combined years of handicapping wisdom was now $320 in the hole with two total crap shoots dead ahead: full fields of "non-winners of two lifetime" older horses and Florida-bred three-year-old maiden filly $5,000 claimers.

Ordinarily, these were Doug's favorite kinds of races. "Proven bums" and "bums-in-training," he called them. Surefire price shots. Only this day, in a dramatic form reversal, Doug was not quickly scribbling gimmick combinations all over his program. Nor, as was his style, was he busily addressing the conundrum of translating and comparing track variants from faraway racing surfaces for use at Gulfstream. Instead, as the horses were being led onto the track for the fourth, he sat staring, seemingly transfixed, by the infield odds board.

"I don't much like anything here," said Peter, noticing his trackmate's sudden apparent lack of enthusiasm, and assuming it masked dark, faraway thoughts.

"What are we doing here, Peter?" responded Doug in a soft, quizzical voice.

"Huh?" gulped Peter.

"What is it that makes this game so compelling? So ... alive. So ..."

"So powerful," interrupted Peter. "So ... elegant."

"All of those," said Doug, taken aback by Peter's choice of words. "Yep, all of those."

This did not have the makings of your basic Doug and Peter conversation. Especially not with eight minutes to post. Sure, every year they'd filled each other in on personal stuff: kids, health, work, and the like. In recent times, the state of their nest eggs and consequent investment strategies were much-discussed topics. Catherine O'Neill—the drop-dead gorgeous track waitress who turned Peter into a walking sweat gland in the summer of 1971 and destroyed his first marriage in the process—always got a mention, too. A lot of words had been spoken over four decades. But "elegant" had never, ever been among them.

It was time, Peter saw, to stop handicapping. Doug wasn't searching for the winner of the fourth. He was searching, at the moment, for answers to larger, far more complex questions: Had this abiding passion for horse racing all been a pathetic waste of time? What, after all these years, was the point here?

To Peter's knowledge, Doug had never addressed such questions. Doug loved to sit around and shoot the breeze, to talk trash. Except for the time he confessed to longing, just once, to sprint Secretariat across the Cliffs of Mohr, he was a surface kind of guy. Not one to look inward, to seek himself.

Peter, by contrast, had asked the questions, had formulated answers, had sought an understanding of his attraction to and relationship with the sport of Thoroughbred horse racing. He knew his conclusions were deeply personal, but he guessed that his friend, on what realistically was their final lap around the track together, needed to hear them.

"I don't remember if I ever showed this to you," said Peter, knowing full well as he pulled a worn laminated card out of his wallet that he had never shown it to anyone. "I picked this thing up in a junk shop in Saratoga about six or seven years ago. Remember that day they shut down the track when lightning blew up a transformer in the middle of the clubhouse turn? We won the last race that day, remember? He paid $9.80, and it was raining so hard you couldn't see him until he ran by the eighth pole. Anyway, I saw this thing in the store. I thought it made sense at the time. It still sort of does. Here, read it."

The card, the size of a driver's license, contained a saying, attributed to Englishman Robert Duncan, entitled "The Horse." Doug dropped his head, held the card in his lap, and slowly read it. Then he read it again.

Where in this world can man
find nobility without pride,
friendship without envy,
or beauty without vanity?
Here: where grace is laced with muscle,
and strength by gentleness confined.
There is nothing so powerful,
nothing less violent.
There is nothing so quick,
nothing so patient.

"This guy makes some valid points, doesn't he?" mumbled Doug.

"Of course he does," said Peter. "You know and I know there are plenty of players out there who'd bet on the length of a lizard's tongue if they could get long enough odds.

"Obviously, horse racing is about gambling and trying to make money. But there's a higher plane, a whole other dimension, a reason why all the time and all the money and all the energy we've invested over our lifetimes have been nobly spent."

Peter could see that Doug was listening, and that he wanted more. Otherwise, with five minutes to post and the lowest price on the board standing at a plump 4-to-1, Doug most certainly would be scrambling to spot overlay three-figure perfecta payoffs.

"Okay, listen," continued Peter in an increasingly confident voice. "I'm not saying this works for everybody, but I figure there are two what I'd call 'grand' reasons why this sport is so extraordinary. First, it's like Duncan says. There's intrinsic sensuality here. A universality, an elegance that's every bit as valid, every bit as palpable as any Brandenburg concerto or Rubens nude.

"Second, there's the intellectual struggle. Every horse race is a self-contained maelstrom of facts and figures. A maze of statistical inconsistencies. To place the right bet is to crack the code. To solve the riddle. To master the unknown.

"Horse racing, as I figure it, is about contemplating unequaled beauty. About straining to divine its inscrutable course. About deciphering truth. And I defy you to name one other hobby that offers more than that."

Doug slowly turned his gaze away from the starting gate, where a field with the combined total of 12 wins in 258 races was now entering their stalls, and fixed it onto Peter. "I'm trying to decide whether that's the biggest load of B.S. I've ever heard, or if it actually makes sense," he said.

"Well, I believe it," answered Peter.

"Then I believe it, too," smiled a suddenly reinvigorated Doug as he pulled out the Old Crow. "Here's to whatever it is that keeps us coming back for more."

The transcendental meaning of horse racing resolved, Doug and Peter hoisted, clicked, and downed their shots in glorious unison.

"Now," shouted Doug, "let's beat this game."

THEY WERE too late for the fourth, and it was just as well. Sterner, a "dead slug" sporting a maiden $4,000 claiming win at River Downs 18 months ago as his sole conquest in life, had crawled home first.

But the rest of the card was another story. It doesn't happen often, but horseplayers every once in a great while slip into a consciousness that allows them to see only that which matters and do only that which is right. Professional athletes call it being in a "zone." No one has ever been able to explain how one gets into a zone, or why one leaves it. But all athletes, and horseplayers, too, know one when they're in one.

In the fifth, Doug determined that the jock switch on a singularly undistinguished colt named Halpernicus was the critical factor. He pulled away by two, and paid $14.40 on top. First Lasix for Redline was all Doug needed to see in the sixth. Redline paid $28.20.

The seventh, a mile-and-an-eighth allowance affair resulting in a $58 perfecta payoff with the second and third favorites, was simply a matter of accepting that the 1-to-2 chalk was a stakes-winning monster at a mile and a sixteenth, and a "pot roast" at anything longer.

The featured eighth, a $50,000 stakes for nine older horses contested at a mile and 70 yards on the dirt, demonstrated conclusively that when a horseplayer is in a zone, he is invincible. The top four choices had 15 career ungraded stakes wins between them. The next two choices had both closed fast behind the two favorites in their most recent starts, and were dropping five pounds apiece.

But all Doug could see—all that mattered as he scanned the *Form*, the Sheets, and his memory—was Karl the Great, dying of disrespect at a constant 8-to-1. Karl had won nearly $250,000 and eight races in 34 starts, but he had always come up short in stakes tests, usually dying in the final sixteenth. He'd been beaten at least twice by five horses in the race, and four times by the favorite.

And yet, Doug knew this was Karl's day. He knew the horse had won five allowance races in the past three years off 45-day layoffs, as was here the case. He knew that while Karl had been soundly beaten by today's competitors when they'd gone around Belmont's and Arlington's one sweeping turn, he was a different horse in races of the same distance contested around two sharp turns, as at Gulfstream. He knew that Karl, carrying 118 pounds today, had pulled most of his fades at 120 or higher. And finally, Doug just sensed it was, at last, Karl's turn to win. He could envision it all in tomorrow's newspaper results chart. It was that simple.

And so it was. Karl the Great charged to the lead, and the rest sucked dirt. All the way around the track. To the tune of $19.80, $10.80, and $5.40. And a $73 perf with the favorite.

It's difficult, if not impossible, for a non-horseplayer to truly comprehend the intense satisfaction and sense of accomplishment generated by a win crafted out of handicapping virtuosity. Both Peter and Doug had tried without success over the years to explain the feeling to their skeptical wives and curious acquaintances.

The pair was now up a combined $4,800 for the afternoon, but both knew that wasn't the point. Over four decades, they had managed maybe two-dozen winning years between them. Both knew, always, that money was not the end, or even the means. It was strictly a way of keeping score. Whether, at the end of each year, either had won or lost didn't much matter. When they won, they usually gave most of it to their kids, anyway.

What counted, what mattered, was the chase. The struggle. The conquest.

"You did it," said Peter resolutely, as the sweating, snorting, brazen bay Karl pranced into the winner's circle. "You reached in, separated the light from the darkness, and grabbed the truth."

"We did it together, Peter. This, I think, is our finest moment," declared Doug.

The flush of mastery is not a sense easily dispersed. And by the time Doug and Peter had collected their winnings, scarfed another Old Crow, and relived the subtle manipulation of the race's statistical tumblers, the ninth and last event of the day was six minutes away.

As quickly as supreme elation had struck, so now despair was at hand.

"This is it, isn't it?" Peter said.

"I'm done betting," Doug answered. "I feel good about Karl being my last winner. Our last winner. There's a symmetry to it that appeals."

Peter took a deep breath, then stared nervously down at the concrete between his feet. "It's going to be okay, Peter," said Doug, a ten-second eternity later. "Maybe the treatments will work, maybe they won't. Either way, I've come to terms with it. And either way, the family's taken care of."

Another pause. Another eternity.

"You know, I sure as hell hope, that you've been one of the important moorings in my life. I mean that," Doug continued.

The last time Peter had cried in front of another man, or anyone for that matter, was at his father's funeral in 1982. Until now. He tried not to. The way men always do, looking away and pretending to clear their throats and busily smoothing their hair back. But Doug's mooring had been his mooring, too. An emotional constant. A "sure thing."

Peter tried to speak, but couldn't. So Doug did.

"I've had a good run, Peter. Really. I've done everything I wanted to do, except maybe take that run across the Cliffs of Mohr."

"Yes," nodded Peter, in a sniffled chuckle. "Yes. Yes. I believe you have. You're right. You're right. A good run. A damn good run."

"I just want one more thing," Doug quickly added. "Alex is going to take me back to Boca tonight, and I know you were planning on seeing Daniel tomorrow, but I think he and Alex were going to play golf this afternoon, so I suggested they meet up with us at Rick's for dinner, if that's okay with you."

"Great," said Peter. "You know, they remind me of us 30 years ago."

THERE'S A GAME some people play. They say to themselves: If I knew I was about to eat my last meal, and I could have anything I wanted, what would I eat?

Peter didn't know if Doug had ever played this game. But Peter had. In his "last supper" were a chicken wing from Smitty's Birdland in Rochester, New York, deep-fried clams from his mother's skillet, the burned crust off his first wife's macaroni and cheese, and two eggs over easy with baked ham sliced fresh off the bone at Rick's Restaurant, located directly across the street from Gulfstream Park.

Rick's was greasy. It was loud. It was crowded. And as far as Peter was concerned, it was The Diner From Heaven. You could buy tomorrow's *Form* there today, and trough down in silence. Or you could instantly strike up a lively debate with a surly waitress, or the table next door, over the day's racing results. Whenever the two came to Gulfstream, they rarely ate anywhere else.

"There's something about cholesterol and horse racing that just seems to fit," Peter said to Doug as the two sat down in their favorite booth, the one in the back corner underneath the faded black and white glossies of Kelso and Native Dancer. Alex and Daniel, fresh off the golf course and a couple of hours in the 19th Hole, glided along momentarily, and joined their dads.

One-liners, back slaps, and laughter quickly flooded the table. Followed by a dietary holocaust of three-egg omelettes, butter, slab bacon, more butter, grits, ham, Greek roast, more bacon, more butter. And coffee blacker than Seattle Slew.

Absent from the table were tears, remorse, pathos. Doug and Alex had come to terms with the future. So, through Alex's understanding, had Daniel. And so, too, in the afterglow of Karl the Great's preordained run, and with Doug's guidance, had Peter. At least partially.

Doug was on his third cup when Alex reached under the table and pulled out two boxes the size of coffee table books, wrapped in week-old *Racing Forms*. One, he handed to his dad. The other to Peter. "To you guys," he smiled, somewhat nervously. "To your enduring friendship."

Neither knew what Alex was up to. But they both liked the sound of it. "I know," laughed Peter. "One of Doug's pot roasts!"

"Nope," said Doug. "A bound volume containing every losing trifecta ticket I ever bought."

"Open it, Dad," said Daniel.

"All right, all right," answered Peter, bending his head to study the *Form* wrapping. "Just let me see who I like in this race on the front, first."

"You, too, Dad, open it," said Alex.

"Okay, then, let's do it together," said Doug.

Peter unwrapped his first, and at once held it up in front of his face. Then Doug did the same. For the amount of time it took Personal Ensign to mow down Winning Colors inside the eighth pole in the 1988 Breeders' Cup Distaff, both men sat silently, staring at their gifts.

Each was an 11-by-17 portrait, framed in gold, of the two of them standing arm in arm on a balcony overlooking Santa Anita's finish line, the San Gabriel Mountains standing snowcapped and suncovered behind them. Doug had asked a fellow player to take the shot four years ago, then promptly thrown the picture and negative into a closet drawer full of old *Forms* and programs, which is where Alex had found it.

An inscription was etched along the bottom of each frame:

The tradition shall live. The legacy is passed. This we promise.

We're off to Saratoga in '94. Your loving sons, Alex and Daniel.

Both fathers instantly realized what this inscription and this moment meant, and were at once humbled by it.

This was not an end, Doug and Peter suddenly knew. But a beginning. Not the dying of a ritual. But a regeneration of it.

A bond of friendship, unbroken by time.

A passing. Father to son.

Peter gently placed his prize on the table, then stood up with coffee cup in hand, determined to face the last moments with strength. "A toast, gentlemen," he barked.

All rose.

"Doug: To our sons, who honor us by this extraordinary gift. To the beauty and power and struggle that is horse racing. And to us, joined through our mutual love of this sport in lifelong friendship."

Doug equally driven to end the leaving with a winning move, barked right back.

"To you, Peter. And the 37 magic weekends in our past.

"To you, Alex and Daniel. And the 37 magic weekends I hope are in your future.

"And may you often need to borrow my wheelbarrow!"

The Saratoga Derby

by K. M. Jones

WHEN LONGACRES ran its last race, my job as a research librarian was snuffed out as callously as the years of history surrounding the track. So many great horses had run there, but no more.

In the months following, I tried other jobs but they were not what I wanted. It was like trying to work a jigsaw puzzle with different pieces thrown in—the pieces just didn't fit. With Longacres closed, there was nothing left in Seattle to keep me there, so I moved to Saratoga Springs.

I had spent these last few weeks searching for work and a place to stay. Someone with my experience should have had no trouble finding work in Saratoga Springs. But, everywhere the response was the same: "Thank you so much for thinking of our company, but we are not hiring until August." It seemed the entire town had an adequate labor force until the racing season began. However, that was still two months away, and I needed something to do right now.

I walked up Union Avenue toward the racetrack. The shady elms lining the street made the hot June day seem almost pleasant beneath their branches. To my left I saw the white pillars of the National Museum of Racing and Hall of Fame. It was the first place I had applied. "We already have a researcher, thank you," was their reply.

I continued along until I stood before the gates of the historic Saratoga racetrack. They were closed, which brought another twinge of depression to my already low spirits. I leaned against the iron gates and to my surprise they swung open. Glancing around, I looked to see who, if anyone, might be watching, and to my relief saw no one. I closed the heavy gates behind me and walked cautiously down the deserted lane.

I relished every moment, for however long the moment would last, fully expecting security officers to escort me off the grounds. The serene beauty of the elms yielded to a grand clubhouse with its great doors open. Inside, through the darkness, I could see vague images of chairs stacked upon tables awaiting the happy days of August when they would be put to use. But there were no people to be seen.

The darkness surrendered to a racetrack bathed in brilliant sunlight. My throat felt tight with the overwhelming significance of the moment. The sense of history was so thick here that it was almost smothering. I took a place on the rail near the winner's circle, or at least where the traditional chalk circle would be drawn in a couple of months. I breathed in deeply the earthy fragrances of freshly mown turf and well-groomed loam. My gaze turned to the pond in the infield. The canoe was gone, but I knew it would be returned sporting the colors of Thunder Rumble, last year's Travers victor, before the front gates officially opened.

I had read accounts of the Saratoga races throughout my career, but they were only stories before today. Now, being here and seeing the track made it all real. Forty Niner and Seeking the Gold had staged their famous duels here in this stretch, as had Jaipur and Ridan. There on the backstretch was where Alydar was cut off by Affirmed and nearly wrecked in their final meeting. And there at the head of the stretch was where Thingamubob died on a sad day in 1938.

I stood there motionless for what must have been an hour, envisioning the great races I had read about, not daring to move lest my paradise be swept away. I knew I was at home here, but it couldn't last. It was sadly ironic that I belonged here yet did not belong here. My depression had returned and I quietly left the grounds.

The remainder of that Friday afternoon in June was spent in walking. I do not recall on which street I discovered the estate sale, but it was the event that changed my life.

"ARE you looking for something in particular?" a young woman's voice asked as I stood among boxes and tables scattered with trinkets and old racing magazines.

"No ... just looking," I replied. I didn't even know what I was doing there. I should have been looking for work, not for dusty old knickknacks that had outlived their owners. The young lady walked away but promptly returned with a glass of lemonade that she offered to me. I thanked her for her thoughtfulness and accepted the glass.

She introduced herself as Helen Hathaway. Although I probably would have discouraged any attempt at conversation, the name had caught my attention. "Really?" I asked. "My name is Hathaway also—Christopher Hathaway."

"Isn't that odd?" she said with a pleasant smile. "I think my grandfather's name was Christopher, but I don't really know. The only name anyone ever called him was Kit, and I never thought to ask Grand-mama what it stood for. Most of this stuff was his. He loved racing. I don't mean he went to the track now and again, I mean he really loved racing."

So there were at least two of us.

"I opened the sale at eight this morning and most of the good stuff was gone by ten minutes past." The good stuff, I learned, was furniture and books from the library. As she spoke, I found myself wishing I had come by earlier to see what kinds of books an elderly race enthusiast in Saratoga Springs would have kept in his library. I imagined that many of them had been racing books. Racing books had been my life's blood. As a research librarian, they had been invaluable to my profession, and essential to my private interests, as well.

We continued to chat away the afternoon as chummy as two old friends. At five o'clock I helped her bring a few boxes indoors and take down the sale signs at the curb. She invited me to stay for dinner and go through what was left of Kit Hathaway's belongings. Throughout dinner I studied her face. Something about Helen's eyes reminded me of my own. The more I looked, the more the resemblances grew. We had considered that we might be distant relatives, but that was difficult to ascertain as Kit had always refused to speak of his past. Helen thought her grandfather was probably illegitimate and his Victorian ethics kept him from discussing it. Any secrets he knew about his parents, he took with him when he died 30 years ago.

"Thirty years ago?" I asked. "But I thought ... the estate sale ..."

"... was prompted by the death of my grandmother, Anna Hathaway," Helen explained. "She died just recently. Grandfather Kit passed away long ago."

"How old was he?" I asked without thinking. Something about Grandfather Kit intrigued me.

"I think he was in his 70s. Grand-mama was 92 when she died."

Helen's grandfather Kit had died in 1962, the year I was born. I began to wonder if his passion for racing had not died with him, but found a newborn soul to occupy, namely mine. However, metaphysics were never my long suit, so I dismissed the thought as merely coincidence.

In a hall closet we discovered a dusty bowler derby that Helen said had belonged to the old man. She had seen countless photographs of him wearing the hat, and Anna had held onto it sentimentally until the day she died. Helen had not put it out for the sale since no one wore derbies any longer and she doubted anyone would buy such an old and well-worn relic. Beneath the hat lay a small green book with a decorative zig-zag trim on the spine.

Helen took it down and explained that this had been her grandfather's journal. She had glanced through some of the pages long ago but the contents had not particularly interested her. The journal had also been kept from the throngs of sale-goers as it was the one thing of her grandfather's that Helen wished to keep. Upon examining it for myself, I discovered that the journal was not a log of a man's days, rather a notebook filled with dates and names of stakes races and their winners.

Helen told me that Kit had always had exceptional luck at the track. His picks invariably won, and he and Anna never lacked financially. Even after he died, Anna had continued to strike fortune after fortune as though Kit were still guiding her selections. He had used the journal, Helen explained, to log the winners after each day's racing was done.

I looked more closely at it, flipping the pages slowly. Most of the entries appeared to have been written with the same pen, as though many pages covering many years had been done all at once. But that could not be right.

The book began with a page dated August 13, 1919, on which the famous results of the Sanford Memorial Stakes were spelled out. Upset defeated Man o' War by a half-length. What a shocker that had been to the race-going public of the day! Page after page the history of racing unfolded in my hands. Jim Dandy beat Gallant Fox in the Travers at odds of 100-to-1. Discovery won the Whitney for three straight years. On the date of August 27, 1945, there was mention of a $2 daily double on Buddy Bones and Junction City resulting in a record payoff of $4,313.90. How exciting! The book revealed all that he had witnessed.

I flipped through the pages and the names that jumped out read like a roll call of champions—Prudery, Zev, the great jumper Beacon

Hill, War Admiral, Whirlaway, Shut Out, Kelso, Buckpasser, Dr. Fager. ...

Dr. Fager? "Wait a minute," the name struck me like a slap across the face. "When did you say your grandfather passed away?"

"1962. I was very young at the time, but I have been to his grave. The headstone says 1962." She looked at me in confusion. "Why? Is that important?"

I snapped the book closed to punctuate the mystery. "Dr. Fager didn't run until 1966."

HELEN brewed some coffee while I perused the latter pages of Kit's journal in greater depth. The mystery grew deeper as each page turned and the years grew closer to today. Secretariat, Alydar, Runaway Groom, and countless other names were penned in ancient ink. My head swam with confusion. He could not have known about these horses, let alone the dates they ran, and the odds, and the times of the races, and the names of the also-rans.

The final page was dated August 22, 1992. The old ink clearly spelled out the name Thunder Rumble as the 4½-length upset winner of the Travers Stakes with Devil His Due second and Dance Floor third. The time was also noted—two minutes and four-fifths seconds. The following page was missing, torn from the book.

"I don't understand." I cupped my head in my hands as I tried to make sense of it. "I don't understand. Are you certain that this was your grandfather's journal and not maybe your grandmother's? It ends with last year's Travers."

"I doubt it." She brought the coffee to the table and poured. "I've seen photos of Grandfather Kit and in nearly every one he's wearing that derby and carrying that book. If it were Grand-mama's, why should he have kept it all the time? Maybe the book was his, but Grand-mama took over the notekeeping after Kit died? It is likely, isn't it?"

"I would tend to agree, except that the entire book was written in the same hand."

"Well, the handwriting is definitely his," she offered. "I've seen the same handwriting in other books he kept. Household expenses, bank books, and things like that."

I shook my head. Every possible explanation was shot down in the end. The man had died in 1962. How could he have known or even guessed that 30 years later a horse named Thunder Rumble would run away with the jewel of all Saratoga races?

"Have you any photos of him still?" I asked, wanting desperately to put a face with the name.

"There's one hanging in the library." She showed me the way down the hall and into the now near-barren room. "It was taken shortly before he died. There are a few much older photographs, but I wouldn't know where to start looking for them."

What I saw was astonishing. The resemblance was overwhelming. There was no doubt about it. We were definitely related somehow. The face was old and withered but the eyes were bright and friendly, and they were mine. This, I imagined, is what I will look like at his age.

I left shortly after that. Helen would not sell me the journal, of course. Now that it made her grandfather such a puzzle, it was even more dear to her. She did, however, give me the bowler derby. It was apparent that we were related and she wanted me to own something of his. She had regretted that she had not learned more about him. I regretted it also, because now I wanted to know so much more.

The following day, I headed straight for the city library and delved into the microfilm that contained copies of all the back issues of the local newspaper. Selecting a reel labeled August 1945, I scrolled forward to the 28th day of that month. A few pages into the issue a headline blared "Local Man Hits Record Double." The story that followed spoke of the previous day's track results and the daily double that I had seen recorded in Kit's journal. As I scrolled the page downward to read the remainder of the article, a photograph of Kit appeared. He was wearing the bowler derby, which was highly unusual for 1945, and carried in his left hand the little green book with the zig-zag trim on the side. The article indicated that Kit Hathaway was a regular at the track and wore the derby for good luck. His face was much younger than the face I had seen the previous night on the library wall. I still could not get over the resemblance. Staring at the newspaper photo was almost like looking into a mirror, with a few decades tacked on, of course.

I knew now what he looked like as an old man and as a middle-aged man. I could guess that as a young man, he was another me, at least in looks and interests. But, to find a younger photo of Kit was not the only reason I had come. I put the reel away and consulted a master index of newspaper articles. In 1962 I found an obituary for Kit Hathaway.

As he had been more than an average citizen of the town, the story of his death was more than an average obituary. It spoke of Kit as a legend among handicappers and there were several photos of him and Anna at various stages of their lives. In nearly every picture one could clearly see the little green book. Although the article said that Kit never told anyone the secret of his remarkable success, I knew it was the book.

Kit had definitely died on September 9, 1962. The newspaper verified it. He had written literally a "wealth" of information into the book over a course of 43 years. It still baffled me that I could not explain how the later races came to be in the book, written in his own hand. If the answer were simply a case of foresight, then his had been extraordinary.

I returned to my apartment and stared at the derby for a long while. If anyone had the answers, it was Helen. I scooped up the derby and headed for the Hathaway house. It was not that I desired to possess the secret and use it to get rich; the book was no good to anyone now. The final entry had already passed and the pages were silent after that. I simply wanted to know how the puzzle fit together. Suddenly I remembered something I had said about my own life—the pieces didn't fit. For Kit Hathaway, as well, the pieces definitely did not fit!

Only a few blocks away from destination, I crossed Union Avenue. I looked both directions and stepped out into the street. The traffic was incredibly light. No cars could be seen for several blocks. The sun caught my eyes halfway across, and I set the derby on my head to act as a shield from the glare.

A horse very nearby screamed in my ear, and I found that I was only an instant away from being run down by a horse-drawn coach. Without stopping to learn where the obsolete vehicle had come from, I dashed out of its path. The driver shouted Victorian obscenities at me. "You cretinous idiot! Have you any idea what these horses are worth? What do you mean by jumping in front of my team? Are you attempting to kill yourself?"

"No," I responded while gasping for breath.

The driver stared at me as though not knowing what else to say. "Well ... good then. See that you don't." As he drove away, I noticed that he was dressed in a very old style of clothing. Perhaps he was part of a historical troupe, or maybe there was a driving competition nearby. More likely the latter.

I dusted myself off as I walked to the edge of the road and saw with a shock that I was dressed from head to toe in clothes that were not my own. These were not the shirt and blue jeans I had put on this morning. I was now clad in a dark suit and the collar of the white shirt was stiff and uncomfortable. Where there had been Nikes, I now sported black dress shoes covered by white spats! In my right hand—an ivory-handled cane.

What on earth had happened?! Union Avenue was no longer an asphalt street but a busy dirt road upon which several varieties of coach and wagon traveled. There were also fine gentlemen on horseback. The road was much more crowded now than it was a minute ago. Everyone was clothed as though it were before the turn of the century. I could not believe this! I could have believed many people suddenly appearing in old-fashioned clothes, because people often dress up to show their horses and carriages, but I could not believe the road changing to packed dirt, or my own clothing transforming to what I now wore. Perhaps it was the trauma of very nearly being run over by the coach.

"Pardon me," a husky voice boomed. "But you appear to be lost." A young, rotund gentleman dressed very much like myself was addressing me.

Although shaking slightly from the moment's confusion, I was able to reply to him honestly. "Yes, completely lost."

"Are you going to the races?" he asked.

"Races? In June?" I replied.

I must have appeared quite insane to him. He cocked his head a bit and raised an eyebrow. "June? You are mistaken. This is August!"

I wanted desperately to ask what year this was, but he would only think worse of me. Instead, I explained that I had nearly been killed while crossing the road. That seemed to satisfy him. Any foolish thing I now said could be explained as disorientation from the accident.

He asked again if I was attending the races, to which I replied, "I would not travel to Saratoga in August just to miss the races."

He laughed loudly and said he felt the same way. He seemed to me to be in his early 20s, but dressed in a fashion that spoke of a well-monied family. We walked together toward the track, and he showed me the program he had bought that morning at the Grand Union Hotel. The date on the front sapped the strength from my legs. The month and day were insignificant, but the year! The year was 1885!

I was dreaming all this, certainly that was the answer. This was a dream, or worse. Maybe I had been struck by a car while crossing the street and now I was lying in some hospital in a coma dreaming about 1885. Or maybe I was dead! Saratoga Springs had always been my idea of heaven, so to speak, but I never envisioned death to be quite like this.

I pinched myself hard enough on the arm to raise a bruise in a few hours. If it were all a dream, I had not yet awakened. 1885 was still there.

I walked a step faster to catch up to the burly gentleman who had made my acquaintance. He introduced himself later as Mason Vander Holden. I did not recall having heard the name before, but it seemed vaguely familiar. Perhaps I had come across it at the library, or maybe read the name while researching Saratoga races any number of years ago. I introduced myself to him as we neared the main gates.

He had come by train from Baltimore to see the races. There was one horse in particular he wished to see run and that was the Kentucky freak, Bersan. "Freak? What do you mean?" I asked. "Does he have five legs or three eyes or something?"

"Horns," Vander Holden replied. "He has horns. I can't believe you don't know that! It's all the papers are talking about these days."

"Horns?" I had read accounts of Bersan. He had been the best son of his famous father, Ten Broeck, the Kentucky superhorse. I had read of many victories by this racer, but I was certain I had never read about any horns. "You mean horns like a bull?"

"No, certainly not. More like a strange bony growth above his eyes. It's not truly noticeable unless you are looking directly at it. I think the New York newsmen are making too much of it, if you ask me. But you know how they like to degrade Kentucky-breds. Anything to make the local horses look better!" I gathered from his words that he liked Bersan and would probably back him at the races today.

We made our way under the elms to the paddock, to where Bersan was being walked under saddle. Sure enough, horns. It gave him an unusual look, like a helmeted charger from the middle ages. I wanted a closer look, so I removed the derby from my head.

Suddenly, everyone was gone. I stood alone beneath the trees, dressed in jeans and tennis shoes and holding the derby in my hand. No Vander Holden, no Bersan, no thousands of other people who were there only a second ago. I looked at the hat. Had it been the hat?

I thought back. The "dream" had all started when I put the derby on halfway across the street, and had ended when I took it off.

"You there! How did you get in here? How did you get past the gates?"

I turned around to see a security officer approaching me. Apparently it was June once again and I was definitely unwanted on the grounds. I could not explain to him that I was here to wager on a horned horse. I knew I was in trouble and resigned to whatever fate the guard would condemn me to. I decided to raise my hands over my head as a show of non-hostility, but had to replace the hat in order to do so.

Instantly the crowd returned. The bay colt, Bersan, paraded by me and the horns, although not the type that could spear anyone, appeared to be still dangerous if the horse made up his mind to use them. I turned to look for Mr. Vander Holden and found him right beside me still talking about the unfair way New York breeders were persecuting Bersan. He had never missed me. As he continued lecturing the points of modern horse racing, I hardly heard a word he said. My mind was too intent on the hat. What a strange power it was that I wore.

The last two days had been bizarre indeed. First I learned of relatives I never knew I had, then of a man who knew the winners of races that were run 30 years after his own death, and now I possessed a bowler derby that was some sort of time machine.

Why had it taken me to 1885? How is it controlled? Does it work on anyone?

KIT HATHAWAY! Of course! Kit had worn this hat and knew the winners of every race he wagered on. Kit had used the hat to travel through time just as I was now doing. That's how he knew the winners and the odds. Things were beginning to make some sense. The pieces were falling into place.

"Come with me, Hathaway." Vander Holden grabbed me by the arm and led me to the bookmakers' stands.

From atop a wooden crate, a wizened man asked us, "Who do ye like for the Travers?"

"Who's the favorite?" I asked him without skipping a beat.

"At the moment, that'd be Irish Pat. Son of Pat Malloy and Ethel, by Leamington. And a faster racehorse ye never did see! I'll give ye 35-to-100 on his nose," the bookie replied in a heavy foreign accent.

Now I knew from my years of research that Irish Pat was a good horse. In his three-year-old season, he had won the Kenner Stakes and was a decent second in the Foxhall. But he had finished out of the money in that year's Kentucky Derby, which was won by the undefeated champion Joe Cotton, who beat Bersan by only a neck. I could not absolutely remember the outcome of the Travers of 1885. But going back over the list of names in the program seemed to help. I knew Irish Pat would be better at four than he was at three, so I settled on the one horse whose name I had read in print more than the others.

"What will you give us on Bersan?" I asked casually. I tried to exude an air of indifference as though we probably would not bet on him after all, to see if the bookie would raise the price.

He seemed disgusted by our selection. "Bersan? That horned freak? I wouldn't bet him to win a one-horse race!"

Vander Holden harrumphed. "My good man, your opinion is fascinating, of course, but what are the odds?" My friend knew as I did that Bersan was an excellent runner and the New York bookie's prejudice against him was more likely a case of prejudice against Kentucky-breds in general.

"Ahhh ..." he peered through round little spectacles to consult his chalkboard. "I've got him at 12-to-1 if yer so inclined." The other bookies were giving far less, so we accepted the 12-to-1. That is to say, Vander Holden accepted the odds as I had no currency.

We took a box seat that belonged to my new friend's family. He said his parents came to Saratoga nearly every year, but family business had forced them to return to Baltimore early, leaving Mason here alone on Travers day. He was happy for the company, as was I. My first view of the stands was one of surprise. They seemed much smaller than they did yesterday. But I quickly reasoned out the difference. In 1885 the stands did not include the additional seating areas that were added decades later.

"Have you ever been to Pimlico?" I asked just to make conversation.

"Ever been?" he beamed with pride. "I've seen the Preakness every year since its inauguration in seventy-two."

"Amazing," was the only word I could utter.

"Not so amazing," he protested. "They've only been running it for 14 years."

"Mason, there's a two-year-old I've heard about named The Bard. If I shouldn't be able to attend the race next year, I'd like you to place a bet for me on him in the Preakness."

He stared at me with a smile. "How do you know he will even be entered?"

"He's already nominated and I think he'll make it there." Vander Holden shrugged, but repeated the name to me and made a mental note of my orders.

The horses took to the track and paraded by as beautifully as any modern horse I had seen. The stirrups seemed longer than I was used to, and the jockeys' clothing dated the race as absolutely un-modern. Other differences caught my attention. Among them—there was no gate. The horses began from a standing start, which saw Bersan off a step slowly. Irish Pat took the lead immediately and drew away from the field. The group charged by in a cloud of dust as hordes of people at the rail cheered and announced the chestnut colt, Irish Pat, as the leader. This was apparently their version of a public address system.

Irish Pat continued to dominate as they flew up the backstretch. Somewhere in midpack, Bersan maneuvered between horses and edged up to the chestnut's flanks. The jockey aboard our pick was some kid named Spellman whom I had not heard of. He drew his whip and struck Bersan a single crack. The horned son of Ten Broeck darted past Irish Pat in a matter of seconds and increased his lead into the stretch. Irish Pat attempted to stage a comeback but Bersan, toying with the field, burst away again and came home an easy four lengths in front. The cheers that greeted him proved that not all New Yorkers hated him. He boasted many more supporters than the bookie had implied.

Vander Holden let loose a yell of triumph as he had placed $100 on the horse. I was happy for him, and happy for myself as well. I had chosen the winner. Better yet, I had remembered the winner! I let loose a whoop of my own and absentmindedly tossed the derby into the air.

I KNEW it was a mistake the second I had done it. Suddenly the stands were dark and empty. The echo of my victory cry bounced off the shell of the vacant grandstands. It was night. I swallowed hard and rushed to find the magical derby. As I stooped to retrieve it from where it had fallen, I was suddenly aware of the fall of footsteps approaching at a quick pace. The darkness cloaked me sufficiently as at least two security officers ran past.

"I swear I saw someone up here. He couldn't have gone far," one of them announced to the other.

"Damned vandals!" the other spoke. "We'd have never known he was here if he hadn't hollered at us." The footsteps ran off past me.

"He must have gone out this way," I heard one of them say in ever-diminishing volume. Soon, they were both gone. I stayed put a few minutes more, then found a way down to the front gate through the darkness. No more derby-wearing tonight.

The selection of Bersan was a fortunate fluke. I could just as easily have chosen Boot Black, the horse that finished third. I would have to be prepared in the future, in the past. Tomorrow, I would buy a book and do some research.

I FOUND a bookstore that sold sports almanacs and they would do in a pinch. But it was not what I wanted. It would never do to take a book published in 1992 to a racetrack of 100 years ago. What if someone else were to see it? How would I explain that? No, what I needed was a book that would be inconspicuous, a plainly covered, blank book that I could write in. Something like Kit had taken with him.

On the way out of the bookstore I found it. There among other blank journals was a simple, green volume decorated with a zig-zag trim on its spine. It was so much like Kit's that I had to have it. It was perfect.

I spent the next two months in the library, reviewing the microfilm and taking notes until I had a serious case of writer's cramp. My funds were quickly exhausting themselves, and I knew I had to find employment soon. But "one more day" at the library became another week, and then another month. I had never read racing articles so closely or so carefully. Before I knew it, I had gone completely through all the available reels, all the way through 1992. I stopped and closed the book. It was not filled yet and there was room for more to be written later if I wanted to.

I made a stop at my seldom-used apartment and collected the derby on my way to the racetrack. I came to a halt at the front gates. They were wide open and the crowd of people astonished me. I had no idea that so many people could fit into this small town. Where did they all stay for a month? I was certain there was not enough hotels to accommodate this many racegoers.

An hour later, and still clutching the derby with a death-grip, I reached the grandstands and found an unoccupied corner in which to stand. I wondered what family owned the Vander Holden box these days. I took three deep breaths, checked for the hundredth time to see that I had the book, and gingerly placed the derby on my head.

Suddenly every man in the stands was wearing a white panama hat, a seersucker suit, and a skinny black tie. This was not 1992, nor was it

1885. Where was I? Or more correctly, when was I? My clothes matched theirs, more or less, with the exception of the bowler derby.

I located the book inside the jacket pocket and replaced it quickly as I made my way down from the stands. No sense opening it until I knew what page to turn to anyway. My first task would be to acquire a bit of money.

"Programs!" a young huckster shouted. "Get your programs here." I needed a program desperately, both to discover the date and to review the field. But I had no valid currency, and except for the hat and the book, nothing that I considered valuable enough to pawn. This was going to be a problem! What a Catch-22. I needed money to buy the program and make a bet, but I needed to win a race to get some money.

"Is your name Hathaway?" a familiar voice spoke in my ear. I turned to see an equally familiar face, that of Mason Vander Holden, now in his mid-50s.

"CHRISTOPHER HATHAWAY," I announced my name, then wished I hadn't.

"It can't be," he stared in disbelief at me. "Time has scarcely touched you. How long has it been? More than 30 years!"

"... Junior. Christopher Hathaway Jr." I looked him over, guessing he had put on another 80 pounds since I had last seen him. I would have liked to hug the stuffings out of him, but it was all I could do to pretend I didn't know him. "Do I know you?"

He produced a deep baritone chuckle. "No, I suppose you don't. I knew your father once. We had a wonderful day at the races here back in 1885. I recall the date precisely because it was the day that the horned horse won the Travers Stakes."

"Oh, yes, I remember him speaking of that day to me. You must be then, Mason Vander Holden?"

"Yes, yes indeed. How pleased I am that he told you of me. Is your father here with you? I have so much to tell him." He looked over my shoulder and around the stands, hoping to catch a glimpse of a much older me.

"No, I'm afraid he couldn't attend this year. He wanted to, though, but he had business in ... uh ... Seattle. He said he would have to make do with the horses at the Alan track in Idaho."

"Well, that is a shame!" he harrumphed in well-known tones. He reached into his vest pocket and withdrew a wad of paper money. Peeling off several large bills, he handed the remainder to me.

"What is this for?" I asked the saint who stood before me.

"You'll find $200 there. It's something I owe your father. Will you make sure he receives it?"

I thumbed through the bills, and true to his word, there were ten twenties. "Certainly," I assured him. "But why do you owe it to him?"

"A long time ago he told me to make a bet in the Preakness Stakes. I put my usual $100 wager on him, and would you believe it? The horse won. I got 4-to-1 odds, and I figure your father deserves half."

I smiled uncontrollably. "The Bard."

"Come with me, Hathaway. I've someone I'd like to introduce you to." He took me by the arm, as he had done 30 years ago, and we tramped off toward the rail. The someone he had mentioned turned out to be a raven-haired, young woman clothed in a calf-length white dress and a hat that I felt did nothing to flatter her beautiful features. The dress indicated the late 1910s. The hat, which must have been on the cutting edge of fashion at the time, reminded me of something I had seen my grandmother wear.

She smiled sweetly at me as Vander Holden introduced her to me as his daughter, Anna. I tipped my hat instinctively. I had never tipped a hat to a lady before, but the polite atmosphere was contagious and it seemed inconceivable not to.

As I replaced the derby on my head, it struck me that I had not been immediately transported back to my own time. I was happy that I had not gone, but was also at a loss to understand why the hat was no longer working. Or maybe I had simply not removed it far enough to trigger the jump. Either way, I was thoroughly confused and not paying a bit of attention to my hosts.

"Christopher?" Vander Holden spoke. "Are you all right?"

"I'm sorry?" coming back to the conversation as he spoke my name.

Mason raised an eyebrow. "Does disorientation run in your family?"

I laughed at his smiling eyes. "Yes, I think so." He left us alone at the rail while he searched for liquid refreshment. Anna spoke at length of her father's admiration for mine while I stole a look at her racing program. August 13, 1919. How strange. That was the day of Man o' War's loss in the Sanford, the first page I had written in the green book. I had started with that date because Kit had. Strange that I should have arrived on that same date. I had been thinking about that first page when I put the hat on. Maybe that was the secret to determining the arrival date. Had I been thinking about 1885 two months ago?

Anna was still talking politely about one of the horses on today's card and what a sin it was that he should have to carry 130 pounds even though he was only two years old.

"I'm sorry?" I came back into the conversation. "Who's carrying 130 pounds?"

"Why, Man o' War is! Don't you read the papers?"

"Man o' War?" I feigned ignorance and thumbed through the program looking for the day's fourth race in which he would run.

She was shocked with incredulity. "Don't you know who Man o' War is?"

I pondered the question. "Isn't he that brother of Masda that's been doing so well lately?"

"Doing so well? He's undefeated!" She looked into my eyes, and I saw a smile start to form. "You're just teasing me, aren't you?" She laughed, and a blush spread over her cheeks.

"According to this," I waved the program slightly, "he's won with 130 before. And he's not the only juvenile in the race with that impost. Golden Broom gets 130 today also." I read from the program and felt chills at the names of the racers and their pedigrees. Man o' War by Fair Play out of Mahubah, by Rock Sand. Golden Broom by Sweeper out of Zuna, by Hamburg. Captain Alcock by Ogden out of Mallard, by Star Shoot. I never dared to dream that I would read those words in a program.

The program indicated that Captain Alcock, if he ran at all today, would do so as an added starter. However, the entry of Man o' War had frightened away enough of the other scheduled competitors, Peace Pennant among them, that Alcock would be given the chance to compete against the soon-to-be champion.

Vander Holden returned, looking much refreshed, and told me excitedly that Captain Alcock could be had for nearly 200-to-1 on the totes! I calmed him down and explained that a late-running horse like that would have little chance at six furlongs, and no chance at all against the likes of Upset and Man o' War.

"But Man o' War's at 9-to-10. I can't make any decent profit on odds like that!" he protested.

"If you bet Man o' War to win, you won't make any profit at all," I stated calmly.

Anna had heard and now thought me to be entirely bonkers. "Man o' War not win? Of course he'll win! He's undefeated. He beat Upset 11 days ago, and carrying 15 pounds more besides."

I shrugged. "Upset will win." She laughed in my face and announced that she was going at that moment to place her $5 on Man o' War and that it was as safe as in a bank. Meanwhile, Vander Holden studied my face and saw that I was entirely serious.

"Where's the best value?" he asked quietly.

"Upset to win. Should be about 10-to-1 right now." He commented again that I was the image of my "father" and he could not possibly turn down my tip after the killing he made on The Bard.

Ten minutes later, the famous race was about to start. Man o' War looked great, but smaller than I had imagined him. I had seen photographs of the legendary runner, but had always envisioned him as towering over his rivals. He walked by me, alert and eager, but no larger than the rest of them. I had to remind myself that he was only a juvenile. There was a gleam in his eyes I had not expected, and I heard him snorting and champing at the bit as he passed by. He was alive and real. He was ten feet in front of me and he was real! Vander Holden looked nervous as he watched the epitome of equine physique parade past.

As they went to the start, I was more and more aware of my pulse. They lined up at the tape as the thunder of my heartbeat pounded in my ears. Man o' War was still circling behind the others, about to come into position when the tape flew upward and the horses bolted away from him. Surprised at the unexpected start, he gathered himself together and shot like a bullet toward the departing pack. He caught the late-running Captain Alcock and The Swimmer before he had gone 30 yards and was pointed at the leaders.

After two furlongs, he had worked his way up to fifth and was skimming the rail to save every inch of ground. Armistice, in fourth, decided on the same route and trapped the chestnut champion on the rail. Johnny Loftus pulled up severely on Man o' War to avoid a collision and maneuvered him around the troublesome colt.

Upset and Golden Broom had swapped first place a number of times already, and Golden Broom currently claimed the lead with Upset only a half-length behind him and pressing hard. Donnacona, whom Man o' War would humiliate in the Belmont Stakes next year, was third, and the favorite, having shook Armistice, was now fourth. The Swimmer had only one horse beaten and that was Captain Alcock who was still trailing the leaders by a dozen lengths.

They swung into the homestretch toward the deafening roar of the crowd. Vander Holden and I watched in silence as the drama unfolded, while Anna and a thousand others shouted for Man o' War.

He drew toward the leaders, third now and closing with every jump. Upset led at this point and appeared to be unwilling to let anyone pass him. Golden Broom was falling behind. The 130 pounds he bore was proving too much. Captain Alcock was finally in gear and flew up from the back of the pack, passing horses one by one, but it was apparent that he had no real hope of reaching the leaders.

Only Man o' War was within striking distance of Upset. Every stride brought him nearer to the leader. Two lengths away. A length and a half. One length away. He had reached Upset! Half a length to go! But there was not enough time. Upset crossed the line. Man o' War had lost.

The crowd stood in shock as Vander Holden celebrated. Anna turned to face me in surprise. "How did you know?" was all she could say for the next several minutes.

Mason was positively buoyant. "Did you see that Upset? What a horse!"

He knew as well as I that, had Man o' War been given a fair start, he would have won easily. But something in me was happy for Upset and Harry Payne Whitney who owned him. Upset was a good horse. Had it not been for Man o' War running in the same year, Upset would have been a great horse. He would win a few other major victories and finish a close second to Man o' War in the Preakness.

I had seen it all before in Secretariat and Sham. I thought back to the Belmont of 1973. While elated with the thrill of Secretariat's victory, I remembered feeling a strange pang of disappointment for Sham. It seemed ironic that I should have witnessed the races in this irregular order. Upset's win today struck a blow for all the Shams of the world.

The greatest irony was that in all the excitement, I had forgotten to place a bet myself.

After the sixth race, in which we found value in the show horse, we retired to the clubhouse and Mason treated us all to dinner. I told Anna that I knew someone in Saratoga Springs with her first name, and who would be about her age, but failed to mention that it was Grand-mama Hathaway.

She confessed to also having known a Christopher elsewhere, but I was nothing like him. She spoke most unpleasantly of the other Christopher and to be honest she wished I didn't have the same name. Through a spoonful of soup, I suggested that she call me something else. She said she would call me Kit.

I dropped the spoon.

A FEW hours later I removed the derby, but it required another 20 minutes of hard concentration to get home. Whatever the hat had, it was losing it.

I sat in my quiet apartment considering the events of the day. I was not merely a person who looked like Kit, carried a book like Kit's, and wore Kit's bowler derby. I was Kit. Anna called me Kit. She was Grand-mama Anna, or would be. Helen was my granddaughter. That is why I had seen resemblances between us.

I had come home to sort things out. The Kit revelation had left me virtually senseless. The thought of being trapped in 1919 had been terrifying at the time, but now, being there seemed the most natural thing in the world. I had the derby in my hands and if there were any magic left in it, it had to make just one more trip.

I had no family, at least not yet, so there was no one to say goodbyes to. I brought the book and hat to the front gates of the track. Racing would not begin for hours, so no one was around. I tucked the book into my pocket and put on the hat slowly. Cars streamed by for over a half-hour. With closed eyes, I tried to picture 1919 and Man o' War and Anna Vander Holden.

Eventually, the mist of the 1990s lifted, revealing the reality of 1919. I rushed through the elms toward the stands. I had made it home! The pieces finally fit.

Dearest Anna,

This will be the final entry in my journal, my darling, for I shall die tomorrow. Use this book as I have shown you. There will be adequate pages to cover the remainder of your years. I have been blessed with the wonderful gift of living a perpetual existence with you. But I must leave now, for I will be born in a few days, and will direct my life to that moment when I return to you in 1919. If you must abandon all else, keep this journal and my bowler derby. I will need them again. Promise me that you will tear this page from the journal. This letter was meant only for your eyes.

I used to believe that racing was my destiny and reason for being. Although I shall never lose my fondness for the sport, with its thrilling dramas, tragedies, and ironies, it is not my reason for being. That, my darling, is you. I have loved you, and will love you, forever.

The Passing of the Torch

by Avalyn Hunter

They will come back—come back again—
As long as the red earth rolls.
He never wasted a leaf or a tree,
Do you think He would squander souls?
—Rudyard Kipling

THE OLD HORSE shifted restlessly in the thick straw of his stall, his legs twitching as he dreamed. Abruptly, he woke, listening, then heaved himself to his feet, disregarding the old, arthritic aching in his knees and ankles. The dull clank of a water-filled bucket being hung in place sounded loud in the quiet, old barn, a relic of other days that was now filled mostly with memories, living and otherwise. Like himself. He swished his tail, feeling the straw caught in it tickling his hocks, and pricked his ears toward Thundercloud's stall.

As he had anticipated, an elderly human emerged in a moment, flipping a rag playfully at the once-gray head—now white with age—that poked out after him with a mischievous attempt at a nip.

"Hey, you! Git back there. You done had your rub, an' you cain't have this rag neither. I still got ol' Torchbearer to rub."

He got the door safely latched in spite of the gray's half-hearted attempt to shoulder past him, and gave an affectionate tug on the animal's forelock.

"You just git back an' eat your breakfast," he ordered. "Mebbe later, if it ain't too cold, I can take you out on a shank an' let you graze a bit. Y'all could use it, I's sure; it's been an awful long winter."

As if he understood, Thundercloud's head bobbed once before vanishing back into his stall. In a moment, the steady sounds of munching drifted out, as they had already been doing from the other two occupied stalls. Torchbearer's nostrils flared at the scent of grain as the old groom refilled a bucket from the bin in the tack room next to his stall, but he did not feel accompanying hunger as he would have even a few days ago, only a sluggish dullness in his belly.

When the man unlatched his stall door and stepped inside, he moved aside patiently and stood, waiting. He heard the rustle as the oats poured out of the bucket and into his feed box, and after the man had taken his water bucket and gone out to fill it, he turned and nosed the grain languidly, but did not begin eating. The short, shuffling footsteps came back, and the scent of water trailed into the stall as the bucket was rehung in its place in the corner. He flicked his ears as the man whistled slowly through his teeth, a soft, easy sound, before pulling the curry comb from his pocket and beginning the job of grooming.

"This is the third day runnin' that you ain't hardly touched your feed, Torch. You ain't sickening, is you, boy?"

The curry comb moved behind the withers, scratching an itchy spot that Torchbearer had not been able to reach for himself, and the old stallion leaned into the strokes with a contented sigh. He turned his head slightly, listening to the flow of talk, though he understood none of it.

"Time was when you had to have a bridle on when you got your feed, to keep you from givin' yousself the colic with your gulpin'. But now you ain't eatin'. And you been lyin' down an awful lot lately, too. Now, don't tell me you hasn't," he added as Torchbearer shook his mane, trying to dislodge a particularly annoying piece of straw.

The man reached over and pulled the offending straw away.

"Used to be that I'd come in here and you'd be the first one stickin' your head out the stall door. Now I comes in an' you're laid out flat. Dreamin', mebbe."

He worked in silence for awhile, then dropped brush and comb into the empty feed bucket.

"Well, you're done, boy. I'll look in on you later."

He gave the old horse an affectionate and worried slap on the neck, then shuffled out. Torchbearer listened a moment longer as the slow, uncertain footsteps receded, nosed his feed disinterestedly, and let the weariness of the last few days wash back over him. With a long, slow sigh, he laid down again in the straw, and the dreams rolled over him like a rising tide. ...

Sometimes the dreams were of other lives, other days. Like dim, half-remembered shadows, he felt the legs of a Mongol warrior around his barrel and heard the wild cries as they met the Kharesmian lines with lance and sword. ... Saw the other stallion, a paint, challenging for his mares, and feinted and bit and kicked in the ancient war dance of his kind until the other fled over the Western prairie with head and tail low. ... Felt the weight behind him as he leaned into the collar and pulled the great wagon. ... And once, tasted sugar in a child's hand as he peered at his young mistress through a pony's thick forelock.

But, more often, and far more vividly, he dreamed of more recent days, when he had been young and strong, and the men had fussed over him like the king he was, leading him out to be shown to others of their kind, or taking him to the shed where the mares waited.

He grunted deep in his throat, remembering the urgency and the pleasure. But it had been long seasons since he had gone to the shed. He stirred, his legs twitching, and the old pain in his legs half-roused him before he settled back into sleep. It had been a long time, a long time indeed since he had taken a step without that nagging pain. ... His legs stirred again, but this time the pain never touched him as he fled far into memory.

VOICES WOKE him suddenly from a slack-hipped doze: low voices, sharp-edged with an unfamiliar urgency. He snorted softly, uneasy. The barn had been filled for several days now with the smell and feel of tension: not danger, precisely, but an undefined something that kept him from lying down to sleep or ever completely relaxing. It had not helped at all that the unseasonable cold had kept him stall-bound for two days, leaving him with entirely too much pent-up energy. No bits of apple or carrot, no visits from the sweet-voiced, soft-handed woman that the grooms called the "Missus." He missed that. And now these voices, moving down the shedrow much earlier than the normal hour. Small things, all, but upsetting to the sensitive colt. He pawed the floor of his stall, and snorted like a rifle shot when his door swung open.

He knew the humans who came in, of course; even in his unsettled state of mind, he had a nicker and a nudge of his nose for old Smoke, the ex-jockey who usually rode him in his morning workouts. But this time Smoke did not return the affectionate gesture. He turned to the boy beside him.

"He fit? Nothin' wrong with him?"

The young groom—little more than a half-grown boy—bobbed his head as he slipped on Torchbearer's bridle and clipped a lead to the bit.

"Fit as a fiddle, suh, and full of hisself. You sure Mistah Sanford want him out, though? At this hour?"

"He said saddle the best horse in the stable and git ready to ride with a message," the old rider snapped. "Torchy's the best. Lead him over by that mountin' block, will you, so's I can get the saddle on."

"But he's only a colt! What 'bout Foxfire?"

Smoke snorted. "Fust time I'se ever seen a groom say the hoss he rubs ain't the best! Torchy could give Foxfire ten lengths over a mile and beat him, even if Foxfire is risin' five. 'Sides, Foxfire won't stay the trip we's got to ride." His voice softened. "I know—you're worried 'bout this here colt, ain't you? Well, so's I. But it's got to be him. Mistah Sanford said it was life an' death."

The boy's eyes widened to two saucers. "Where you goin'?"

"Doctor's," Smoke answered tersely. "Hold him steady, now."

Torchbearer had seen excitement in Smoke many times before, but never fear. The smell of it was acrid in his nostrils as the old rider laid the saddlecloth on his back. Nervous, he danced sideways, causing the boy at his head to take a sharper grip on his bridle to bring him back beside the mounting block. Once on, the saddle felt strange, and he shifted about, his ears flickering.

"That ain't his regular saddle," the boy objected.

"No, it ain't." Smoke's breath came out of him in a sharp grunt as he tugged the cinch tight. "But a racin' saddle ain't good for long ridin', and it ain't got no place to fasten a saddlebag. This ol' Army saddle does."

The boy's eyes widened. "You useta be in the Army?"

Smoke tugged the saddlecloth smooth and gave the girth another inspection. "Now, when would I have been in de Army, boy? This was my uncle's. He went west fo' a Buffalo Soldier after the war—brought this with him when he got mustered out. Just lucky it fits ol' Torchy here well enough."

"But why—"

Footsteps hurried toward them, cutting off the boy's question in mid-breath. "It's Mistah Sanford!" he whispered, his eyes going from saucers to dinner plates. “At this time o’ the night? What’s goin’ on?”

“Didn’t you hear nuthin’? It’s Miz Sanford—shhh!” The ex-jockey straightened respectfully as his employer came up. “He’s ready, suh. Sweet Lord, you all right? You looks like a ghost.”

The white man choked on what sounded like a sob before mastering himself. “Never mind me. Here’s your message.”

Torchbearer sniffed curiously as a paper passed from the white hand to the brown one, releasing a faint, familiar scent of vanilla and roses as it was handled.

The old rider tucked the note into his jacket and vaulted from the mounting block to the saddle. Freed from the ground lead, Torchbearer danced expectantly. “Ground’s hard as a rock, suh. Hope this don’t ruin him—there’s a lot ridin’ on him this spring, ain’t there?”

“Can’t be helped, Smoke.” The white man’s face was agonized, but his voice was firm. “Don’t spare him. It’s Death you’re racin’ tonight, and if it takes this colt to bring the doctor back, do it! God speed, Smoke—if you an’ Torchbearah can’t fetch him in time, no one can.”

“Yessuh!” Legs squeezed against Torchbearer’s sides, sending him forward, and suddenly he was galloping out into the night, away from the stables, away from the track, away from everything he knew. He shook his head, confused, then lengthened his stride as the wild exhilaration of speed began to take over.

“Steady, Torchy.” He flicked an ear back to catch the familiar voice, and felt the supple touch on the reins. “We got the turn onto the road to make. Steady, now—”

The hands gathered him in and he slowed, changing leads to negotiate the turn. Frozen clods skittered from underfoot as he fought for purchase and won. He snorted, the frosty air cracking in his nostrils, and lengthened stride again as he straightened into the road. Now he could run! He picked up speed, surging into the bridle, and felt a vague sense of disappointment when he was checked.

"Not so fast, boy," Smoke's voice said along his neck. "Got to pace you—it's seven miles out and seven back. Mov'n 'bout a two-fifteen clip, an' you'll be done before the trip is. We won't help the Missus by lamin' you before we git to doctor's place."

The words meant nothing, of course, but the calming tone and the gentle, immovable hold on the reins did. Torchbearer pulled a moment more, begging for more speed, then resigned himself and settled to a steady gallop.

Luckily, the dirt road was smooth, with only a few small dips and holes. Torchbearer ran easily, his blood pounding with the rhythm of his long stride: the coiled thrust of strong loins and haunches; the stretch of long forelimbs reaching for ground and then sweeping under him as the haunches gathered for their next leap; the bellows-sweep of air in and out of his lungs; the familiar feel of Smoke balanced on his back, almost as much a part of him as his own muscles.

The wind rushed by, washing away any sense of time; it was almost with surprise that the colt saw lights blooming out of the darkness, and Smoke's hands pulled him up in a lantern-lit courtyard. A Negro boy scurried out of the little stable, his mouth making an "O" of surprise. Smoke didn't waste time on conversation. He swung his leg over Torchbearer's back and slid to the ground, flinging the reins to the startled boy.

"Keep him moving," he said curtly, and ran to the door, pounding briefly before it opened and he vanished inside.

Torchbearer circled uneasily, ignoring the feeble clucking sounds that the boy was making to soothe him. Another horse whinnied from the stable; he ignored that, too. Now that he was no longer galloping, he could feel the stinging in his legs from pounding the hard-packed, unyielding surface of the road: nothing severe, but uncomfortable. Steam rose from him in a cloud, and he shivered, feeling the wind searching his sweaty sides. He switched his tail sharply, his ears flicking as he tried to make some vague sense of it all.

The door reopened abruptly, sending Smoke and another man, tall and white, spilling out into the courtyard. Torchbearer stopped his circling and pricked his ears as they approached, his nostrils dilating with an unfamiliar prickling scent. It came from both men—or did it?

"You're sure you want me to take him?" the stranger asked as Smoke threw loaded saddlebags across the colt's back. "He's already come a long way to get here, and this frozen road has to have been rough on his legs. Lucy's fresh."

Smoke stood on tiptoe, fastening the bags. "Mistah Sanford said so, suh. An' you know he's faster'n Lucy, fresh or not. If he cain't get you there'n time, ain't no hoss can. Now git up there! I'll bring Lucy 'long behin' fo' you."

The stranger mounted, and Torchbearer danced nervously as he felt the unfamiliar hands gather up the reins. The prickling smell was stronger, filling him with uneasiness. Then the man loosed his hold on his mouth and he was away, back up the road by which he had come.

No easy gallop, this time; Torchbearer felt the urgency of his rider, and responded with such a surge that a blur of words gasped out and the reins tightened. But this man, though a good rider, was not the master Smoke was. The colt pounded on, faster, faster, until he reached the limit that his flesh would endure, until his lungs and legs burned with pain. But the prickling scent came faster still, rising along the wind.

Hoofbeats sounded in Torchbearer's mind, galloping, galloping. And out of the wind, out of the vague starlight, the other horse came: a pale horse, the merest of flickers in the colt's side vision, but gaining. The strange scent was tenfold stronger now, as if it had found its focus in the horse, or perhaps in the black-cloaked rider that bestrode him. ...

Animals do not fear Death the way Man does, for they lack the anticipation that makes him a horror to our kind. But Torchbearer felt an apprehension strange to him nonetheless as the pale horse and its dark rider surged closer, now at his haunches, now at his girth, now at his neck.

He dug in stubbornly, the inbred desire for dominance greater than any fear. The pale horse's advance slowed, slowed ... but still on it came, inch by painful inch. Half a mile, perhaps, to go—breath burning in his lungs, eyes glazing with effort.

He slewed into the farm lane with a great scrambling of hooves, barely keeping his feet. The pale horse was nose to nose with him, moving as easily as the ghost it was; yet it could not shake him, though his feet and lungs both screamed with pain. All through the last two furlongs to the barns, he battled on, refusing to quit even after the pale head thrust in front and slowly, slowly crept away.

Lights and buildings loomed out of the darkness, and suddenly he was hurtling toward a solid wall of people. The weight on his back shifted back, and hands pulled hard at his mouth, bringing him to a desperate, slicing stop as the grooms and servants scattered; then the man flung himself from the saddle, grabbed his bags, and hurried toward the house. Torchbearer watched him go with dull disinterest. It did not matter, any more than the fussing of his groom or the excited swirling of the other humans. The long race was over, and he had been beaten. Now there was only pain, and the waiting.

Before him, just below the steps, the pale horse waited also, riderless. ...

News came with the dawn, and it was the master himself who brought it. He came stumbling to Torchbearer's stall like a blind man, nearly kicking the bucket of icewater in which the colt's near forefoot soaked before Smoke could steady him. Torchbearer scarcely took notice, his attention consumed by the pain that throbbed from hoof to knee in both forelegs.

"How is he?" the white man asked, his voice rough and unsteady.

Smoke shook his head slowly, his eyes wet. "Bad, suh. I sent Two-Bit fo' the vet, but I'se seen enough bowed tendons to know this one ain't goin to heal enough to race again. He done foundered, too. Mebbe we can save him fo' stud, but his racin's done fo' sure."

The man reached out a trembling hand to stroke the colt's rough, black mane. "I'm sorry, boy. You did your best, I know. But death had the heels of you. Death had the heels of you!" He stifled a sob as Smoke locked gazes with him, a terrible understanding in his eyes.

Outside, on the edge of hearing, hoofbeats passed by. Torchbearer did not need to look to know what—or who—moved slowly away. Only this time, the pale horse carried a double burden.

The hoofbeats faded, and were gone.

OR WERE they? Memory shaded into present awareness of the sharp, ringing sounds of a horse's feet on hard ground. They were coming back, stronger, faster; in fact, they were stopping just outside his stall door. He felt a shiver go through his frame, and stirred feebly in the straw. Outside, he heard the soft rustle and thump of someone dismounting, and then the lighter steps of a riderless horse fading away.

"Torchy! Hey, Torchy!"

His eyes flew open, and in a sudden rush of energy, he bounded to his feet—ignoring the worn and useless shell he left in the straw. With a joyful whicker, he stretched his head out to the man who waited across the stall door for him. It was Smoke, unmistakably Smoke, but somehow changed from the worn, old man he had last known years ago. Bent and crippled with age at their last meeting, now he was a shining and ageless god from whom boundless energy flowed. Torchbearer whuffled affectionately against his chest, feeling the loved hand scratching just behind the ears where he had always liked it.

Smoke grinned, showing teeth that would have been the envy of any pearl fishery. "So you remember me, do you, boy? It's been a long time—if you can say there's any time here, that is. And it's high time you were free from this life." He vaulted to the horse's back. "Let's go, Torchy!"

He reared eagerly, troubling his laughing rider not in the least, and sprang away through barn walls that faded like smoke even as he leaped.

In their place, green meadows surged and billowed like waves around his knees, and the ground had a glorious give to it that invited speed and more speed. He neighed joyously as he ran, feeling the effortless give and play of his muscles and the current of delight between himself and the man. It was marvelous, this new sensation of boundless, inexhaustible speed and energy, and when he pulled himself up, it was not for weariness, but for the simple joy of the change.

"You like it?" Smoke's voice asked as the man slid from his back. He snorted his agreement; odd, now, how the sounds suddenly made sense. "These are the Summerfields, where beasts go 'tween times—though they usually don't stay long."

Torchbearer's ears flicked a question at him. "You want to know where you're going?" Smoke grinned. "Why do you think I'se here? I did want to jus' have a visit with you, but I'm also yo' guide."

The horse reached out mischievous teeth, nipping, and danced away, clearly inviting a game. Smoke laughed, but did not follow.

"Sorry, Torchy. I'd like to play, but our time here's growin' short, and I'se got other work to do. And so do you, now I think 'bout it. Come on, boy. I'll show you where you's 'sposed to go." He walked away, down the long gold-and-green meadow, and Torchbearer followed.

They walked what seemed a long way through the sweet-scented, rolling grass. The horse sensed rather than saw the change at first: a faint wavering in the golden air that gradually coalesced into a passageway of glowing green. He looked an inquiry at the man, who understood.

"Yes, boy. That's it. You just walk in there, and the rest will follow." He looked up at the golden sky, his eyes full of something that even now Torchbearer could not understand, and then looked back at the horse. "It's time, Torchy. Go on."

The green glow pulled at something deep inside the horse, beckoning. He took a step forward, then hesitated, looking back at Smoke. The man laughed softly.

"No, boy. I cain't go with you, not this time. You see, Adam's chilluns, we only passes through the world once, and then them that believes goes home to Jesus, hallelujah! But hosses, they's bound to the earth till world's end, and they pass through agin and agin."

Smoke laughed again, a rich, deep laugh that rippled the grass and set the light itself dancing.

"In the ordinary way o' things, the turn of the wheel's a mite random, and you could come up as anything from a cart-horse to an Injun pony. But I asked a favor for you, Torchy. You gave your racin' life fo' one of my kind, though you couldn't understand that. Now, you'll get it back ... and this time, the world'll get to see the racehorse you was born to be. So go on, big fella. It's waitin' for you down there, and I think you're goin' to like it."

Smoke's hand clapped him on the haunches, and Torchbearer found himself—walking?—no, drifting into the green passage. As he slid forward, the walls constricted and darkened, and a strange feeling came over him: not frightening, but oddly familiar. The last of the green shimmered down into black, and waves of pressure rippled along his sides with increasing immediacy and intensity as the darkness closed around him. He found himself stretching his neck out along his forelegs as though he was diving, and felt himself impelled forward ...

Light! Not the golden light of the Summerfields, but brilliant enough after his journey through the darkness. A firm grip on his ankles pulled him further, and suddenly he was out, lying on warm straw, and shaking and snorting his head to clear his nostrils of fluid. Beside him, a dark mare nosed him interestedly and licked his rough new coat, then heaved herself to her feet.

She gave off a rich, promising scent that filled him with an instinctive need, and he wobbled to his feet. His legs sprawled awkwardly, and the two men watching him laughed as he fell in a tangle, but before they could move he was back up and wavering to his dam's side. Hungry lips fumbled for, then found, the teat, and in the urgency of his first meal, the other life he had known faded away, until there was only the here and now. At last, his small belly filled, he collapsed into the straw and slept, and if he dreamed, he did not remember. ...

"WELL, what do you think of him, my dear?" the man asked his wife.

She smiled, watching the chestnut colt playing beside his mother. "Oh, Mahubah's done well by us, I think. Such a big, strong rascal, and only two days old!"

She laughed as the colt frisked up to her where she stood by the fence, sniffing at her outstretched fingertips, and then whisked behind his mother in a sudden fit of shyness. The mare flicked her ears and continued grazing, unperturbed by her son's antics. After a moment, the colt's white-starred head peeked out from behind his dam's haunches, and then he was suddenly off, bucking and kicking as both humans laughed.

"Well, what do you think of him, Mr. Belmont?" the woman challenged, her eyes twinkling impishly.

"Hmmm, he does seem lively enough, and a good-looking fellow, too," the man observed. "I'd certainly like to continue working with the Fair Play—*Rock Sand cross; we've had a couple of good ones out of it already, and the trainer says this colt's sister, Masda, looks to have a lot of speed if he can only settle her temper. She's a bit of a Tartar, it seems. By the way, dear, I did promise you that you could name the next one; now that you've seen him, do you have any ideas yet?"

"Oh, I don't know." The March wind chose that moment to send a chill gust blowing over the nursery pastures, and the woman drew in closer to her mate, who obligingly draped an arm around her shoulders. She looked up at him, her face half laughing and half serious.

"Since those awful Germans started the war in Europe, and you've talked a good deal about rejoining the Army—well, if you do, perhaps I'll name him after you, my man o' war."

"Man o' War?" he said, tasting the name consideringly. "I like that. It has a good ring to it; a name people could remember."

The woman tucked herself in closer under her husband's arm as they turned away from the pasture and started the walk back to the house. "Oh, they will, love. They will."

MR. BOJANGLES

Mr. Bo's Last Dance

by Alan P. Henry

THERE'S a special sound a frigid October downpour makes in a maple forest: a kind of muffled, frantic roar caused by rain pelting dead and dying leaves. There's a special smell, too. A slight mustiness, yes. But a cleansing odor as well, made all the more so at dusk, as the raw night air rolls in.

So it was as the three darkened figures stood shoulder to shoulder, bodies hunkered against the storm, at the wooded edge of the paddock-sized clearing. All three wore hooded parkas and beat-up rubber boots. None spoke, preferring instead to stare quietly down at the muddy burial mound spread before them, and the glistening black marble tombstone behind it.

Words later. Private thoughts now.

The stone had been Jed Porter's idea. At 77, and with a bum ticker, such things had been heavy on his mind lately. And besides, he hated those flat grave markers. "Seems to me a final resting place deserves something upright, something proud," he'd told the local mason a week earlier. "And make sure you gimme one with some space on it. I got a few things to say."

The mason knew Jed well enough to know he couldn't have paid for such an extravagance. Forty years of collecting tolls on the New York State Thruway had left the gaunt, craggy-faced old man just enough pension to afford a simple lifestyle and basic upkeep on his two-room cabin and small barn a hundred yards up the hill from the grave.

No, the money for the stone was Claire Pemberton's contribution. Only a year out of Cal State, she was already into low six figures and climbing at a Seattle computer firm. "The bill's mine," she'd insisted, when Jed called with the news of Mr. Bojangles's death. "After what that old boy did for me, it's the very least I can do."

Then there was Hutch Griffin's part. Sixteen years earlier, he more or less had adopted the two-year-old colt. Now, the barrel-chested Finger Lakes trainer figured it was his duty to bury him.

It had taken Hutch's considerable ingenuity, and the brute strength of three farm hands from down the road, to dig the hole in the rocky earth and move the body into it. The farmers had never buried a horse before. But the job had been done, neatly, and on time. Claire, flying in for the occasion, had requested sunset as the time to convene. And sunset it was.

For ten minutes, as the rain poured on, the unlikely trio remained silent. Claire, whose ready tears mixed freely with the water streaming down her face, was the first to audibly address the dead. "I'll always love you, Mr. Bo. Always."

Jed followed, his voice wavering at the edges. "I figure I'll be seein' you soon, Mr. Bo, makin' that bran mash just the way you like it. We'll find ourselves some of them Granny Smiths, too. As many as you want."

Hutch figured he'd better say something next, though he didn't know what that would be, until it just sort of blurted out of his mouth. "The hell with all this funeral talk," he snapped. "We shouldn't be standing here despairing over Mr. Bo's death. We should be remembering the good times, and being thankful for what he did for each of us when our turn came to take care of him."

Another moment of silence passed, as Hutch's words took the others somewhat by surprise. Then Jed spoke up again, this time resolutely. "You know what, Hutch is right. I've got a jug of brew and a pot of hot chili back up at the cabin. I say we go drain 'em both and send Mr. Bo off in style."

Hearing no argument, and suddenly overcome by a sense of eagerness, Jed turned away from the grave and led the group single file onto a trail that quickly disappeared into the forest night. "We've got a lot of storytelling to do tonight," whooped a newly spirited Claire from the rear of the line. "We sure do," Jed shouted at the darkness ahead of him. "A lot of manure to shovel!"

Back in the now-empty clearing, a gust of wind blew a swatch of dead maple leaves in a swirl around the tombstone. Some of the leaves slapped up against the stone's polished base. Others pressed atop the mound, and into the mud.

AS PROMISED, the pungent aroma of simmering onions and chili powder greeted Jed, Hutch, and Claire as they walked into the cabin and shook off the weather. A maple log fire supplied light and warmth.

Spare would have been a charitable way to describe Jed's plank and shingle home. A big old ragamuffin green sofa, flanked by a couple of rickety wood rockers and a standing lamp circled the face of the large stone fireplace. A pile of black and magenta horse blankets lay stacked on a cot in one corner. A propane stove, a relic of a refrigerator, and an old wooden cabinet stood in another. The fire completed the decor. Always, the fire. Jed couldn't very well fix the leaky roof anymore, but he could still split wood. And the feel of a fire pleased him. More than that, actually. It kept him company.

"Help yourselves to food and drink and relax," demanded Jed, as he threw another log on the glowing embers. Hutch and Claire complied, and took their places in the rockers. Then Jed poured himself a double into a glass jelly jar and sank into the stuffed sofa.

What to say, where to begin, Jed and Claire momentarily wondered to themselves. Not Hutch. He knew where to begin. At the start, which meant the 1979 Genesee Valley Breeders Association fall sale for horses of all ages. Hutch had kept the sales catalog all these years, and had brought it along because he didn't think Jed had ever seen it.

"Why, you sentimental old pack rat," laughed Jed, as he gently thumbed the catalog's yellowed pages. "Let's see what we've got here."

Neverwas—Neverwillbe, by Neverheardof. That's not exactly how the sales brochure listed the breeding of the bay colt identified as Lot #36. But it would have been close. The colt's sire, Ivan the Terrible, and dam, Cathy O, had singularly undistinguished careers. Black type, what little existed, was three generations removed.

"Why in hell did you want this one?" Jed wondered out loud, as he scanned the page, looking in vain for clues to genetic worthiness.

"Well, I'll tell you," Hutch shot back. "The auctioneer started at $500, then dropped to $250, then to $100. No one made a sound. The colt was smallish and back in the knees. He had a short hip. And the owner hadn't even given him a registered name. I figured all that made him worth zero. Seeing as how I'd just gotten my training license back, zero was all I could afford, so that's the offer I made, and damned if the owner didn't take it after the sale ended. I guess he figured he was cutting his losses. As for me, I'm not sure what I was figuring. Another shot, I guess."

Another shot, indeed. In 1974, the New York Racing Board had banned Hutch Griffin from training for five years. They'd said the small-time conditioner was hooked up in a race-fixing scam at Finger Lakes. Not true, he'd said. Even his two alleged co-conspirators called him innocent. No matter. Justice, or the lack of it, needed doing. At age 38, he was gone, and so, shortly thereafter, was his wife. And when the ban was up, he was still gone. No one with a horse to train wanted to get near him.

The subject was not one Hutch liked to talk about. But now, as Claire and Jed hunched toward him, it somehow seemed a comfortable thing to do, and so he continued. "I had no job, no prospects, and no owners beating down my door. But I still had the desire, I still went to all the sales, and there was just something about the look in that colt's eye when I checked him out before the auction that told me he had some guts inside.

"Nobody else wanted to take a chance on me, and nobody else wanted to take a chance on him. I kind of figured that made us a team. Besides, neither of us had anything to lose by at least trying."

"And the name?" Claire asked. "You've never really told me why you named him Mr. Bojangles."

"That was easy," said Hutch. "I'd gotten a stall back at Finger Lakes, and the first morning I had him, I just wanted to take him out for a short gallop. You know, to see what kind of way he had about him. It had rained hard the night before and the track was total soup, so I was wrapped up on him real good. And what he did when he got out there on that water has stuck with me ever since. Just like Mr. Bojangles did in the song, when he ran, 'He lightly touched down.' It was like all the other horses were slopping around in hip boots, and he was dancing on air. I had him named before we hit the far turn."

"C'mon, Hutch, get to the winning," Jed loudly interrupted, reaching for a refill from the jug.

"I am, I am," Hutch barked back. "So there's Mr. Bo, which is what everybody in the barn started calling him right away, with the usual 'baby' problems: fever, skin rashes, that sort of thing. He really was an ungainly looking thing, but I kept believing that if I could hold him together, the way he skipped across the track would some day count for something.

"In the meantime, I'm working nights at the country store back home in Websters Crossing to pay the bills. And then comes the first Saturday in May 1980. Not at Churchill Downs, but at Finger Lakes. What a day."

Hutch paused for another gulp, then quickly got back to it. "The talk was all about whether Genuine Risk could beat the boys in the Derby. Not by me, though. Mr. Bojangles in the third. New York-bred maiden specials at six furlongs. A sloppy track, just like the one I first galloped him over. Man, it was perfect. He just did that dance, wire-to-wire, and it was all over. Those other horses, they didn't know what hit 'em. Then we came back in three weeks, on a fast track this time, and Mr. Bo did it all over again."

He didn't have to go on. As Mr. Bo's racing career took off, Hutch kept a scrapbook containing newspaper articles chronicling the horse's successes. And each time, in later years, that Hutch, Jed, and Claire crossed paths, the leather-bound volume inevitably came out.

This night was no exception. In the unlikely event that Jed or Claire had forgotten any of the details, Hutch happily began turning the scrapbook pages on the floor before them, in front of the fire.

"Local Trainer Rides Comeback Trail," trumpeted the headline in Hutch's hometown weekly, the Websters Crossing *Gazette*, after Mr. Bojangles had won the sixth sprint of his three-year-old season, racking up $58,000 in winnings under the black and magenta colors of his owner's newly coined Dime-A-Dance Stables.

"Rags to riches: Mr. Bojangles Keeps on Dancin'," *The Thoroughbred Record* headline read a year later, following Mr. Bo's fifth consecutive win at Finger Lakes, this one a $35,000 overnight stakes. A paragraph toward the end of the story bore good news as well: "Griffin now conditions 15 horses for five owners, thanks to Mr. Bojangles's success."

"Mr. Bo goes to Saratoga," the *Daily Telegraph* wrote in August 1982, as the five-year-old was again on a Finger Lakes win streak.

"You must have felt like you were in heaven when you made that trip," said Claire, seeing the clipping once again.

"Yes, I believe I did feel that way," Hutch grinned. "I think Mr. Bo had won about 17 or 18 races by then. A stakes, a whole bunch of six- and seven-furlong conditioned allowance races, lots of starter handicaps, too. And $280,000. I never wanted to race him over his head. But I got a call from the racing secretary over there, and he said he'd been hearing all sorts of stories about this overachieving little horse at Finger Lakes. 'The Little Engine That Could,' someone had called Mr. Bo. And the racing secretary wanted me to bring him to Saratoga.

"Well, I told him I was flattered, but unmoved. So then he tells me he's got this race I might be interested in, but it's open company, and he understands my reluctance. After all, he says, Finger Lakes allowance horses don't ordinarily measure up to better-bred stock from bigger tracks, anyway. Mr. Bo and I were in the van that night, headed east.

"Two days later, we're in a $56,000 allowance race. There's a couple of Chicago ungraded stakes animals and a bunch of hard-knocking sprinters like us, except they're from Belmont. A Seattle Slew, a Buckpasser, two Bold Reasonings, that sort of stuff. Well, I had checked the weather before getting in the van. And, of course, it had rained like hell all that week.

"So there we are, saddling up in the paddock, with all these blue-blood horses and megabucks owners all around us. And out of nowhere some fan leans over the fence and lets out this yell in our direction: 'Put the hurt dance on 'em, Bo. Put the hurt dance on 'em.' Boy, that got me even more pumped than I already was. It must have pumped Mr. Bo, too, because put the 'hurt dance' on 'em he did. Gate to wire. Drawing away."

The emotional electricity generated by horse lovers when they start swapping racing stories—all arms and grunts and uumphs—now crackled inside Jed's smoky cabin.

"Hurt dance!" Claire screamed in joy, as she and Jed slapped a high five on each other. "Put it on 'em, Bo!"

"Wait, wait, wait," Hutch shouted. "Here comes the best part. So then I see the racing secretary the next morning, and I look him straight in the eye and this is what I tell him: 'Thanks for the easy win. Check, please. We're goin' home now.' Just like that." A flourish of raucous foot-stomping and fist-pounding followed, after which Hutch wrapped up the saga.

"I gave Bo a long rest after that race. His knees had started acting up, and I figured he might not have too many races left in him. Obviously, I figured right. He came back about six months later, at six, and won one out of four races. But by late summer, the well was dry. Both front knees were bad. The tendons, too.

"We'd had one helluva great ride together. Because of him, I was training about 25 horses by then, some of them good ones, and I actually had some money in the bank. The horse had given me the chance I needed. Labor Day weekend I figured it was finally time to let him retire.

"That next Tuesday, that's the day I took Mr. Bo over to the Loving Arms. And met you, Claire."

The fire, the company, and the moment all felt just right to Claire. All felt like home. Which is why the tall, lean, fire-engine redhead was a bundle of smiles as the focus of conversation shifted her way.

"The Loving Arms," Claire mused, tossing shoulder-length ringlets off her full face of freckles. "Boy, was I a mess back then."

Indeed, all the girls at the Loving Arms were a mess, at least when they got there. The syndrome was more or less the same. No one cared about them, least of all their parents, if they had any, and that rejection had hardened them into "social problems." Truancy, drugs, petty theft. The usual social dysfunctions. It was the job of the state-supported Loving Arms, located 15 miles south of Finger Lakes in Scottsburg and just up the road from Websters Crossing, to try to get the girls through a special high school program and back out into the real world in some kind of decent emotional shape by the time they were 18.

Horses were a part of the therapy. Hutch knew that, and knew the place was always looking for older horses, because over the years a few of the "graduates" had turned up as hot walkers at Finger Lakes. They'd all seemed like good workers to him. Respectful. Not stealing anything. Hutch had never figured to breed Mr. Bo, so putting him together with some girl on the mend seemed like it might be a good fit.

Claire had never touched a horse before the morning Mr. Bo showed up. In fact, the brooding 15-year-old with the penny-ante rap sheet had made a point of telling the facility's director that she hated horses. What the girls professed to hate or not hate didn't matter, though. Her new job, whether she liked it or not, was to become Mr. Bojangles's personal groom and exercise girl.

"We didn't really get along so well the first fall and winter," said Claire, smiling into the firelight. "Mr. Bo still had a lot of that racehorse swagger in him.

"When the other horses walked by him in the barn, he'd start nodding his head up and down and kicking at the sides of his stall, like this was his castle and they were interlopers. And when I walked him, it would always be at his pace, not mine. It was so bad in the beginning, I was literally yanking him around the ring.

"Eventually, though, we came to understand each other's habits and needs. I started looking forward to taking him on long walks in the fields, and getting my back nuzzled, and having him be glad to see me in the morning. He loved getting his chin scratched, and being curried, and he even began following me around without a lead.

"It took almost a year, I figure, but I finally got him to where he wasn't always being such a self-centered brat."

At that last comment, Jed broke into a wide smile. So did Hutch. Claire understood the irony of what she had just said, as well, and chuckled to herself.

Indeed, through constant companionship and caring, she had coaxed out of Mr. Bo a new, gentler sense of self-worth.

Just as Mr. Bo, through constant companionship and caring, had coaxed out of Claire an equally transforming, gentler sense of self-worth.

"The thing is, it didn't really dawn on me what the point of taking care of a horse was supposed to be until almost two years later, at the Fourth of July parade," Claire continued.

"Tell the story, Claire," Jed said. "I've heard Hutch's version, but not yours."

"I suppose it can't hurt," Claire answered. "The *Gazette* reporter who had written about Mr. Bo when he was racing at Finger Lakes happened one day to ask Hutch what had become of the horse. Hutch told him where Mr. Bo now lived, and the guy called the Loving Arms and the Scottsburg Chamber of Commerce and talked them both into putting Mr. Bo in the Fourth of July parade. Kind of a local hero thing.

"I was told by the director of the Loving Arms that since I had such a wonderful relationship with Mr. Bo, I would lead the horse down Main Street, all three blocks of it, and that we would in effect be representing his institution to the public.

"Well, I freaked out. But like everything else there, I had no choice. I was really embarrassed that the Loving Arms van was driving behind us with a loudspeaker blaring the song, 'Mr. Bojangles.' And I hated the banner in front of us that said: 'Mr. Bojangles—Finger Lakes stakes winner and fan favorite—rides again at Loving Arms.' But that apparently was part of the deal the Chamber and the Loving Arms had worked out.

"So there we are, on this perfect 'mom and apple pie' July 4th morning, walking down Main Street, and two or three hundred people are on the sidewalks clapping and smiling and cheering at us. Yah, it was hokey. But all of a sudden, as we passed the little makeshift reviewing stand in front of the police station, I felt this incredible sense of accomplishment, like there really was some merit in being responsible. Like I mattered. It was an awakening.

"Mr. Bo was into it, too. I had him all shined up, with a checkerboard water brand on his rump, and a racing saddle on his back. He couldn't go six furlongs in 1:11 anymore, but you could tell by the way he strutted and cocked his neck and swished his tail that he was all Thoroughbred.

"I knew you were going to be there, too, Hutch. The director told me you said you were coming down. And I wanted you to be proud of both of us: Mr. Bo, and me, too."

"Proud?" sniffed Hutch, who suddenly had contracted an uncharacteristic lump in his throat. "I don't think I ever felt prouder. Of any horse. Or any person. You were perfect together. Just perfect."

With the help of two more logs, the fire was now in full flame, spitting embers, letting off loud snapping sounds and requiring no accompanying conversation. Claire, Jed, and Hutch obliged, content to sit back and stare into the heat.

Claire was thankful for the long silence. It meant she could stop talking about herself, and the lucky bounces her life took after the parade: the high school equivalency diploma and subsequent graduation from Loving Arms a year later; the admission to Cal State because her natural mother was a California resident; and an apparently natural aptitude for computers.

She knew she lived in a different world now, far from the Loving Arms, far from Mr. Bo, far from Jed and Hutch. But that was okay, she thought to herself. Through the occasional phone call or letter or visit back East over the past ten years, all had become family.

That's the magic, Claire pondered, as Jed faced the fire and broke the quiet.

"YOU KNOW, I ain't got much," he spoke softly. "But what I've had, I'm grateful for."

No, Jed didn't have much. Always a loner, never married, Jed had his cabin. And, up until a week earlier, Mr. Bo.

A couple of years after Claire left the Loving Arms, Hutch had gotten a call saying Mr. Bo was not well and that state regulators were insisting that the horse be removed from the facility. The illness wasn't life-threatening. Nothing more than arthritis, really. So Hutch called Jed, a fellow dinnertime regular over the years at the Websters Crossing Diner who'd always said he'd love to look after a horse. Hutch had called Claire, also, to tell her about his plan, and she'd flown out special to meet Jed.

"Do you remember what I said to you that day I brought him over?" Hutch asked Jed.

"Sure do," Jed answered, after pulling another swig. "You told me we were a couple of high-mileage old guys who could look after each other just fine.

"And you were right, too. Seven years, by my figurin'. Seven good years. The thing about it is, Mr. Bo had that Thoroughbred heart, that Thoroughbred bearing. And no matter how bad his knees got, or how bad the flu got that finally killed him, you sensed that he always knew his kind is something special.

"I'll tell you what else he knew. He knew I needed a friend. Someone to cook mash and pick apples for. Someone to walk down to the clearing with. After morning feed time, I'd go up to him and he'd just put his chin on my shoulder and keep it there for a minute or so. Like he was dreaming.

"And I'd just stand there and let him dream. That's what I'd do. I'd just let him dream."

Jed's voice dwindled to silence, as he saw Claire's eyes again begin to tear. Hutch, too, seemed suddenly lost in reverie, or whiskey, or both.

As the others nestled in their rocking chairs, Jed moved to the fireplace and rustled the fading embers, hoping to coax another hour's warmth from their midst. In the dimming light, he shuffled back to the sofa, pulled one of Mr. Bo's black and magenta blankets up over his chest and closed his eyes.

Down the hill, in the clearing, the night stillness and a crimson carpet of newly fallen leaves covered the burial mound. The rain had stopped. A half moon now hung high in the cloudless sky, its light casting directly upon the shiny face of the black marble tombstone—and upon the delicately chiseled "few things to say" Jed had insisted upon penning.

Mr. Bojangles

Jan. 6, 1978-Oct. 28, 1995

The fans, they cheered your racing chart:
Some twenty wins, done in a prance.
But you meant more, as with fine art,
To those who took a deeper glance.
To one, you gave a brand new start,
A lease on life, a second chance.
As for the next—a mended heart,
A peace of mind, a life's romance.
And at the end, you did your part
To break an old man's lonely trance.
Now as you ride death's heav'n-bound cart,
Know we on earth loved ev'ry dance.

Teaser

by Scott Travis Hutchison

WHEN YOU'RE in charge of a farm's stallion barn for long enough, you sort of get used to the way people see you: You're supposedly a rugged, hard-necked son-of-a-gun who handles the kind of Thoroughbred that wants to breed and wants to run and wants to stomp you into dirt. And not necessarily in that order. They believe you assume the attributes of the animals you work with, and, since no right-minded person would trust a rank-minded stud horse, people naturally assume that you're the kind of guy who might kick or bite them, given the chance. That's the way the horse farm workers say it, whatever it means. Even if you aren't exactly that kind of person, you live with people seeing you that way just the same.

Kristi is an exercise girl on the farm I work at. Hanover Stables is a notable Thoroughbred facility, in the business of breeding, boarding, breaking, and training. Three hundred and fifty horses to maintain. She's up in the training barn with a shedrow of six horses all aiming at the track. Some she broke, some she got back in shape after a racing hiatus. Kristi's a fine-looking woman with no ring on her finger, and I'm a single man. A good single man. She's like me, bumping up in the 30-years-of-age range, about ready to stop the farm- and track-hopping and settle into one place. And though I've been trying to stir up a little interest, trying to get her to maybe give me some consideration, she's got her opinion of stud men; says stud men are insensitive brutes on a par with the headstrong horses they work with. Maybe I shouldn't respond by telling her she's green and giddy as the horses she saddles up, but I can't always help myself.

I'm not sure of how it sounds to say it, but our farm's teaser stallion is all mixed up in this. You understand his job, I'm sure: I take him up to the mare barns from late January to early April, leading him around to various broodmares, trying to get them in the mood, or accepting verification when they squeal and kick out at him that they most assuredly aren't in the mood.

His name's Richmond Charger, and he's never led me to think that he's anything less than up for the job. Sorry about that. Now that I've said it, I hear the pun. Folks are always finding puns and innuendo in the speech of stallion handlers, even if it isn't intended. Hell, that's the exact problem I'm aiming at when I tell you that people have got stud men pigeon-holed on being the grand possessors of testosterone-enhanced attitudes and macho senses of humor. I say things and people see all kinds of male crudities in it. But, to tell the truth, I'm not that clever.

So I take Charger around, sometimes up to a stall door, sometimes out in the mares' field while they're grazing. He's game enough. He knows the manner in which a stallion is supposed to present himself, and he's out there trying to stir up a little hormonal curiosity amongst the ladies. For his troubles, he gets to go up near a broodmare and sniff a little. For his troubles, she sometimes breaks down showing she's in season or sometimes she fires out a hind leg trying to connect with something she is not in the mood for. And sometimes she connects. Either way, I lead him on out of there with nothing, or with nothing to show for it but a nice hoof mark in the dust of his neck.

Kristi's got her opinions. She says that the number-one worst job on the farm is cleaning out the washrack traps, where water and manure and horse hair all collect and percolate. I pretty much agree. Which I'm learning is a good thing to do with a woman. But then she says that the second worst job on the farm is being the teaser stallion. Kristi has it in her head that a teaser must live a life of frustration, seeing so many females each day, feeling the fire, and then having me shank him back at the moment when things are looking most promising. She can't understand why the fire ever comes back, day after empty day.

The first day I ever met Kristi, we got off to a bad start. She was fresh on the farm and putting her nose into every corner of the place, seeing what was what. So, she came jouncing her five-foot-tall jockey-firm frame into my stallion barn to check out the "old track retirees," as she called them.

Kristi had a little blush going across her spackle of freckles and had a comment at every stall, comparing her shedrow of hopefuls to my proven winners. But I held my tongue. Still, as she moved through the barn the studs all started acting up, nostrils flaring, pawing at the floors, biting at the bars of their stalls. Stallions have a keen sense of smell, and they know when a female, even a human female, is going through a cycle. I'd seen it before. I'd been polite toward Kristi the whole time, but my charges were out of sorts. I was in God's-own earnest when I asked her if it was that time of month for her, but Kristi took it all wrong—jabbing a pointed finger in my chest before I could even finish my sentence, calling me a few choice names even I hadn't heard before, and kicking buckets as she exited the barn.

I've had a devil of a time getting past that one over the course of this past year. I had to apologize and admit to stupidity in choosing my words about a hundred thousand times. Took six months before we ever really got to a conversation level, and a few more months of fixing her truck, offering to help rake her lawn, and finding all sorts of odd reasons to take me up to the training barn on errands before I could get her to go out with me. Might not be too smart, but I'm patient.

It so happens that Kristi and I have the same time-off schedule. Twelve and a half days on, working Saturday mornings, then Saturday afternoon and Sunday off. Half the crew gets one 36-hour reprieve on a given weekend, then the other half gets it the next. With free time being so precious, I try to make something happen with Kristi. Sometimes she'll go out to a movie with me. She likes an earlier show, because she wants to get some sleep later. I'm the same way myself.

Sometimes she'll go out to Bonanza with me, and I'll order the T-bone and she'll order the petite filet, and we'll fill our plates at the all-you-can-eat salad & fixings and we'll try to illuminate our particular views of the horse world to each other. There's other times she won't go with me at all, and I stay at home on Saturday night and try not to think about the fact that at 7 p.m. my best bet for TV is 24-year-old reruns of "Lawrence Welk" or "Hee Haw."

I've tried to explain to her that I'm not like other stud men, that if I'm not out with her then I'm not going into town and to Andy's Pub trying to see what else is out there. I'm not going to say that in my younger days I wasn't racing around and doing all right for myself, but those times simply don't have the same pull for me anymore. I've pretty much put such notions behind me; I like a slower life, and I'm not looking to be back in that kind of position again. I've said that to Kristi when we're out having dinner, and she shuts her eyes and takes a bite of blue-cheesed lettuce and shakes her head saying, "God, what a stud man." Coming from her, I pretty much know that's not a statement of attraction.

But I stand up for Charger when she starts getting down on his job. I've got million-dollar stock in the stallion barn—one Derby runner and the others solid moneymakers—and they've all got serious cases of the ornerys even though they're paddocked daily as well as led up to the breeding pen once or twice a day to cover mares. When the season is in, that is.

They're a bunch of hard heads, but I know how to handle 'em. Some of them you've got to put the shank chain over their nose, others you put it in their mouths for a little teeth filing, while others you've got to put it on their gums occasionally for a reminder. Then there's one nasty character that I simply have to muzzle before I take him anywhere. Some folks say it's harsh treatment. I say it's survival when you've got a thousand-plus-pound animal who'd like nothing better than to prove on you that he's still got the rigor and the vigor to bust you in half. I give good for good when they're behaving, and dirty for dirty when they get into their attitudes.

But Charger isn't like them. Though he's got the last stall at the end of the barn, he knows who he is, and he's got as much heart as any of their bloodline and stat sheets protest to. I bought the brass name plate for his stall door myself.

Four years back he was a sharp-looking, two-year-old chestnut with three white stockings, paying his dues in the training barn. I was working layups at the time, but I liked to go up to the training facility when they were working Charger. Everybody was hot for him. Said he had the real-deal shot, a Grade 1 stakes runner for sure. The whole foot crew would get up in the observation tower to watch the jockeys breeze their horses, and Charger was something to see. He knew how to pace himself and hang in the top three the whole time, biding his time, but what made him special was when he was asked to take the lead. I never saw a crop put on him. A hand nudge, a little leg squeeze, and he knew what he was supposed to do. We were all saving our money just so we could bet it on him one day.

He was out in a back paddock by himself—some Sunday crew worker was giving him a little exercise—when the Thoroughbred bad-odds caught him. It had rained the night before, and Charger was just being his young, fiery self, cutting across a field at full tilt. And when he went to put on the brakes with the usual distance to spare, that soft earth and mud kept him right on going through a wire-weave fence with a top-board. The board snapped on impact and stabbed over a foot deep into his chest.

I got the call to come help the vet work on him, even though he was a training horse. Doc always liked me holding for him because he trusted me to keep him safe. If a horse acted up, Doc knew that I'd pull the horse on top of me and get stomped or crushed on a wall before I'd let anything happen to him. He knew, no matter what, I'd stay by him. I've still got that kind of reputation as a horse handler—it's not something that holds true for just everybody. Kristi's told me that some of the other handlers have said that to her. She begrudges admitting it, but I like her smile when she finally allows for the fact that I might be solid that way.

Working on Charger, removing board and splinters and going in and sewing up on multiple levels of muscle took over three hours. Even though we had some serious painkiller in that horse, I think he'd have let us do what we needed to do for him without much of a fuss. It's like he knew we were simply trying to do right by him. The boss put in calls to the insurance company, and we took before-and-after pictures. When all got said and done, the insurance people covered the medical cost, and that was it. They said the way they saw it was we still had a live Thoroughbred. Any chance of that horse's chest coming back into racing form was shot to hell, but their position remained the same: live horse, they'd pay the vet bill, but no big money to cover the loss of potential. I get it—I just don't like it.

Charger has some fairly decent bloodlines. Even so, the boss didn't have to pay much for him, seeing as how Charger's former owners were more than happy to unload him for whatever they could get. And that's when his career as a teaser began. It tore me up inside to see that horse so limited, when all he really wanted to do was what he was born to do: He wanted to run. But becoming a teaser kept him from a worse fate.

I've noticed lately that Kristi's taken to wearing some kind of perfume, both in the barns and when we go out. I couldn't tell you the name of it, but I know it beats the hell out of anything else I'm accustomed to smelling during working hours. She comes down to my barns still sweaty from knocking out her own chores, and I catch that whiff of sunshine on new-cut hay or whatever it's supposed to be—some fancy Frenchy label, probably—and I forget about my back or the load of feed coming in or the head-butt our big horse gave me while I was washing out his automatic waterer. I try to act all crusty like she expects me to, but when I get to telling her about the plans I've put together for Charger and that scent is hanging on the wind, I get kind of strange inside, and I don't suppose I've got her fooled very much.

Kristi appreciates the fact that I've made the effort to call every little two-horse farm in the tri-county area, seeing if people want a free breeding for their school ponies and plugs. All told, I round up five or six mares a year for Charger to cover, and the owners get a foal that's better than they could have ever afforded and Charger finds a reason to keep the fire. Kristi says that a good stud man knows how to work hard to bring in the ladies. And me, I'm not sharp enough to figure if there's anything inside of what she's saying, though I've hurt my brain a couple of times trying. But one thing I do get is how I can look in Charger's eyes and sometimes I see a dullness, I sense something like a sadness in that horse. I think he knows he's moving on in years and he wants more, and certain runs just aren't available to him.

It was last Saturday night that I think I finally got through to Kristi. We'd come back to the farm after a late KFC run, and I popped the question. Full moon was out, and I asked her if she'd do me a big favor. I asked her to ride Charger. There was risk involved, to be sure. He hadn't had a saddle on since the accident, four years ago, much less a bit. And it was night. Don't ask me what possessed me. Somewhere over the mashed potatoes, perfume, cole slaw, and original recipe, Kristi kept talking about what it meant to a Thoroughbred to be ridden, how you could tell that their hearts swelled all big in their chests when you asked them to pick it up, and how horse and rider—when it was right—were one fluid animal racing in the wind.

We were driving in her truck, a half-mile from the farm when I asked her. I said I'd lead her around in a breaking pen and make sure Charger was okay with it, told her I'd protect her if she felt she was game for a ride. And she stared at me for the longest time without saying a word. I was getting pretty nervous, not knowing what I'd said this time. But then she pulled into the barns' driveway rather than going on to the workers' houses, and I guessed she'd made a decision.

We got out at the stallion barn. I went to turn on the spotlights while she reached behind her seat for the old saddle and tack she liked to haul around with her. She gave me a tired look when I made sure she had a helmet along with everything else. When I backed off, said it was her show, I liked the way she laughed when she said we were both dumber than stud horses.

Let me give it to you this way. Charger looked surprised when we started putting the saddle on him, but he sniffed at the bridle and then took it when I put the bit in his mouth and pushed the leather up over his ears. His ears suddenly perked up, and he stood up straight, and he didn't even move when Kristi cinched up the girth or when I gave her a leg up on him. I slowly led the two of them out of the barn, and they both looked fine with it. My plan was to have them go in a breaking pen for a little jog, but Kristi set me straight on her plan. She's one strong-minded woman. And I respect that. After only a little protest on my part, I nervously led them the quarter-mile to the training track. My mind was all afire with what I might have started.

Charger has a serious hitch in his stride. When he's been turned out and you see him running around in a field, you can tell that his front end doesn't extend quite right. He fires out those front socks best as he can, but the muscle mass just isn't there like it's supposed to be, and it's an odd pull. I explained all that to Kristi on the walk up the lane to the track.

To the right of the lane was the mare and foal field; the ladies were snorting and walking up to the fence, checking us out, while some of the babies were lying down in the field and sleeping under the moon. I went on a second time, making sure she understood the dangers of going forward with this enterprise; she cut me off midstream with an icy "I know." By that time we were at the oval. So, I clamped my mouth shut, let her loose, and took myself on up into the observation tower.

It's hard for me to relate what happened from there. Maybe what lit my eyes up was on account of the light and shadow tricks of the full moon. I was gripping the whitewashed wood of the tower rail. Blood was coursing hard in my veins. Watched Kristi get Charger warmed with a little jog, watched her ease him into a canter, and I could see that her weight was a different element for him to coordinate in his gait. Still, it was like I was seeing a little dance to his step—like there was something in him that had waited for this opportunity. And when she gave him a little squeeze, I couldn't believe what I saw: they were moving. Fast moving. Taking the circle. A blur along the rail on the backside of the track. Hoofbeats. Heartbeats. One gray form. Straightaway. Laying it down. Making the turn and flying. Ghost-mount. Drumming. Tearing it up in front of me. Gone.

I was down out of that tower in a flash, running to get out on the track and catch those two. They weren't supposed to go that fast. They weren't supposed to tap into anything like that. Charger could pull a muscle, or stumble, and Kristi might get dumped forward and roll under a falling horse. Hadn't moved that fast in years. I was running. I was yelling her name.

And then, right out in front of me, they emerged from a moonlit steam cloud, darkness haloing all around them. She was patting him on the neck and talking nice to him. I led them both on back down the lane, past the mares and their foals all lined at the fence. All of us looking at one another, taking in this new power. And Charger, hot and tired, but his eyes looking like sadness wouldn't ever visit him again.

I wish I was smart enough to know where I stand with Kristi. But I got my opinions. We worked together untacking Charger, and washing him down, and then took turns walking him. I was waiting for Kristi to say something, but we were pretty quiet, except for the little business stuff we were taking care of, asking for the sponge and passing the scraper blade.

Once Charger was cooled out and put back in his stall, we both stood there looking at him as he satisfyingly munched on his hay. Then my heart started beating fast. Kristi actually put her arm around me, and let me put my arm around her. We stood there in the stallion barn and watched that horse for another hour. We started talking then, telling the story four different ways and laughing at all of it.

And I don't care what anybody thinks—I'm telling you I was perfectly content when she kissed me on the cheek. I was happy for her. I was happy for Charger. I was happy for me. I could have stayed there all night.

Phoenix

by Caroline Nesbitt

PEOPLE WILL TELL you it isn't safe to dream, because dreaming invites destruction of the dream. I could never believe this. Maybe because I'm a Pisces, the zodiac's ultimate dreamer. Maybe because dreams give me something to live for. Maybe because I've always held tightly to the notion you can have the thing you dream, if you dream it hard enough and long enough—if you aren't afraid to work.

So I dreamed of owning a horse that could run at Saratoga.

And I watched my dream die in the middle of the stretch in the third race on a sunny Wednesday afternoon the first week of August.

She was named Phoenix, after a movie star who self-destructed. This was not my idea of a good name; partly because the star in question was male and the horse a filly. Partly because I had the idea that the phoenix was a mythical bird that, unlike the movie star, resuscitated itself. But I'm superstitious enough to think changing a horse's name invites bad luck, and I only owned about 15% of her anyway, so Phoenix she stayed.

She was as pretty a two-year-old as I could ever hope to see—a clear, striking bay with a white stripe and a couple of diagonal socks that gave her some flash. She was nice and square, too, with decent bone and an eye that said she wasn't brainless or wily. I couldn't look at her without thinking what a nice hunter she'd make, and how I'd like to be the one to do it.

But for the moment she was a racehorse. Not a fancy racehorse, mind you, but looking like she might be the useful kind that pays back most of the extravagant bills presented to cardiac-arrest-prone syndicated owners every month, whether the creature is running or just standing around eating its head off.

And she was good enough to run at Saratoga.

So there we were, half a dozen shareholders and what seemed like about a thousand family members, boyfriends, girlfriends, cousins, aunts, neighbors, and who knows what-all standing around in the paddock like the monarchs of a very small nation, watching our dream filly. It seemed a little crowded out there to me. It also seemed there was a lot of preening and giddiness going on that wasn't strictly speaking a part of the actual horse. But I was the only person in the group who'd ever known horses up close and personal. And this was my only route to a dream, so I'd taken it.

"You're out of your tiny mind," my husband, Steve, had asserted when I'd told him what I'd done. "You are out of your extremely whacked-out, imbecilic mind." The soul of tact, Steve is. And practical, too, which I am not.

Obviously. Because here I was in the paddock, watching this perfect filly gleaming her way around the shady tree with our number pinned to it, instead of installing the new septic system our elderly farmhouse sorely needed ... and which the cost of this filly could have provided.

"What do you think?" asked Steve beside me. He's not so practical that he doesn't want to join in the fun.

"I think she looks like a racehorse," I said. My nerves were tingling. Our filly. Saratoga. Our trainer was saddling her. She shook her head and reared straight up, scattering syndicate members and their hangers-on like confetti. She came down hard, shook her head, tried to go up again, the trainer and groom yelled a little, and she decided to stand still instead. I avoided the temptation to go in and help. Unlike my hunters, this filly didn't know me from the dog rifling the garbage across the street. It felt odd, owning a horse I'd never handled.

"What do you mean, she looks like a racehorse?"

"I dunno," I said, in nervous exasperation. "She has that kind of slinky walk, like a cat. I like the way she uses her hind legs. She just looks like a racehorse, okay?"

"Should I put money on her?"

"Sure. Why not?" I grinned the reckless grin of a gambler looking at the stake of a lifetime, equal parts fear and bravado.

When the bugle sounded, I stayed in the paddock to watch my filly mince out to the track. It struck me that she looked a hair—just the slightest hair—off in front. I wondered if she'd done some damage landing so hard after she reared. Stung herself, maybe. I mentioned this to the trainer. He looked at me dismissively. "It's nothing," he said. "Don't worry about it."

And she sure looked good cantering down the track, glossy and gleaming in the sun, a groom's delight, black mane and tail like plumes framing her mahogany coat and white markings. She loaded into the gate like a professional and when the bell clanged and the doors crashed open she broke ahead of the mob and streaked down the track like a thousand demons were on her tail. The crowd was roaring away and the other owners were shouting and carrying on, but I was worried.

She was going too fast too soon, but still she was in front and holding off all comers around the turn and still holding them off as they came toward home with the crowd shouting her number, shouting her name, the announcer saying "and it's Phoenix, Phoenix still holding on by a neck at the head of the stretch," and all of a sudden she bobbled, that's all—bobbled and slowed and the crowd groaned and shouted again as the rest of the field streaked past her like thunder and her jock pulled her down, fought her down, until she hopped to a three-legged halt and he jumped off and I realized that I had run out on the track right behind the trainer. My horse, breaking down, was all I could think. My horse at Saratoga, breaking down. I ran and ran toward her, to touch her, calm her, feel her legs, wait for the ambulance in stunned disbelief while the ecstatic crowd cheered a winner home in a distant universe.

IT WAS a serious fracture, the vet said. We all sat in his office, the other owners and the trainer, Frank Hobbes, and me. No more giddiness and no more hangers-on, just a bunch of somber people looking at money swirling down the toilet.

"What's that mean?" asked the guy called Harold, a banker in real life.

"Sounds to me like it means she's finished," said Bill the insurance tycoon. "Isn't she?" he turned back to the vet.

"Well ... maybe, maybe not. We can pin it, we can drill it, we can turn her out. There's a lot of options. ..."

"That all takes a lot of time and money."

"Money depends on the route you take," offered Frank. "But time ... you're looking at close to a year, easy."

"A year! A year doing nothing but eating?" This from Tanner, the lawyer who'd gotten me into the syndicate.

"Yeah."

"Will she run again?"

"Well ..." said the vet. "It's too early to tell. Some do; some don't. It depends on a lot of things."

Bill the insurance tycoon grunted. "Better sell her quick and cut our losses."

"She's not worth much on three legs," said Frank.

There was a long silence. I suggested that maybe we should all sleep on it and meet again tomorrow, which seemed to be a relief to everybody. We straggled out. The others left clustered around Frank. I hung with the vet.

"I'd like to talk to you some more," I said. "I'd like to look at the filly." And then I added, since he was looking at me the way horsemen always look at rubes, "It's okay. I've seen a couple of legs." I told him about the rearing episode, about my vague feeling that there'd been something wrong. And the nagging sense that serious fractures don't happen just because a horse comes down hard after rearing, or because the track was too fast.

The vet looked at me funny some more and said something neutral that only increased my suspicion that there just might have been a hairline fracture in existence before the filly ever walked into the paddock.

Oh, I know it's not that uncommon, it happens all the time that a tiny fracture won't show up on an X-ray or that the pressures to run a syndicate horse are greater than the ability to follow vague notions that aren't borne out by standard medical procedure. Human oversight? Human greed? I don't know. But I looked at the filly in her stall, dull from painkillers and tranquilizers, and I felt sick.

"I owe you, babe," I said into her silky ear. "I'll make it good, somehow."

THE NEXT day, I offered the rest of the syndicate a sum of money that bordered on the absurd. They took it, patently relieved to get out so easily. One or two were derisive, and made cracks about women thinking with their tear ducts, which I pretended not to hear while I ground my teeth. Tanner the lawyer did the legal stuff, and we all agreed sort of emptily that it had been nice doing business and Frank Hobbes said I knew who to call if the filly came sound and I said yeah, sure, and as soon as she was fit to ship I took Phoenix home.

I told Steve I was going to fix her, school her, turn her into the dandiest little hunter you ever saw, and make my fortune selling her. I was serious, too.

LAYUPS are layups, not too interesting. While I showed hunters and schooled hunters and sold hunters and bought hunters, Phoenix hung around in her stall, getting well.

When she started jumping out of her skin, I hand-walked her until she pulled my arms out. Then I ponied her beside my old standby, a 20-year-old gelding I'd bought at Suffolk Downs 15 years before and had so much fun with I'd never sold. He was solid, forgiving, and slow. When the snowpack was deep enough to cushion the ground, I turned the filly out with him.

All this time my own vet monitored her. "Tincture of time," he cautioned after every visit. "She's doing great, but don't screw it up by pushing her."

Spring is slow in New Hampshire, which keeps people like me from doing stupid things with recuperating horses. I taught the filly to ground-drive and longe. I tacked her up and let long stirrups clank against her sides and towed her around with me while I set up jumps in the ring. By the time I got on and rode her down the road with Steve beside me on her baby-sitter, she never turned a hair. She just clomped along like a nice old horse with her ears flopping.

When my vet gave me the green light, I spent a long time walking and jogging on the roads, the way we legged-up field hunters in the old days before everybody got to be in such a hurry. I took her for long strolls across the fields and taught her how to cross water and ditches. I have to report that she stayed remarkably sensible. If I hadn't seen her on the track a year before, I'd have sworn she was dead between the ears. Which is a nice quality in a Thoroughbred hunter, if you ask me.

One day, trotting down an old log road, we rounded a corner to find a substantial tree downed across our path. My reflexes are quick, but not as quick as Phoenix's. Before I had time to pull her down and find a way around, she took a couple of easy canter strides and jumped the sucker, then tried to buck me off on the landing side.

I was panicked about her legs, but I had to laugh. "Think you're pretty special, huh?" I said, when I had her back under control. And truth to tell, she was looking smug. I had my hunter, all right. She was going to be just the nice little horse I'd always imagined, except for one overriding problem that kept getting in the way.

I wanted a racehorse.

"THAT'S GREAT," enthused Steve when I related the jumping episode that night. "You should get a lot of money for her, she can jump like that. Especially when she's such a pretty girl, too."

I crawled into bed and looked at him, troubled.

"What's the matter?" he urged. "That's what you wanted, right? You did a great job. You took this busted-up filly and fixed her and gave her a new life and she looks great and she's going great. So, sell her, happy ending, new septic system, everybody wins." He climbed in next to me and turned over with a sigh, ready to drop instantly off to sleep.

"Uh," I said. "Yeah. That's what I wanted. Yeah."

I stared at the ceiling and told myself again that was what I wanted. That was why I'd done what I'd done. I listened to Steve's breathing, already deepening toward the regular rhythms of unconsciousness.

"Steve?"

"Mmmph."

"Do you ever have passionate dreams? I mean, dreams about stuff so far beyond the realm of possibility that your heart aches like a five-year-old kid looking at a puppy through a pet store window?"

"Uh-huh."

"You do?" I leaned up on one elbow and looked in amazement at what I'd thought to be the most down-to-earth man of my acquaintance. "What do you dream of?" I expected him to say something standard, like pitching for the Red Sox. But he surprised me even more.

"A cream-colored Miata," he said thickly. And then he began to snore gently.

I lay back and laughed out loud, astonished at the things people admit when they're too asleep to protect themselves. And I wished I could buy Steve's cream-colored Miata, present it to him, see his face when he discovered it in our pot-holed drive with a red ribbon wrapped around it. Then I sighed.

"I dream of owning a horse that can run at Saratoga."

The next day the septic system backed up and sent the entire disgusting contents of the toilet into the bathtub.

OKAY, I admit it: I was doing the one thing professional horsemen are never supposed to do. I was falling in love with Phoenix.

I was also getting some nasty little ideas, and I was galloping her on the sly, 'way back in the far pasture. And she was putting her head down and galloping like a racehorse, she was good and fit, and she was staying sound. She liked the grass, too.

I called my friend Ray Boulton, who trained at Rockingham, and took the filly down for him to see. He watched her move, he listened to her, he watched her work, he didn't say much, he listened to her, and watched her move some more.

"Well?" I kept demanding, on tenterhooks. "Well?"

"She can run a little bit," he acknowledged, finally. "She might do okay."

I grinned all over my face. "Great! That's great! I'll bring her back ..."

"You'll leave her here."

"Oh, no. Ray, I gotta keep my eye on this filly, I can't let ..."

"You want me to train your filly? You gotta let me train your filly. I mean, Christsakes, Molly, how long have we known each other?"

"Twenty years, something."

"Right. So trust me with your damn filly. Okay? Or take her home and don't come back. You know you can't be in control of this part, you know better."

So I left Phoenix whinnying after me and cried all the way home. And had a blistering fight with Steve.

The following week I traded one dream for another and sold the hunter I'd been winning everything in the region on, the one that was going to be my ticket to the big indoor shows in the fall. I pestered Ray daily. He responded with a lot of blue language and said I was the worst pain-in-the-ass owner he'd ever had. Then one day he invited me to come see my filly make her comeback start.

Phoenix broke slow, got bumped, tripped, recovered, and ran a gaining fourth. Ray was pleased. "She's tough," he said. "I thought for sure she'd quit when she got bumped, but she just dug in."

"So ..."

"So what?" All innocence, the s.o.b.

I took a deep breath. "So ... uh ... What's next?"

He grinned slyly. "Dunno. I'd like to run her on grass at Suffolk, see how she likes it."

We did. Phoenix liked it, and placed.

"So ..." I said again.

"So, what?" Baiting me to the max.

"So ... so ... so don't be doing this to me! What do you think? Is she ... do we have ... Is she gonna ...?"

He laughed uproariously. "God, I love you when you're out-to-lunch. Yeah. She's going to Saratoga, been booked for weeks." I whooped and hugged him and looked at my beautiful bay filly, fit and sleek and powerful, with that sharp gleam in her eye that said she was ready to eat wildcats.

And I knocked wood.

NOTHING BEATS Saratoga in August. The way the stands are all tarted up with the fancy grillwork covered in new white paint, shady trees making the grounds cool with dappled light, families from everywhere in the world having picnics and watching monitors, and the stands crowded with die-hards and partyers and the whole town looking grand and elite and goofy, all at once. Flowers everywhere. People everywhere. I paid homage on Fourstardave Way and hung around the barns and attended swank art galleries in a sort of happy daze.

Phoenix settled right in and worked well. In a panic over the thought of losing her, I infuriated Ray by refusing to contemplate claimers. So he found a spot on the grass for non-winners of two. "She could be out of her class here," he warned. "No promises, okay? We'll just give it a try and drop her back if it doesn't work."

"What are you going to do if she's a washout?" asked Steve.

"She can't be a washout," I said, dizzy with nerves. I didn't tell him how far out on a limb I'd gone, about the bank loan or the money borrowed from my family. I knew I'd have to send my filly to the sales if she was a washout, because I was going to be washed up. And if she broke down ... I bit my fingernails some more and cursed the dreamer that got me into these messes.

By the day of the race I was so twisted that Ray banned me from the barn. I aged ten years in two hours. I watched the odds on my filly soar from 20-to-1 to 60-to-1. Lameness problems, the buzz went. Out of her class.

And finally I was in the paddock again, under the trees again, watching Phoenix stalking around the tree with the number seven on it, led by somebody that wasn't me. Saddled by somebody that wasn't me. Ray grinned, thumbs up. I hyperventilated a little more and tried to smile.

"So, what do you think?" asked Steve, at my elbow. "Does she look like a racehorse?"

"Steve, I dunno! I dunno! Yes, okay? Yes, she does. She looks like ... she looks exactly like a racehorse. Okay?" I was wringing my hands. My teeth were chattering.

"So? Should I bet on her?"

"No!" I turned to him in alarm. "The odds stink! Don't ... don't ..."

"Don't what? Waste money? Jinx her? What?"

I took a deep breath. "Don't ... don't ... don't ... boogey me right now. I ca ... ca ... n't stand it." He shot me a funny look, and stared at Phoenix some more. Then he said I was a hopeless case and excused himself and went someplace else.

In my few lucid moments I had to admit Phoenix did look exactly like a professional racehorse. She wasn't washy, she stepped around with her long, slinky catwalk and just a hint of a dance here and there, and her eyes were bright, alert, shining, full of fire. She kept looking over to the track. She couldn't wait to run. I could hardly stand looking at her, she was so beautiful. When the bugle sounded and she headed to the tunnel, I wobbled to the nearest rail and propped myself there, praying hard that she wouldn't get hurt that she wouldn't get hurt that she wouldn't get hurt and simultaneously drank in the fluidity of her stride, her confidence, her rippling muscles.

When I looked at her rivals, fear clutched my heart so hard I could barely breathe—two coppery chestnuts and a gray and two bays, a couple of big rakey mares and one mincey filly that looked like a little rat but gave the impression she could fly. They cantered down the track and out onto the grass and time went into slow-mo' while they milled around and loaded into the gate and all at once the doors clanged open and the announcer shouted that they were off and you could hear their thunder, see their mighty bodies bunching and stretching until they began to string out like multicolored geese streaming over bright green turf.

The mincey filly was flying, all right, a blistering pace with the gray hot behind her and somewhere trailing was Phoenix and into the turn they stayed like that until another chestnut came up and I couldn't see Phoenix anymore, she was somewhere boxed and invisible with heaving bodies all around her and the gray overtaking the liver chestnut. And then they got to the top of the stretch and there was this incredible roar from the stands behind me and I strained my eyes and saw Phoenix, Phoenix on the outside, Phoenix streaking down the outside racing three wide as if her tail were on fire with her eyes blazing and her ears pinned back and she was in fourth and edging into third and I was screaming and crying "PHOENIX! PHOENIX! GOGOGOGO MOVE-YOURBAYASSPHOENIX!" until I was hoarse and she was nudging the gray mare and the post was almost on us and she was—was she? WAS SHE?—edging closer and closer and they flashed under the wire like one horse and the crowd was insane and the announcer was shouting something about the incredible race run by the little mare who'd had such bad luck last year and the board was saying PHOTO FINISH.

I staggered out to the track to find my filly. Ray met me there, grinning like a child, caught me by the waist, squeezed the breath I'd barely caught right out of me, and we met the filly and her rider jogging back. She was panting like a bellows, steam rolling off her, fire in her flaring nostrils, her rider pounded her neck and said great, what a great race, what a game little mare.

The board flickered and it was our number, Phoenix's number seven up on the board in the win spot, and there was this huge roaring shout from the stands, and the announcer was saying that she was going to pay some really lucky people a whole lot of money for betting on her, a Cinderella story for a hard-luck filly. We went crazy then, and Steve caught up to us on the way to the winner's circle and spun me around so hard, laughing so hard, that I fell over when he let go. When I got myself up and dusted off we tried to pose gracefully for the win picture, but I think we all looked a little drunk.

And that's all it takes for dreams to come true in the end, about five minutes. A lifetime of dreaming and months of pain and untold labor and then poof ... and that's your dream. I looked around me dazed, wanting to savor it, stop it, make it last as long as the buildup had. Too soon! I wanted to cry out. It's gone too soon! I wished I'd thought to bring my camera, to take stupid out-of-focus photos of all this delicious frenzy to reminisce over at leisure and bring it back to life, to capture the numbers on the tote board forever. Then I turned to follow my beautiful, weary filly back to the barn, to walk her and wash her and care for the reality that was her.

I looked at the board again on the way out and shook my head wistfully. "Look at that payout! Makes me wish I'd put some money on her." I grinned at Steve sheepishly, expecting him to tell me not to be so greedy. But he didn't.

"I did," he said instead, and started to laugh again, his face pink and excited. "I put a hundred bucks on her to win!"

I stopped dead, slack-jawed, and tried to wrap my mind around the figures this meant. "A hun ... Oh my God, Steve. That's ... that's ... that's enough for the septic system!"

"Oh no, ma'am, it is not," said the most practical man I have ever known, still laughing like a lunatic and actually hugging himself in glee. "But it is one hell of a down payment on a cream-colored Miata."

Time Exposure

by K. M. Jones

THE Time Police interrogated me for what seemed like days about the disappearance of Numitor. No, I didn't know what had happened to make it all go wrong. Yes, I knew I was involved, but I didn't know what had caused it. No, no one had paid me to do it. No, of course I didn't know anyone who might profit by the horse's disappearance; my interest in racing was merely as a railbird.

The captain, who had been sitting quietly through most of this, finally spoke. "You know, this is just the type of thing that could shut down time travel forever. Didn't you stop to think about that before you intervened?"

I shook my head. "I don't even know what I did! I followed all the rules."

"Repeat them." He stood and waited for me to recite the rules that are drilled into any potential time traveler prior to departure.

"One—observe only. Two—do not participate. Three—do not, under any circumstances, change anything." Then I shrugged. To my knowledge, I had not transgressed in any way.

"Okay," he said. "Start again from the top." And I did.

IN SPITE of knowing virtually zilch about the mechanics of time travel, I enjoyed using it nonetheless. By the same principle, I don't really understand how a television works, either, but that doesn't keep me from putting it to use. The papers were all signed and in order and, after a few minutes during which the grounding wristband was carefully applied, I was ready to go. I stood waiting in the chamber while the technicians made some adjustments on their computers, then, in a twinkling, the laboratory vanished and Churchill Downs appeared. Churchill Downs, Breeders' Cup day, 1991.

It promised to be a day of both great excitement and great disappointment, just like any day of racing usually is. If it were in my power, I would find the owners of Housebuster and ask them to withdraw their entry as I knew he was destined to suffer a career-ending injury in the Sprint. But I had signed the contract and I knew the rules. Observe only. Do not participate. Such misfortune lay ahead; however, I had not come to change anything. I had come to witness the Classic and photograph the winner.

Photography was my hobby, and racehorses were my passion. The two often met in the form of portraits—my major source of income. I had recently lost the opportunity to photograph this particular horse as he had been euthanized just last week due to the infirmities of old age. That's why this time travel trip had been scheduled.

For some reason, standard cameras don't operate very well when you take them into "previous time." For that reason, I had been equipped with a technological masterpiece known in time-traveling circles as an NEF camera. The prime letters stand for nuclear-electro flash, or neo-electronic flash, or something like that. And, like most things mechanical, I didn't have a clue how it worked. But I had the latest model available, and couldn't wait to try it out.

I purchased a track program and retired to the clubhouse. Throngs of people filed by me continuously on their way back and forth from the betting windows, an activity that was out of bounds for me. Rule number two—do not participate. The topic of most conversations was, as expected, opinions regarding the eventual outcome of the Classic. They repeatedly uttered names that were very familiar to me, but, oddly, not a one mentioned the horse who I knew was going to win the richest race of the day. What silly people, I thought. Hadn't they been paying attention? Was this their first trip to the track? How I would have loved to blurt out, "You're picking that horse? Ha! You're going to lose!"

Turning the program page to the feature race, I scanned the list of entrants looking for Numitor, but his name was not there. Incredible. It's got to be there. I looked through again, turning pages forward and back in the unlikely event that his name had been placed in the wrong race. Still no Numitor.

What a confounding situation! He was going to win the 1991 Breeders' Cup Classic, yet for some unexplainable reason he wasn't even entered in the race. I made my way out to the rail clutching my NEF and watched the horses parade to the post. Twilight Agenda was full of himself, tossing his head and prancing as though he owned the world. Chief Honcho seemed intent on biting his pony. Black Tie Affair walked by as the picture of composure, but took the time to notice the crowd beyond the rail. The afternoon sun caught the red coat of Festin, lighting him up like a bright penny as he cantered by. But the familiar jet black of Numitor was missing.

"Excuse me," I nudged the fellow beside me, "I thought Numitor was going to be here today."

He stared blankly at me for a few seconds. "Who's that?"

"Numitor?" I couldn't believe his ignorance. "You must be kidding. He won this race last year."

The stranger shot an eyebrow up and laughed a little. He pointed toward the track at a bay colt with blue and yellow silks. "Unbridled won it last year."

"Not Numitor?"

"Who the heck is Numitor?" he asked, peering over his dark glasses.

I cocked my head to one side, still not believing that this man had not heard of one of the greatest horses of all time. "He was a Triple Crown winner, a son of Swale."

The stranger laughed louder this time and pushed his glasses back up his nose. "Swale? Swale didn't sire anything. You don't know much about racing, do you?"

The remark caught me like a punch in the stomach. Don't know much about racing? He could not have been more wrong. I had followed the sport of kings all of my life. Not only could I quote the names of all the major race winners for the past 50 or 60 years, but also for the next 20 or so to come. But I certainly didn't tell him so. I smiled weakly, shrugged, and walked away from the rail, leaving him chuckling to himself.

Something was wrong. The words of the stranger had left me deeply concerned. Swale didn't sire anything? Did he mean Swale didn't sire anything important, or Swale didn't sire anything, period? Either way, he might as well have said Northern Dancer was gelded, or Secretariat never raced, because I knew those were equally unbelievable.

Suddenly the Breeders' Cup Classic was irrelevant. It didn't matter to me who won this sham event. None of it was real. Numitor was supposed to be here, and he was supposed to win the Classic for the second year in a row.

I left the grandstand area and found the track library, where the answers would certainly be forthcoming. The woman behind the desk was surprised to see me there, since everyone at the track at that moment was waiting for the last race of the day to begin. She drew her eyes away from the television. "May I help you?"

“I need help tracking down a particular horse.” But even as I spoke, the bell sounded and the gate clanged open and her attention was right back on the race. “I’ll wait,” I offered. She glanced back at me with a thankful smile.

This was the first race of the day that I did not already know the outcome, so despite my earlier denouncement, my curiosity was slightly piqued. From what I knew of the others in the field, Twilight Agenda was my pick, but the librarian cheered Black Tie Affair all the way down the stretch, clutching her winning tote ticket. Although I knew the result was a false history, I was happy for her. Why spoil her fun?

Finally she turned the set off and addressed my inquiry. “Okay! What’s the name of the horse?” she asked as she punched a few keys on her computer terminal.

“Numitor,” and I spelled it for clarity.

She waited for the computer to offer some answers. “Hmm. ... I show an Argentinean horse born in 1960. Is that it?”

“No, American, born in ... uh ... 1986, I think.”

She shook her head and typed the name again, double-checking the spelling. “Nope ... nothing else by that name. Did he race in this country?”

“Well, I thought he had,” I replied.

“If he ran in this country, he’d certainly be in the computer. Who’s his sire?” she waited for me to answer.

I paused, then figured I had better tell her. “Swale?”

She rested her fingers immediately. “Oh, it couldn’t have been Swale. He never went to stud.” When I asked her to explain, I was surprised to hear another false history.

“Swale died at age three, following a morning workout at Belmont. It came exactly eight days after his Belmont Stakes victory and caused quite a stir because no one knew what had caused his collapse. There were speculations, of course, ranging from heart attack to poisoning. The autopsy didn’t really point to anything.”

"Swale died at age three?" I put my head in my hands and rubbed my temples. That was all wrong. That wasn't the way it happened.

She punched a few more keys. "All right then, let's try his dam. Do you know who she is?"

"Squander, by Buckpasser. She was being boarded at Claiborne Farm back then and was among the first mares to be sent to Swale. ... I mean, she was going to be sent to Swale in the spring of 1985."

The woman listened to my story politely, nodding, then entered the named Squander on her keyboard. Immediately a listing of Squander's offspring scrolled up the screen. "This is interesting. I don't see any foals named Numitor, but you were right about her being boarded at Claiborne. She was taken to Mr. Prospector in the spring of 1985, and he's a Claiborne stallion. See here? In 1986 she produced a bay colt by Mr. Prospector. Oh, that's cute—they named him Lost Opportunity."

Lost Opportunity. How profound. If Swale died at three, they certainly lost the opportunity to take Numitor's dam to him.

I thanked her, congratulated her again on Black Tie Affair's thrilling wire-to-wire victory, and left the library. I glanced around at Churchill Downs one last time and snapped off the wristband. Instantly the racetrack was gone and the laboratory returned.

AFTER a quick explanation to the technicians that the trip was not yet finished, I was soon sent on my way again and within a few minutes found myself in the year 1984. Belmont Park this time. Early morning of June 17. I hoped I had the date correct. The librarian had said "exactly eight days" after the Belmont Stakes. She seemed pretty sure about the eight days. She had also said "following a morning workout," so I figured pretty early in the morning was a good guess.

I'm not sure what I thought I could do to stop whatever was going to happen, but at least Swale was alive at this point. Right now, at this second, history was rolling along correctly. My gaze was drawn to the track and the black horse who swept by me only a few yards away. I watched in fascination and felt my heart leap with joy upon seeing him again. How young he looked. He had yet to develop the stallion's girth and bull neck that I remembered when I had first seen him in the Claiborne paddock. He was an old man back then, but now he was an athlete, sleek and fast, his whole life ahead of him. But if the librarian's tale of this timeline was correct, then Swale's whole life now had only a few more minutes left in it. I tried to shake the possibility out of my head.

As he left the track, I followed at a great distance, not wanting to be involved in what might happen, or, heaven forbid, be the cause of it. I had grown up learning an entirely different history, living in an entirely different racing future. If Swale were to die now, there'd be no Numitor. No Triple Crown winner in 1989. No back-to-back Breeders' Cup Classic winner. But more than that—it would compound. If Numitor never lived, then none of his offspring would either. Numitor had gone to stud and died of old age just a week ago. How many foals had he produced? A thousand, probably more. And pretty good ones, too. Three European Breeders' Cup winners that I could think of off the top of my head, two Japan Cup winners, oh—and Numismatist, the filly who won the Dubai World Cup. I stood there stunned. None of them would exist if Swale died.

There had to be a way to stop whatever was about to happen, hang the rules. After all, I wasn't altering history—I was preserving it. So far, everything was okay. It was so frustrating not knowing what the changing factor was going to be.

He was already being bathed by the time I looked up again. It was a perfect image of him—standing there playing with his chain, a light steam rising from his back. What a beautiful picture.

Picture! I had forgotten all about the NEF camera! What a wasted trip! I could have been snapping Summer Squall, Twilight Agenda, and all of those legendary runners I had seen at Churchill Downs. There had been no opportunity to photograph Numitor, the reason I had come, but at least I'd get a great shot of Swale for my gallery. I withdrew the NEF from my shirt pocket, turned on the powering device, positioned the horse in the viewfinder, and pressed the button.

With a shriek, Swale threw his head in the air as his hind legs slipped out from under him. I gasped, dropping the camera, and slapped both hands over my mouth to keep from shouting. The marvelous black horse fell heavily upon the ground and in an instant I knew that he was dead. From my vantage point, I could see the distress on the people's faces as they rushed to offer some assistance, but they were too late. It happened so quickly. No Swale. No Numitor. No Numismatist. All of them gone in a flash.

I had not expected this to happen. In my memory, Swale had lived a good, long life. To see his inert body laying there was terrifyingly surreal. With trembling hands, I picked up the NEF camera and unsnapped the wristband.

HAVING RETOLD this entire story to the captain of the Time Police, the answer became obvious. Numitor was gone because he was never born. He was never born because Squander was bred to Mr. Prospector and not to Swale. She wasn't bred to Swale because Swale never went to stud. He never went to stud because he died eight days after the Belmont. And he died on that morning at the same instant I took his picture. The fault lay in the NEF camera.

There had never been a problem before, the captain commented. "If the NEF camera is the culprit, there'd be famous people dying inexplicably all over the place. We've sent literally hundreds of travelers back in time with cameras just like this one."

"No, not just like this one," I argued. "This is a new camera. They said I was one of the first to get the new model."

The captain ordered the camera to be taken to the lab, and placed an immediate freeze on all further trips until the equipment had been thoroughly examined. He asked me why Numitor should be missing from the Breeders' Cup if I had not yet gone to Belmont to see Swale, upon which I explained to him for over half an hour the concept of nonlinear time. Oh, well, not all policemen are scientists. He didn't get it.

When the lab results were finally returned, the captain told me that there was indeed a fault in the electrical portion of the camera's powering device. This new model apparently operated on the same electrical frequency as the impulses in the equine brain, which is a slightly different frequency from the impulses in the human brain. When the NEF was directed at a horse and discharged, all the impulses in the horse's brain would be interrupted. Immediate death would follow. And it was doubtful that anyone would think to look for that particular cause.

I sat there quietly wondering why I had to be the first person to point the new camera at a horse. And while expressing that thought aloud, the captain and I had the same thought. We raced to the laboratory and checked the travel logs. Two people were currently out on journeys of their own and they both had taken the new model NEF camera with them.

The captain read the log. "The first one is witnessing the arrival of Christopher Columbus in the New World. No horses there. That should be okay."

"And the other?" I asked with trepidation. The possibilities and resulting implications were staggering. Could the death of any horse mean so much to human history? I tended to think so. History would certainly change if a horse suddenly died under Alexander the Great, Joan of Arc, General Washington, or Lester Piggott. Human history has always been written on the backs of horses.

The captain looked up, knowing immediately the gravity of the situation. "He went to Claiborne Farm to see Easy Goer."

The Painting

by Alan P. Henry

CARL GREENE had never really thought of himself as the vulnerable type. Sure, there was the land mine shrapnel in the back outside Panmunjom in 1953, followed by almost three years of jaw-grinding rehab in a VA hospital. And the divorce, which 30 years later blew a gaping six-figure hole in his FBI pension plan. And, of course, half a century's worth of painful 1-2-3-5 superfecta finishes. But that was about it, give or take a few family funerals.

About it, that is, until right now, right here. Dawn, on the backstretch at Saratoga Race Course. Fish-cold hands vice-gripped against the outside rail, midway around the turn for home. A percolating stew in the belly torn between simmering down and shooting straight up the throat. Eyes blank, staring icily straight at nowhere.

One August week a year, every year for the past 15, Carl had begun his Saratoga mornings at this spot, usually with black coffee in one hand, an unfiltered Camel in the other. To one side, the three-sixteenths pole from which the storied likes of Suspended Flight, Look At Me, and Vodka Tonic had launched rallies into Thoroughbred racing history. To the other side, Barn 37.

Why Barn 37, he'd never really figured out. Maybe it was the angle at which early light pricked through the spindly Norway spruces, bounced off the tin roof, and brought to life the 18 horses stabled along the south face of the rickety wooden structure. Or maybe it was the interplay between the sycamores lined in front of the barn, the horses circling the trees, and the steam that rose behind all of them from great mounds of last night's discarded straw. For whatever reason, that particular spot just always felt like the right place to be.

"My private escape," he'd called his adopted sunrise rail-side roost to friends back in Chicago. "Peace," too.

But on this Wednesday morning, 7 a.m. sharp as usual, Carl knew full well there was no escape. Or peace. On this morning, everything was different. Up for grabs. His past, and what it meant. Perhaps his future, and what it held. Certainly his heart, and to whom it belonged.

"I never should have come up a day early," Carl mumbled to himself, nervously pumping both wrists back and forth into the rail. "Why me? Why now? After all these years! Damn that painting! And damn Dark Tuesday to Hell!"

DARK TUESDAY. Yes, there was the culprit. Of all the fifth wheels and perverse concepts in the world, August Tuesdays at Saratoga had to be near the top of the list. Right up there with ice cream in January and Bibles in by-the-hour motels.

After all, Monday's races, and the sundry frustrations they spawned, were already ancient history. And Wednesday's races lay forever away. To call Tuesday, the one day of the week when there was no racing, a "dark day" was being kind. Dark, for sure. More like positively black.

But Carl had flown in a day early this year because the Brunswick B&B across the street from the track had called a month back with a Tuesday cancellation and offered him his "usual" back room for half price.

Why not, he'd figured. Get in around noon, spend the afternoon goofing around on Broadway, do a little handicapping, and be well-rested for a week of racing. Beginning, of course, at 7 a.m. Wednesday in front of Barn 37.

Saratoga Springs had first crossed Carl's consciousness as a teenager, when he read a newspaper article in the San Francisco *Chronicle* about a little town in upstate New York where people came from all over the country every August just to go to the races. A place where schoolteachers and doctors and plumbers swapped laughs and handicapping horror stories while politely lining up at streetside stands on Broadway for early morning delivery of the *Daily Telegraph*. A place where hot tips, workout tabs, and breeding nicks were the grease of the commonweal. As a recent, rabid initiate to Thoroughbred racing at Golden Gate Fields, Carl had sudden visions of the Emerald City, glistening capital of the Land of Oz.

War wounds, family, and work had conspired to keep him away from Saratoga until he'd passed age 50. Nothing had kept him away since.

As an August "regular," part of the daily drill was a walk along Broadway, with its hodgepodge of junk shops, grande dame hotels, biker bars, and highfalutin haunts. That included an annual stop in the Empire State Emporium, a darkly paneled ground-floor maze of closet-sized rooms and hallways, jammed wall-to-wall and floor-to-ceiling with other people's basement rejects. A few years ago, he'd found an old LSMFT lighter there; further back, a Boston *Globe* trumpeting Secretariat's Triple Crown win.

On this Dark Tuesday, the Emporium was as cluttered and claustrophobic as ever. And empty, too. Junk, after all, is junk. As Carl twisted and turned his way toward the back of the store, he found at the end of an unlit hallway a place he'd never before run across—what appeared to be the establishment's pathetic excuse for an office. In one corner of the unoccupied room, a 35-watt lamp was trying to do a 100-watt job atop a worn wooden desk piled high with disheveled stacks of *Daily Racing Forms*. On every wall, yellowed curled posters were tacked helter-skelter to warped wooden paneling. An old, metal four-drawer file cabinet stood in the darkest corner, behind the door, its bottom drawer missing. On top of the file cabinet, behind a jumble of empty Coke bottles, a painting of a backstretch scene leaned against the wall. Judging by the dust on the 18x24-inch canvas, and the dirty wood frame, Carl figured it could have been sitting there for who knows how long without so much as a human glimpse.

But Carl quickly wanted more than a glimpse. Moving the bottles aside, he could see this was not just another painterly Saratoga moment. Through the film of filth, he could see it was a moment he knew well. The backstretch, from the three-sixteenths pole, looking due east at first light, straight at Barn 37.

Carl moved face to face with the unsigned painting, scanning every inch, finally fixating in the dim light on what appeared to be the stable's silks, on a sign, hung on the back corner of the barn. "EW," it read, the blackened art deco lettering surrounded by a reddish-colored circle lost in heavy-handed varnish.

At that moment, a teenage boy quietly appeared in the office doorway.

"I'm sorry," he said. "This area is private."

"But this painting; I'd like to look at it further," said Carl, his baritone voice instantly aggressive, his hands reaching for the artwork. "I might want to buy it."

"Sorry, mister, please don't touch. I'm just the help. All I can tell you is that the owner told me nothing in this room is for sale."

"When will he be back?" Carl shot back impatiently. "I want to look at this painting."

"It's a 'she,' and maybe in a few hours. I don't know."

Over the course of 25 years as a field agent with the FBI in Chicago, Carl had helped put away plenty of oily con men, ham-handed mobsters, and pinstripe boodlers, and being told to get lost, no matter how politely or appropriately delivered, was not something he took well. But the kid was just following orders, so Carl backed off.

"I'll be back later," he said in a thinly disguised huff.

Never one to shirk a challenge, Carl knew the afternoon's mission before he'd left the Emporium. Someone had painted his spot. Who would have done that? And why? And when?

"EW," he rolled over in his mind. "Find them. Find the answer."

IN THE late 1970s, Carl and a couple of pals had raced a string of cheap Thoroughbreds on the Chicago circuit. No-counts, mostly, though You're An Angel and No Discount, a pair of hard-knocking fillies with bad attitudes, had managed to cover expenses before wearing out. Carl knew, thanks to an IRS audit of No Discount's partnership five years after her demise, that the paper trail on a stable, if recent enough, shouldn't be that hard to pick up.

He began at the Saratoga Public Library, a creamy marble homage to turn-of-the-century architectural grace.

"I'm looking for a racing stable that once ran here that went by the initials EW," Carl told the elderly woman at the impeccably polished mahogany reference desk. "I saw it painted in a picture in a junk shop on Broadway and I want to track it down. Can you help me?" The approach was vintage Carl. To the point. Polite but firm. No extraneous banter. Just like at work.

"Well, let's see what we can do for you," smiled Nettie, whose "have a nice day" yellow name tag, stoop shoulders, and matching white hair and fake pearls placed her right out of central casting for the part she was already playing in real life.

"Would that be the owner's initials or the trainer's?" asked Nettie.

"I don't know."

"About what year do you think we're talking about?"

"I'm afraid I don't know that, either. I'm guessing maybe somewhere between 1950 and '80."

"Well, nothing was really put on the computer until the last 15 or 20 years, so that would be out. I suppose you could go through the microfilm of every day's racing chart for every one of those years, and look for something with EW in it. Or maybe ... we could start over here."

As Nettie spoke, she moved with a 70-something shuffle to a thick cardboard three-drawer file that had been shoved on the floor of a closet behind the reference desk. As Carl bent down to pull out the box, Nettie explained its contents.

"Every year from sometime in the 1930s up through, I think, the late 1960s, a gentleman used to do a watercolor reproduction of every winning owner's silks for that meet. He painted them on cards that had around ten silks-shaped stencils on each card. Then he would print the name of the stable or owner underneath their silks. Since you have the design, that might do it.

"You know," whispered Nettie, with the look of an archaeologist on the scent of the Dead Sea Scrolls, "I've been here 41 years and I don't remember the last time someone asked to see these. This is exciting!"

The files, Carl saw at once, were as advertised: catalogued on 4x6 cards by year, starting in 1931, 12 watercolored stencils per page in three rows, four across, with alphabetized stable names neatly inscribed underneath.

Carl started with 1940. At only 14 cards or so per year, the task was an easy one. There was Easy Winners Stable in 1941, but the silks did not use letters; Equine Wonders in 1951, but with just a "W" on the silks; Eva Worthington in 1961, with the letters EW, but in blue block type inside a white square.

Only two years remained: 1968 and '69. A dead end soon enough, Carl thought to himself—but not for long. Flipping to the second card in 1968, he immediately spotted his prey. Top row, right corner. The letters EW, black and art deco style, curved inside a magenta circle, exactly as in the painting. And underneath, in perfect parochial school penmanship: Evening Wind Stable.

"Bingo!" he shouted out over his shoulder in Nettie's direction. "Now we've got 'em in our sights." The thrill of the hunt quickened Carl's pulse. Just as when he'd uncovered the offshore bank account that ultimately sent publishing heiress Kathy Stevenson and her lover, then-Illinois State Treasurer Lee Star, to jail for the 1973 contract murder of her husband.

"Oh, my yes, we do have them in our sights now, don't we?" tittered Nettie, not used to such delicious intrigue.

"To the past-performance charts in the microfilm room!" she chirped, patting her hands together.

Twenty-four racing days, nine races a day. "We'll just start at the beginning," said Carl.

Inside the time it takes to bathe a horse, there it was. The *Daily Racing Form*, August 9. Fourth race, $20,000 claimers. Six furlongs in 1:13. The winner: Bourget Lake. Randall Davey, trainer. Evening Wind Stable, owner.

A shoulder-slumping sigh blew from Carl's nose. He knew Davey, now dead, had been a small-time New England trainer for decades, only rarely venturing to Saratoga. Surely, he wouldn't have commissioned a painting. No, the key was still to uncover the identity of the owners of Evening Wind Stable, but nothing in the official charts had put a name to it.

"Now what, Nettie?" Carl asked, after explaining to her that stable partnership documents would be long-since destroyed or buried in unsalvageable state files.

"There's always the winner's circle picture. Maybe that would provide some clues."

Why, Carl wondered aloud, couldn't Nettie have been on the case back in 1976, when all he'd needed to nail federal tax auditor Julie

Weary for extortion was a simple incriminating snapshot or two. The chances of a picture producing tangible evidence was a longshot, he knew, but worth chasing.

"Yes, I might have made a good Sam Spade," Nettie laughed.

"So, Nettie, where do you hide the winner's circle photographs from 30 years ago?"

"We don't. No one officially does."

"That can't be," said Carl.

"I'm afraid it is. But there's my old friend Talbott Leyden. He took all the winner's circle shots for years then got fired during one of the NYRA shake-ups in the 1980s. He's kept copies and negatives of every winner he ever snapped."

"Yes?" Carl prodded. "And you know where to find him?"

"Of course. We eat breakfast at the same diner. I'll call him right now."

"Talbott ... Nettie ... Listen, I need a favor. August 9, 1968, fourth race. I want the winner's circle picture ... I'm sure that won't be a problem."

"Yes? Yes?" coaxed Carl, knowing he had long since lost all control of his own investigation.

"He says for a $25 darkroom fee, he'll drive the picture over within 30 minutes. I said yes. I hope you don't mind."

"Mind? Are you kidding! Done!"

True to his word, Talbott was along shortly, handed Carl a brown manila envelope, took the cash, and left.

With Nettie standing over his right shoulder, Carl opened the flap and pulled out a glossy 8x11 photograph, in perfect condition.

Carl slowly perused the picture from right to left. There was Bourget Lake, held tight at the bit by trainer Davey, who was flanked to his right by two people. A girl, who looked to be around ten, and ...

An awkward gasping sound jumped from Carl's throat, as though a much larger man had grabbed him in a bearhug from behind.

"Are you okay?" Nettie asked, not knowing what to think.

"Fine. I'm fine," said Carl, quickly composing himself. "Nettie, trust me on this. I have to go right away. I promise I'll let you know what happens. In the meantime, you're the best."

Carl knew he owed Nettie more of an explanation than he had given her. He just hoped that a kiss on the forehead and the promise he'd explain later would suffice, at least for the moment. Because now, there was urgent business at hand.

THERE MIGHT have been a "Yield" sign at Circular and Hansen, and maybe even another one two blocks later. Carl wasn't sure, and he did not care. He only knew he had to get back to the Emporium. Immediately.

As he walked into the store, envelope in hand, Carl spotted the young man he'd seen two hours earlier. "I want to see that picture again," he said, in full FBI mode. "Is the owner in yet?"

"Yes, back here," came a muffled voice from the office at the rear of the store. "Come on back."

Carl moved quickly past the clutter, through the darkened hallway, and into the office, now choking with cigarette smoke.

A 40-ish woman, slender, with matching curly brown hair and eyes, sat at the dingy desk, a pile of sales receipts, half-filled tin ashtray, and calculator in front of her.

"My name is Eliza. May I help you, sir?" She knew full well, of course, why he was there. The teen had told her about his first visit and his somewhat agitated state.

"Yes, my name is Carl Greene, and I'm here about that painting," he said, sitting down at the desk and pointing over his shoulder to the top of the file cabinet. "I have discovered some of the history behind it, and I want to buy it."

"Well, that's certainly interesting," said Eliza, matching his deadpan look with one of her own. "And what is it you think you know about the painting?"

Carl opened the envelope, took out the photo, and placed it on the desk in front of Eliza. "I know the painting was probably done about 30 years ago, and that it shows what is now Barn 37, and that the barn was once used by Evening Wind Stable, and this is a picture of one of that stable's horses in 1968."

Eliza looked down at the photo, still sporting a blank expression, then looked back at Carl. "Yes? Anything else?" she asked.

"Yes," said Carl. "The woman in the picture is Mattie Alloway. We met in Paris on April 28, 1953. In a betting line at Longchamp. She was studying painting and art history at the Sorbonne. I was a war correspondent between tours of duty in Korea. I had not seen her face again in 46 years, until 20 minutes ago, when I saw this photograph."

"My, what a story," said Eliza, now fumbling for a Marlboro in her top desk drawer. "So, I'm still not sure what you want."

"What I want, Eliza, is to buy that painting. That's my spot, where I go every morning. I'd also like to know who painted it, and if you know anything about the woman in the photograph."

Staring straight at Carl, Eliza held the cigarette to her mouth, took a slow, deep drag, then exhaled even more deliberately.

"Here's the story, Carl. I can call the owner of the painting and ask if she wants to sell it, but I don't think she will. It's here, sort of for safekeeping."

Those weren't the words Carl wanted to hear, and he did not trust them. But this war of wills was far from over. Rather, in his mind, it had just begun.

"I need your help on this one," said Carl, who stood up, went to the door, then turned around and faced Eliza. "If Mattie is alive, and someone contacts her, have them give her this message: 'Au vent du soir. Pour toujours.' "

"I'm sure I can't be of much use to you on that last one," said Eliza, remaining stiff in her chair. "But if I learn anything, I'll be in touch."

TUESDAY AFTERNOONS on the covered front porch of the Brunswick were Irish tea and shortbread time—one of innkeeper Catherine O'Neill's special touches.

"Ah, just in time for a spot of tea," Catherine smiled in Carl's direction as he climbed the porch stairs, Wednesday *Racing Form* in one hand, manila envelope in the other.

"Maybe in a few minutes," said Carl. "Just let me clean up first."

"By all means, Carl. And by the way, a woman named Eliza just called for you. I left her number on the desk in the second-floor office. Use the phone there if you like."

A new scenario raced through Carl's head with each step up the stairs. The owner will sell the painting. Eliza's found Mattie. No sale. No information.

"Eliza, it's Carl. I understand you called." All business, as always. At least on the surface.

But the voice on the other end of the line was not all business. Rather, it seemed to Carl a bit erratic.

"Carl, please just listen to me and don't ask any questions. I wasn't being completely honest with you in the shop, but so much was coming at me at once I just couldn't take it all in. The woman in the picture you showed me—her name is Mattie Alloway Andrews. She's my mother. Meet me at 7 a.m. tomorrow at the painting if you want to talk."

"I'll be there," said Carl, knowing exactly where she meant, and knowing not to say another word.

In an instant, each minute seemed to take an hour; each hour, a day. And still there was no time. No time for handicapping. No time for a post-dinner cognac on the porch. Only time to stare at beautiful Mattie in the 31-year-old photograph; to collapse backward through the years and relive the loss all over again; to wonder if he'd stopped searching too soon; to commit every square millimeter of her image, undiminished by age, to memory. The chiseled dimples and tossed, peat-brown hair framing a broad Scottish smile, the inscrutable dark eyes, the strong shoulders and muscled, heavily veined arms draped, he now assumed, around Eliza.

Seven a.m. Wednesday ... A nighttime away. As he dozed in fitful 30-minute bursts, a lifetime away.

"I'M SORRY I'm late!" Carl whirled around, toward sunrise and the voice, hands flying free of the rail.

"Eliza! Forget the time. I'm so glad you called and wanted to see me."

"Me, too, Carl. Me, too. I think we have a lot to talk about."

Tuesday's edge was off her voice. His, too. Standing face to face in worn blue jeans and flannel shirts, each appeared to the other far more human, more approachable than the day before.

As both settled their backs against the rail, facing Barn 37, Carl could feel his stomach suddenly calming and the blood coming back into his hands. Both knew it was truth time.

"Tell me about you and my mother," Eliza said. "Tell me everything."

Carl knew that would be easy to do, because he remembered everything, as if it had just occurred.

"I was 23 and on top of the world. I'd been given six weeks off between tours covering the Korean War peace talks in Panmunjom for the Associated Press. My real passion was horse racing, and when I got the chance to go to Paris I took it, because I knew I could go to Longchamp.

"It was my first day there, and I went straight to the track and hit the winner of the first race. Her name was Le Vent Du Soir. I'm standing in line waiting to cash my ticket and there's this girl in front of me shuffling through her pocketbook. I was semi-fluent in French, but I knew she spoke English because she had a copy of *Ethan Frome* sticking out of her bag. I don't know why, but I just sort of blurted out: 'Le vent du soir.' That's 'evening wind' in English."

"I'll never forget the first thing she said to me when she turned around: 'That's why I bet on her. Because the evening wind makes wonderful things happen. Like magic.' I think she had me from that moment on.

There was just a brash, warm way about her that reached inside and grabbed my heart."

Carl shifted his back uncomfortably on the rail. "Eliza, if you don't want to hear this, just tell me and I'll stop."

"No, I want to hear everything. I have to."

"Okay then," said Carl. "For the next month and a half, we were inseparable. We both loved horses and art and French poetry and Bordeaux wine. I think we went back to Longchamp half a dozen more times, and Saint-Cloud once or twice, and did all the museums. Mostly, though, we simply melted into each other's arms. We were goners: hopelessly, helplessly, timelessly in love."

Eliza pulled out a Marlboro. Carl, a Camel. With shaking hands, he lit both.

"So, what happened after six weeks?" Eliza asked.

"I had to go back to Korea. The night before I left, all we did was cry and make love and wrap our souls around one another. The next morning, at the airport, we whispered the same last words to each other: *'Au vent du soir, a l'amour, a nous. Pour toujours.'* (To the evening wind, to love, to us. Forever.)

"I knew I meant it. I didn't know if she did, but it didn't matter. Less than a week later, I was in a jeep outside Panmunjom when we hit a land mine and rolled over. They didn't think I was going to make it for a while, and the next two years-plus were just a blur of operations and heavy painkillers. We'd agreed to meet again in Paris four months later, but when I finally got well enough to try to track her down through the Sorbonne, they were no help; and when I called her parents' house in New York the phone had been disconnected. I figured I'd lost her and I simply gave up. I didn't have the sense to know it at the time, but in the back of my heart I've known it almost ever since. She was the one."

Carl looked up at the sky, fighting to keep tears from forming. Eliza, too, felt a mist filling her own eyes.

"And then?" she asked. "What about since then?"

"You know. Work, family, divorce, retirement. Nothing out of the ordinary, really. And then I started coming to Saratoga every August and to this spot every morning, never thinking in a million years that she might have been here."

"Well, she was," said Eliza. "Right there, in Barn 37."

"How did that happen?" Carl asked, nervously lighting up a new cigarette with the last one.

"My grandparents owned some horses and had them spread around a few tracks. When Mattie came back from Paris in 1953, she became a painting instructor at the Boston Arts Guild and began hanging around Granddad's string of horses on the Boston circuit. She got married in 1955, and her last name became Andrews. He lasted long enough to have me three years later, and she never remarried. In 1968, Granddad had a couple of decent horses and wanted to send them to Saratoga. She jumped at the chance to oversee them and insisted they be called Evening Wind Stable. To my knowledge, she never told anyone how she came up with that name.

"So that's you in the winner's circle photo?" Carl asked softly.

"Yes. Yes it is. With our one winner, Bourget Lake. A California-bred. Mom named her."

Carl had assumed that already. In the epic 19th-century French love poem *Le Lac*, Alphonse de Lamartine mournfully returns to Bourget Lake, where he and his now dead lover had spent their happiest moments together. Under soft cotton sheets in Paris, Carl and Mattie had read *Le Lac* to one another their last night together. He still had the book.

"And the painting?" Carl asked.

"She did it. That summer of '68 we basically lived right here. And that's when she painted it. Her easel was not more than ten yards from here."

Carl breathed deeply before asking the next question, Eliza even deeper before answering.

"Eliza, you haven't told me if she is still alive."

"I can tell you that she is all around us, right now."

"I don't understand," said Carl.

"The next year, just before the August meet was about to begin, Mom was diagnosed as having an advanced stage of ovarian cancer. She died within weeks. In the hospital, she asked that she be cremated and that her remains be scattered on the backstretch here. The track officials said no, but I wasn't going to let them deny her last wish. The next morning I came here before sunrise and scattered her ashes around the barn, and over here by the rail. We are with her right now. Without knowing it, you've been with her for all these years. As I now realize it was meant to be. For both of you.

"I also know something else that was meant to be. The painting. Until yesterday, I thought it was mine, but it's not. It's yours."

"What do you mean?" asked Carl.

"Wait here. It's in the car. I'll bring it over."

Overnight, Eliza had wiped the work clear of dusty disinterest. As she held it in the sunlight, the frame now had a rich, burled walnut luster to it. The canvas itself was suddenly alive; a chorus of daybreak yellows and golds, lush greens, and earthy browns.

"Read the inscription on the back, Carl. When you left that message for Mattie yesterday, I knew right away who the painting belonged to."

Carl took the painting from Eliza and rested it against the rail. Across the back of the canvas, in large, neat marking pen script, it read:

To the evening wind, which blew our souls together.

To love, upon whose cloud we floated.

To us: hearts as one; lips in lust, kissing the sun.

Forever.

Carl opened his arms to Eliza, and she moved easily into them. Each let the tears fall down their cheeks and onto the other's shoulders. Tears of loss, both knew. But tears of love, as well. Tears that cleanse the past and mend the heart.

Behind them, hard against the inside rail, a two-year-old chestnut filly in long white stockings skipped lightly by the three-sixteenths pole, rhythmic jets of steam shooting from flared nostrils, clippety clops pounding in perfect cadence against the cuppy chocolate earth. Unraced. Unbeaten. On top of the world.

Under the early morning Saratoga sky—one circle joined, another just begun.

Like magic.

Tack Talk

by Dennis M. Patterson

SEEMS LIKE you're always hearing some good story around the racetrack, but I got one to tell you that's a little different. Different in what way? I'm sure you've heard plenty of stories about horses, famous and not so famous, and the people, also famous and not so famous, who guided or misguided their careers. Well, this is the story of a pitchfork. Oh, not just any pitchfork. This is the story of a 120-year-old pitchfork and the travels, people, and places that make up this more-than-a-century-long story. But first, let me backtrack a little and tell you what led me to think this story should be told.

We were all in the tack room one night, talking about what we liked, and maybe some things we didn't like, about our jobs. What's that? Who am I? I'm a halter. And a pretty good one, I might add. Triple-stitched leather. But I'll tell you more about me later. First, here's what some of the others had to say:

"Being a brush has been a good job. Since I'm the soft body brush, I cover a lot more territory than my partner, the stiff brush, who just does the mane and tail. But it takes both of us to make the horse look good. Of course, you can only do your best work if you have a groom handling you who is as dedicated as yourself. I've taken care of as many as four horses at a time, which is hard because if one of them gets a little rash, you're afraid of giving it to the others. Right now, I'm lucky 'cause the girl who's my groom has a team of brushes for each horse. Most days, we get a warm bath when we're through working and get to sit out in the sunshine. The one thing I really dislike is when you bust your bristles getting the horse to shine, and you're barely out of the stall, and you hear the horse down rolling."

"Being a blanket has its share of excitement. I remember how scared I was the first time they put me on a horse. I started to lose my balance and fall off one side. Lucky for me, that hot walker knew this was my first job, and he stopped that horse and eased me back on. I came close to falling a couple more times, but he kept an eye and a steady hand on me, and we made it through that first morning. But I learned that, even with experience, you can still get hurt. Some of those horses get to feelin' pretty good and they're dancing and playing, and it's hard to keep your balance. You get on one of those horses with a hot walker who ain't watching you, and the next thing you know, you're slidin' and fallin' right under that horse. He gets spooked and goes to jumpin' and kickin', and the next thing you know, you're laying on a table in the emergency room at the tack shop with somebody putting stitches in you. I've got some stitches myself. See my back corner there? Been lucky—never got tore up too bad. Seen a real nasty one up at Churchill couple years ago. Wind was blowin' pretty hard, and that old blanket never had much of a chance. Horse got to actin' up real bad, and next thing you seen was that poor blanket fallin' underneath him and gettin' all tore up. Wasn't no trip to the tack shop for stitches. They just gathered him up and took him straight to the dumpster.

"Being a night blanket can really be dangerous. Oh, they're heavier than us and got a few extra straps and buckles to hang on with, but when those horses get to layin' down and rollin', it's hard not to lose your balance. But I don't want to make it sound all bad, 'cause really, I have a lot of happy times. I can't wait for morning to come so I can get on those horses.

"Now the night blanket there works seasonal. Goes to work in the fall, works all winter and into spring, and then is put away for the summer. Actually, I get some days off in the summer also, when they use no blankets or just a flysheet. The flysheet is seasonal also—just works in the very warmest weather. Days of not having to work are often considered a vacation, but not to this blanket, or cooler, as we're often called; it's more like punishment.

"Like I said, I love getting on those horses, although on some days, you only get on one horse. If they just walk, you might get on a couple. But if you get on one that just had a bath, you can figure that will be your last ride for the day, 'cause you'll be too wet to get on any more. Sometimes you get to cool one out after a race. And I've even gotten to go to the paddock, although there's a specialist for that called the paddock blanket. And they're always very neat and clean-looking. They're all fairly small but must have great balance, 'cause I never heard of one getting hurt.

"I guess I've taken up enough of your time with my story, but before I fold up, there's one more member of my family I should mention. That's the rainsheet, tough-skinned and doesn't see much action. But I got to give 'em credit. When that old rainsheet does show up for work, it's always in the worst of weather."

"Speaking of action, no one sees more action than me. I'm a D-bit. Some people say I'm the most common bit—poor choice of words. What they mean is I'm the most popular bit. I see plenty of action morning and afternoon. I can handle most horses. They use me to start all the two-year-olds. Of course, like any class, you're goin' to get some students that become a discipline problem. That's when they bring in my friend, the ring bit. Between us, we handle at least 80% of the action. If they have to go past me and 'Ringo,' they've got a real problem. There are some short-tempered bits out there that take no nonsense, but I never liked to work that way. I find a lot of the success or failure depends on the trainer and rider. If they could see and feel what I do when I'm in there working, they'd know why some of those horses act like they do. I see sharp teeth and cuts on the inside of the mouth. I try my best to avoid them, 'cause horses really hate it when I touch those spots.

"I like all the action in the morning, but what I like best is getting to race in the afternoon. I like being part of the team when we win. I get to where I can pretty much tell who's holding those reins by the way they make me move. I've teamed up with some good riders—Pat Day, Shane Sellers. And I'll tell you one who can make those horses grab me and wanna move is that Donna Barton."

"Donna Barton?" repeated Ringo. "Dee, was you with that D. Wayne Lukas outfit?"

"No way, I ain't wearing none of that white nylon. I'm strictly into leather. Horses like the feel of leather better, too."

"Nylon, you say? You sure Lukas's headstalls aren't leather painted white?"

"Nope, nylon. How about you, Ringo? Which do you prefer?"

"Oh, I gotta say I'm a bit partial to leather. Get it? A bit partial to leather."

"Yeah, we all get it. Real good."

The saddle and girth see a lot of action and are a real necessity, yet pretty much get taken for granted. And how about the saddle pad? Gets pushed down on top by the rider while getting poked from below by a bony backbone. Sort of between a jock and a hard place.

Of course, there are so many more members of equipment that make up a racing stable, but I better get on with my story. We all agreed the little footpick did an important job but got little if any recognition. We also all agreed that none of us would want to be the thermometer. Then somebody said they wouldn't want to be a pitchfork, either. That's when I felt it was time to tell my story.

LAST YEAR, the boss left Keeneland and took about ten horses over to Churchill Downs, my horse being one of them. It so happened, when we got settled into our barn there, my horse was in the last of our stalls. This old worn-looking pitchfork was working for the outfit next to us and was hanging on the wall next to my stall. Right from the start, that old fork was real friendly and made us feel welcome. This isn't always the case when you ship into a new barn.

Anyway, at night when I'd get hung on the door and everybody had pretty much gone, that old pitchfork would start talking to me, asking me where I'd come from, where all I'd been, what I'd seen, and so on. Well, I pretty much told him my story in the first few days we were there. When I started asking him about the same things in his life, he began telling me this wonderful tale of a journey that had taken over a hundred years.

"Can remember most all of it," he began, "but just can't remember when they put me together. From what I can gather, I was made somewhere up in Ohio. The first I recall that I existed, I was riding in the back of a wagon. There was a group of us back there: other pitchforks, some hoes, a few sickles, and some shovels, also two sledgehammers and an anvil. At that first awakening of my existence, I couldn't see much 'cause we were all covered by a large piece of canvas. I could feel a gentle tapping on the other side of the canvas. I was to later learn the tapping was what is known as rain.

"The wagon wasn't moving now. And later, when the tapping stopped, the canvas was thrown back, and I experienced two grand sights at once: sunshine filtering down through those beautiful trees. My roots being what they are, I guess it was natural that I was drawn to the beauty of those trees. The driver waited under those trees until the rain stopped, and then we continued on. Apparently, we had started in Ohio at that tool farm where we were all created, and we were heading south. Southeast, I guess, 'cause we left Ohio, crossed into West Virginia where my awakening took place, and then rolled on into Virginia. After I don't know how long ('cause I couldn't judge time back then), we turned into an opening between some low stone walls and up a lane to a beautiful farm called Kincaid Estate. This was to be my first job.

"The wagon rolled along the lane 'til it turned past some large trees and stopped in front of a great white barn that was to be my first of many homes. We were carried inside and left to experience the wondrous sights, sounds, and smells of our new world.

"The following morning, we were lined up and assigned our various jobs. I heard them say I was to stay at the barn 'cause I was too light to work in the field. That didn't bother me none. I was a four-prong fork that stood five feet from the tip of my prongs to the top of my handle. I figured, in time, I wouldn't be too light to work in the field. But in time, I learned that wasn't so.

"The year was 1877, and I had come along just after two of the biggest events in this country's history—one of great sadness, the other of joy—the Civil War and 100 years of independence.

"I liked working in the barn every morning with Baldwin. That's the man who took care of me. I don't know why he didn't work in the field; he for sure wasn't too light. One day each week, Baldwin would gather me and some of the other tools up, along with maybe a big piece of burlap, and carry us all down to the big house where Mrs. Kincaid lived. They said Clayton Kincaid, her husband, had gone off to the War and hadn't come back yet. He never did come back while I was there. Anyway, Baldwin would take us all down there and we'd work in the garden.

"I really enjoyed these days, except for one annoying habit of Baldwin's. When I wasn't working with him, and there was no place for me to lean against, Baldwin would want to stick me in the ground. But he never did this gently. He would drive me into the ground with a two-handed slam. Sometimes there were rocks under the ground, and if you hit your prong on a rock, you could feel it all the way up your handle.

"I know Baldwin also enjoyed these garden days, especially when Abigail, the housekeeper for Mrs. Kincaid, would come out on the porch. The gardening would come to a halt, with Baldwin up there leaning on that porch railing, until Abigail went back inside the house.

"Then one day after I'd been there several years, Abigail came out on that porch with the most beautiful image I've ever seen. She was a broom with a long slender handle of white ash. Abigail let her dance some leaves off the porch and then stood holding her while she talked to Baldwin. Too soon, we heard Mrs. Kincaid's voice from inside the house, 'Abigail, I need you in here,' and my first and only love was carried back inside.

"From that time on, I could hardly wait for garden day, although I knew from the start it was the impossible dream. She was no barn broom, and I knew no pitchfork would ever see the inside of that fine house.

"Didn't matter anyway, 'cause one day we got the news that Mrs. Kincaid had sold the farm. Soon after, everything in the house was loaded on wagons, and they carried that broom on down into Tennessee, and I never saw her again.

"A short time later, I was on a wagon myself, heading west into Kentucky. I wondered what my next farm would look like. But let me tell you how this story could have ended on that trip out of Virginia. We were going down this road, and I could see that sky was getting black pretty fast. The driver pulled over under a tree and was going to wait for the storm to pass. Then I heard him say maybe he could make it to the next farm and find better shelter and maybe a meal. Anyway, we didn't get too far up that road when there was this sorta blue flash, and lightning hit that tree we had been under. Seems like lightning comes looking for my kin, but if we had still been there, it might have come looking for that wagon first.

"Speaking of my kin, what type of wood do you think I am? I'm pretty sure I know now, but for a long time, I didn't know what my family tree was. I'd heard pine, oak, ash, hickory, even mahogany or maple."

I told that old pitchfork I didn't know all that much about wood, but I knew he wasn't mahogany. I knew some mahogany once, 'cause in this one tack room where I used to hang out, the boss had a desk of mahogany. The desk said his whole family was into furniture—tables, chairs, certainly not tools. Seemed to think he was better than most wood. Said you never hear someone say, "It's getting cold in here. Throw some more mahogany on the fire." You might hear me say it.

I told him, "You're not maple, either. The maple family—they're into furniture, too. Also, they're in the syrup business. No, I'd say you're either oak or hickory."

"You're right. I'm hickory. I just like the sound of that word—hickory. And I'm living proof we're a pretty sturdy family.

"Anyway, when we finally reached the end of our journey, it wasn't a farm, but a racetrack somewhere in Kentucky. We were just moving into a new century, and I most certainly was moving into a new and exciting existence. My good fortune came in the form of a groom named Wendell, my all-time favorite person.

"Wendell had a gift when it came to working with horses. Only two or three horses at any one time were lucky to have Wendell as their groom. He devoted so much time to each horse, that's all he could handle. Sometimes he'd take me off the wall before sunrise and I'd never get back up there until sundown. But I didn't mind. I loved to watch Wendell do his magic. He'd stand me in the corner of the stall in case I was needed and then go to work on those horses. He could get those horses so relaxed they'd sometimes lay down while he was in the stall. Never seen horses do that with anyone else. He loved those horses and they loved him.

"He'd take them out to graze in the afternoon. Out aways from the barn was this oak tree, and under it, Wendell had this whiskey barrel that had been sawed in half. Kept it covered with this piece of canvas. Barrel was filled with something called brine. Wendell would take those horses out there and stand them in that barrel. Said it toughened their legs. Said prizefighters soaked their hands in brine.

"Wendell's prize possession was a pair of deerskin gloves that Isaac Murphy gave him. Sometimes he'd put those gloves on when he worked with me. I never did see Isaac Murphy. He had died in 1896, only 37 years old.

"When I was with Wendell, we always worked with the best trainers—Sam Hildreth, John E. Madden, A. J. Joyner, names you may not know, but they were the best.

"In 1919, we were with trainer H. G. Bedwell. Wendell was rubbing a gelding called Billy Kelly, and we went to the Derby. We ran second, but another horse from our barn won, a maiden named Sir Barton.

"Anywhere you went that year and next, you only heard one name, Man o' War. Funny thing, he was born in Lexington in 1917 but never ran in Kentucky. Kept him up there in New York for some reason. Even carried him over to Canada for his last race. Beat that same Sir Barton in a match race. Came home to Kentucky after he was retired and died in Lexington in 1947.

"After I came to the racetrack, there was no more riding in wagons. Traveled by train or van. Been to New York, up to Chicago, down to New Orleans.

"One day in 1935, Wendell laid down on the straw to take a nap like I'd seen him do many times. Only this time, he didn't wake up. When they came and carried him away, I was glad he had those gloves with him, 'cause it was fall and there was a chill in the air.

"About this time, there was a jock starting to make riding history, a product of Ohio like myself. Many say the best ever—Eddie Arcaro. Rode a lot of those Calumet horses. In fact, after Wendell was gone, I was with Calumet Farm and the Jones boys for a few years. Naturally, we went to the Derby about every year, but my man never won it. Seemed like about every horse in the barn was a Derby contender at some time. Did some work in Whirlaway's stall, though we didn't take care of him. The best horse I worked with at Calumet was the filly Bewitch. She even beat the great Citation."

I told the pitchfork I'd been with some good trainers and some pretty nice horses, too, but never got close to being part of the big races. I don't even wear a nameplate.

He said, "Let me tell you about a nameplate. Know what happens to a halter with a nameplate? When that horse is finished, you're finished. End up in a bag in the corner of the tack room. Nobody wants to wear a halter with someone else's name on it. Oh, they might take the nameplate off and still get some use out of you. Now when they're putting that nameplate on, you probably don't notice there's some pain involved, 'cause you're all proud and excited about being a special halter. But when they take that nameplate off, it's not pretty. Oh, even if they try to be careful, you're still gonna end up with some scars. The bottom line is you're just gonna end up being a shipping halter. Know what that is? Every time a horse is shipped to the farm or some owner changes trainers, you hear them tell the groom, 'Don't send him in that halter, use this old one.' Next thing, you're going from horse to horse, this barn to that barn, and so on. After a while, you get all dried up and start cracking. The other tack sees you and starts talking. 'Remember that halter? Used to be with that nice two-year-old. Thought they were heading for the classics. Colt went wrong before he turned three. When's the last time you think he's seen some saddle soap?'

"No, you don't want no nameplate. You'd be better off being a rope halter on a mule down in Georgia. Oh, it's been nice working around those big outfits and famous horses, but what really matters is just being able to work with horses and those fine people. Like they say, fame is fleeting. Who would have ever thought Calumet could come upon hard times?

"Anyway, I've enjoyed it all and like this small barn I'm with now. Wanna hear something sorta unbelievable? Yesterday, while you were out walking your horse, this man I never seen before comes down the shedrow and introduces himself to my groom. Says, 'My name's Clay Kincaid and I own these horses. What I'd like to do when this meet's over is take them down to my farm in Tennessee for the winter. If you feel like a little change of pace, you're sure welcome to come along and take care of them and stay at the farm until it's time to go back to the track next spring.'

"The groom thanked him and said he'd sure enjoy that and would look forward to seeing Tennessee for the first time.

"Clay Kincaid said, 'If you're more comfortable working with your own equipment, just pack it up and bring it along, although we've got everything there. And I mean everything. When my great-great Grandma Kincaid moved down there from Virginia nearly 100 years ago, she brought everything she had. And, between the barns and the main house, I'd say it's all still there.'

"You hear what I'm saying he said?" the pitchfork asked. "Let me ask you this, Mr. Triple-Stitched Halter. Do you suppose if it was protected from the worst of weather and not asked to work too hard, white ash could last as long as hickory?"

I don't think he expected me to answer this question, which, of course I couldn't anyway. But I hoped this marvelous existence in which he really had no choices and which he really had no control over would produce yet another great experience for him. 'Cause unless he was leaving out a lot of bad stuff, that old pitchfork has been on one great roll for 120 years.

Guess we'll have to finish this talk later. I hear the key in the lock. Let's go train some horses.

The Foundation

by Avalyn Hunter

THE APRIL sun was warm and kind, but Agba had little heart to notice. He sat quietly at his horse's head as he had all night, keeping vigil. The breeze that swirled through the slats of the stallion box brought teasing scents of flowers and green meadows, mixing with the odors of well-kept horses and clean straw.

From the green downs outside, human voices mixed with the sounds of horses: yearlings at play, anxious mares calling to new foals, and once or twice the deeper-throated whinny of a stallion. Sham noticed neither scent nor sound. He lay as he had for hours, his head in Agba's lap, with only the shallow rise and fall of his ribs showing that he still lived.

A shadow darkened the box door. Agba looked up. The sun silhouetted the man outside, but its rays winked on silver trimming and gold buttons and outlined the fashionable wig with a white aureole.

"How does he fare?"

Agba shook his head, not trying to conceal the reddened puffiness of his eyes. The Earl nodded. There was no need for words between the two men; they had been servant and master for over 20 years—or, rather, Sham had been in the Earl's possession for that long, and Agba had served the horse, something the Earl understood if few others did.

The nobleman cleared his throat. "I have had the gardeners make a place for him," he said quietly. "When he has passed, come to me, or have word sent. It is only fitting that the savior of Gogmagog be honored with a proper burial."

Agba nodded, turning his attention back to the horse. After a moment, footsteps faded away as the Earl left him to resume the death watch. The sun slowly crept higher, sending bars of light down onto the thick, golden straw, but the man did not stir, not even when he judged the hour for midmorning prayer had come. He mouthed the traditional words silently, his head bowed, but his eyes never leaving his horse.

As he finished the prayers, he felt the straw stirring by his hip. He smiled sadly, gently reaching a hand to the one companion who had shared this vigil with him. From underneath his mantle, he heard a brief, rusty vibration; then the head of a cat emerged from that refuge, blinking filmed eyes against the light. The striped body followed slowly and stiffly; the cat stretched himself gingerly, then touched his whitened muzzle to Sham's. At that touch, the old horse's nostrils flickered wider, and one ear pricked for just a moment.

Agba watched the two animals, feeling his throat tighten. How long had the three of them been together? Twenty years at least, surely. He could not remember now where the cat had joined them, though he had a vague memory of an awkward catling scurrying about the fringes of a cobbled courtyard. Most likely the inn, he thought. It had been from the drafty stable there that the good Earl had purchased Sham; but it could have been the home of the kindly Quaker who had rescued the horse from a brutal Paris carter. It hardly mattered.

Through all the long years at Gogmagog, Grimalkin had been there, keeping the mice from Sham's stall and sleeping by his side. Sham fretted when his small companion was gone too long, and the head groom had given orders long since that the cat was not to be molested by any of the stableboys on pain of the Earl's displeasure—so even though Grimalkin was now far too old to earn his keep by hunting, he lived on. But not for much longer, Agba knew. Even though the Moor cared for the cat as carefully as for the horse, the hallmarks of extreme old age were there for anyone to read in the shabby coat and sunken flanks.

INSHALLAH, Agba said in his heart. As Allah wills. He reached down to stroke Sham's neck. Even in the thinness of age, the horse still had the high crest inherited from an Arabian grandsire.

"Freak" they had called him in the King of France's court, seeing only the outsized crest on a body half-starved from an arduous voyage, not the grace and speed that had made Sham to be considered worthy of part of a gift from the Sultan's own stables. They knew nothing of his royal breeding, of the planning that had joined the finest Barb strains of Morocco with the blood of a prized Bedouin stallion. Nor had the English been kinder in their assessment—until Sham's son Lath defeated the best they had to offer on the courses of Newmarket, not once but many times. Then, suddenly, the high crest was no longer laughed at. It had become the mark of Godolphin breeding instead, the finest to be found, and buyers came from all over England to seek colts and fillies with the high head and crested neck of their sire.

Agba smiled, for a moment transported back in memory to the day Lath had carried off the Queen's Plate. He had been there with Sham, of course, watching from the stallion's back—the Earl had felt it good advertising to have the horse there, available for inspection by horsemen impressed by the prowess of his sons. But even the Earl could not have anticipated that his horse would be called for by the Queen herself after the race, to receive a plume of the royal purple at her hands in token of Lath's victory. After that, there had been no further questioning of Sham's worth; as the "Godolphin Arabian" he was celebrated far and wide, needing no approval from the arbiters of equine fashion or the certification of a pedigree long lost to mischance. As the Earl had said when asked of the horse's lineage, "His pedigree is written in his sons."

Lath, Cade, Regulus ... Agba recited the names silently, remembering their exploits. It was Cade who carried on the lineage now that Sham was too old for breeding, passing on his sire's qualities to new generations. And even Cade was no longer young, but already he had sons who gave good promise of continuing the line. Still ...

Sham stirred feebly, and Agba leaned forward, voicing the wordless croon that was all the speech he had. For a moment the ears pricked, the dulled brown eyes opened, and recognition sparked deep within, bringing fire and spirit back for a brief second. The stallion raised his head a few inches, and his nostrils fluttered with a faint nicker. Then the head dropped back to Agba's lap, and the horse did not move again.

Grimalkin flinched back, then stretched a cautious paw out to his friend. There was no response. The cat quivered, his whiskers stuck out stiff as wires, and sat back on his haunches. He stared at Sham's body as though willing the horse to move, to rise; then, without warning, his muzzle tipped back and he voiced a long disconsolate wail such as Agba had never heard in all their years together. The sound echoed throughout the stable like a mourner's cry. Before it had died away, the cat was gone, vanishing like some furred ghost.

Agba did not move. For a long time, he sat hunched over Sham's head, only his eyes betraying that he was not a statue: They traveled slowly over Sham's body from nose to tail and back again, blinking occasionally as vision blurred and silent tears spilled over. But at last there were no tears left to cry. Agba wiped his eyes with his sleeve and rose, setting Sham's head aside as gently as if the horse merely slept. His bare brown feet made no noise as he slipped from the stall. Head bowed, he paced slowly up the long stately lane from the stable to the house. The servants there let him pass without comment, long since used to his ways, and he went down the long hallways with their polished sconces and portraits until he came to the Earl's private study. The door was open, but he paused politely at the entrance until the Earl looked up.

"Ah, Agba. Come in." The gray eyes were sad, and for the first time Agba noted the deepening lines around them; the Earl, too, was growing old. At the Earl's gesture, Agba took his usual seat on a hassock, curling his feet under him after the custom of his native land. "So he is gone?"

AGBA nodded. The Earl closed his eyes for a moment as if in pain, then pulled a bell rope. Almost at once, a liveried servant appeared. "My lord?"

"The Godolphin Arabian is no more. Send to Chapman and tell him to move the horse's body to the burial site. Have him send to me when all is ready."

The servant bowed and left. Agba studied the floral pattern of the carpet with eyes that did not really focus until the Earl cleared his throat. The Moor looked up to meet the steady, gray gaze.

"I have wondered what is to be done for you, now that your horse is gone," the Earl began hesitantly. "I would gladly give you the care of any horse in my stables ..."

But Agba was already shaking his head. The Earl eyed him keenly. "No? Perhaps a place in my household, then, or elsewhere on my estate?"

Again the headshake. The Earl nodded slowly. "I feared it might be so. You were always the Godolphin's servant, never mine. But what will you do, then?"

Agba uncurled from the hassock, padding softly over to the ornate globe that dominated one corner of the study. Turning the sphere, he brought the coast of North Africa into view and pointed. Again, the Earl understood.

"You wish to go home." The words were statement, not question. Agba nodded slowly, his sad, black eyes never leaving the Earl's gray ones. "Or, rather, you must go home. Why, I do not know, but I see it in your face." The nobleman sighed deeply, his face aging years in a moment. "Very well. I shall be sorry to lose a friend such as you have become, but it will be as you desire. You shall have passage to Tangier and money to keep you, as well. Also, I shall write a letter testifying to your service. ..."

A tap at the door interrupted the Earl. He turned toward the newcomer. "Yes, Chapman?"

The head groom shifted awkwardly from foot to foot. "Begging your pardon, milord, but you did say to send when the burial was ready."

"And it is? Very well." The Earl rose slowly. "Come with me, Agba. It is only right for you to be there."

For a moment, Agba wanted to refuse, not sure he could bear the sight of his Sham's body consigned to cold earth. But the Earl was waiting, and he made himself put one foot ahead of the other, following the old nobleman down the long, carpeted corridors and out onto the flagstone walks. The scent of early roses flooded his nostrils as the Earl stopped, blending with the smells of sun-warmed grass and freshly turned earth, and he looked up to find himself standing by a deep pit. He swallowed hard, knowing what lay within.

"I hope the place pleases you," the Earl said softly, in a voice meant for his ears alone. "I like to think that the Godolphin would have liked it, here in the sunshine with his sons and daughters close by."

Agba nodded, though he only half heard. He looked at the roses that surrounded the grave, at the surrounding pastures, at anything but the awful hole that held what was left of Sham. Then something caught his eye: something small and gray, huddled beneath the roses at the head of the grave. His eyes suddenly blurred. He walked quickly and jerkily to the place and bent. His hands touched fur, and he bowed his head, knowing before he lifted that the life was gone. He turned and knelt at the edge of the grave. He could scarcely see but needed no sight for this; he lowered Grimalkin's body gently. One of the gardeners stepped forward, words of indignation beginning to sputter from his lips, but the man was abruptly stopped by the Earl's own cane extended in front of him.

"Let him be." The Earl's voice sounded strangely thick, as though he too was only a breath away from tears. "I recognize the cat. Such faithful friends should not be parted."

Agba laid the cat's body next to Sham's head and rose, resuming his place by the Earl. Someone pressed a clod of earth into his hand, and he mechanically followed the Earl's lead, letting the lump drop into the grave. It made a dull thud as it struck. There was a long moment's silence; then the Earl slowly turned away, and as he did the gardeners' shovels began a slow rhythm. Above, as if the sky itself mourned, gray clouds drifted in.

Agba did not follow the Earl back to the house. He stumbled away, not really seeing where he went until he fetched up against a fence. Far away, the bells of a village church tolled the noon hour and he sank to his knees in prayer, for a moment setting aside grief. But he remained on his knees for a long time after his prayers were finished.

HE KNEW what he should do, of course. He should be gathering his small possessions, preparing for the return to Morocco according to the orders of the Sultan given so many years ago. That Sultan was likely long dead now, but the habit of obedience still remained; only a decree from Allah Himself would have set those orders aside in Agba's mind. So, the Moor would return home. But what then? Would he return to the stables, be given other horses to tend? Would he be executed because of the failure of that long-ago gift to France, or honored because of Sham's success in England? Would he ...

Agba shivered as he realized he had no answers. For nearly 30 years, his life had been tied to Sham's. The horse had been all the purpose he had ever needed. But now Sham was gone. Grimalkin, too, had passed away, and for the first time in his life, Agba found himself alone and without purpose.

His throat tightened—this time not for Sham, but for himself. What would be the reason for his life, the legacy he would leave behind? He had long since accepted that he would never marry. There would be no sons to carry on his memory. With the money promised by the Earl, he might be able to complete the hajj to Mecca, but there could be no scholar's honors, no veneration as one wise in his faith: not for a mute. He had no wealth and no means of acquiring it. He could not make a name for himself through great charity. All he had was his integrity and the long years of faithful service to his horse. Yet what would they matter to others? Would anyone remember, or care?

A curious whuffling noise interrupted his brooding. He lifted his head. From across the fence, bright, inquisitive eyes met his. The colt snorted as the man moved, stepping back on quick nervous feet, then pricked his ears and posed. At that moment, the sun broke through the shifting clouds, illuminating the colt in golden light.

Agba gasped. For a moment, the years spun backward. It could have been Sham there looking at him, with golden highlights shining from his dark bay coat and his fine-boned head held high. The colt's small movements were Sham's; his eyes were the same rich purple-brown. Looking in them, Agba saw his horse's spirit. And more. For one shining moment, he saw others looking out of those eyes—bays and grays, chestnuts and blacks; horses stretched flying in the wind, running over the green downs of Newmarket and Ascot or the lawns of Chantilly; horses carrying the silks of kings and nobles; horses of every size and description, but all with Sham's spirit looking through their eyes.

The vision trembled, then shattered. Agba found himself back in the sunlit world. Across the fence, the colt tossed his head, only a colt again. Or … was he? He nickered softly, with a questioning note, and to Agba's astonished delight, a young cat came trotting up, touching noses fearlessly with the larger animal before turning to look at the watching man. The green-gold eyes blinked, the striped body quivered. And then the cat stalked right up to the Moor, butting against his hand with a familiar rusty purr.

Agba threw his head back and laughed his silent laugh as his clever fingers scratched deftly behind the catling's ears. Then he rose from his kneeling, the movement startling both animals into flight. He stretched creaking legs, watching the colt run, and seeing Sham's speed in the young, strong legs. What did it matter that he had no voice, that no man would ever hear his story or know the full tale of his life? Allah had heard His servant's need and had answered.

SEE? A voice seemed to say. These are your memorial: not cold stones or empty words but swift sons and daughters of the wind, running free. So long as Sham's line lives, so long will you be remembered.

He looked out over the pastures one last time, seeing the young horses there with new eyes. Across the field, the dark bay colt had caught up with his mates. Bucking and playing, they raced away across the meadow, their tails flagged as if in salute to the quiet watcher. He lifted a hand in a gesture that was half blessing, half farewell as they vanished over a gentle rise.

"Agba?" Footsteps hurried up behind him. He turned, a smile still touching his lips and his sad, black eyes. "Ah, there you are," Chapman said, his face flushed with sun and evident hurrying. "His Lordship sends for you. The man sent to the inn says there's a coach leaving for Plymouth tonight, so if you step smart, you can be on your way this eve." The head groom swallowed hard and thrust out a hand. "I've a deal of work to see to, so I'll not likely see you again before you go. Godspeed to you, Agba."

Agba took the proffered hand, shook it, and turned away, leaving the pasture without a backward glance. Suddenly eager, he hurried toward the manor house, pausing only once as he reached Sham's grave. Where the gaping hole had been, green turf had been laid, and amidst the turf a plain slab of granite without inscription or marking. Agba frowned, wondering at the lack of words.

"He needs no inscription," a familiar voice said. Agba jumped, only then realizing that he was not alone. On a bench amidst the roses, the Earl of Godolphin sat, a smile of understanding in his gray eyes. The nobleman waved a hand at the surrounding fields. "Out there is all the memorial he could ever need. He has laid the foundation for a new and noble breed, and in that he will be remembered. Nor do you need graven words to hold your memory. The Godolphin Arabian may bear my name, but he was ever your horse. You and he will be remembered together. Or so I think."

Agba bowed deeply, his eyes shining. In a few simple words, the Earl had unknowingly confirmed the message he, Agba, had received by the pasture fence. It is a sign. Whatever comes to me, my life has been fulfilled. Praise be to Allah. He straightened, his eyes full of all the gratitude he had no speech to voice. And, to his surprise, the Earl rose, bowing to him as if to another noble.

There was no need of further words. Hours later, Agba watched out the back window of the coach as the Godolphin manor dwindled in the distance, then turned. As if in escort, colts and fillies raced the coach in the pastures to either side of the lane. Agba watched them, seeing his beloved Sham in every lifted head, every silken stride, and found himself content. As the coach rattled past the last fence, he lifted a hand in farewell and, sinking back against the cushions, slept.

Third Jewel

by Bill Melzer

"I'M GOING to pretend I never heard that." There was a prolonged silence on the line, and for an instant L.T. imagined that Denham Peck's feelings had been hurt by his tone ... but just for an instant.

That's like expecting ice to take offense if you imply that it's cold, L.T. thought.

"Look," Peck finally said. "It was just a suggestion."

"First," L.T. replied, "I won't have you trying to dictate my colt's schedule. The race in Nairobi is too close. Second, to 'suggest' that I run Rime Or Reason and not really try with him ... that's incredibly callous, even for WorldWideRacing. So you can take your under-the-table 'appearance fee' and ..."

L.T. swallowed the balance of his retort. He had long ago resolved never to let Peck rile him, and that determination was especially important now.

After all, it's not every day that you got to go for the Triple Crown.

"Please," Peck said, "you misunderstand WWR's position. We're just thinking about what's best for racing. If you win the Belmont today, imagine the goodwill an appearance in the East African Cup would generate ... and you could still make the Travers."

What's best for WorldWideRacing, you mean, L.T. wanted to blurt out. *At first, WWR had looked to be an ally, a white knight. What happened?*

Peck seemed to take his silence as tacit acceptance.

"Good, good. I'll see you at the conference," he said before disconnecting.

Let him think what he will for now.

L.T. glanced at the dark vid-screen above his dresser. The call had jolted him from a fitful sleep, and he hadn't had a chance to check the clock before Peck had started in.

"Time?" he asked aloud, and the screen came alive in soft, glowing green: 5:07 AM - 08 Jun 2019.

Geez ... doesn't he ever sleep?

L.T. shifted to the edge of his bed and sat with his eyes closed.

"Today is for you, Nicholas," he whispered, as always.

Inevitably, when he spoke with Denham Peck, L.T. was reminded of Nicholas—both so persistent, both so hardheaded. Nicholas had spoken incessantly of his dreams to work with horses. Despite that, L.T. had been proud of himself for being a "good parent," as he railroaded his ever-more-distant son toward college instead.

L.T. shook his head, struggling to keep the painful memories at bay.

Why is it, when you finally realize you weren't listening, it's always too late?

He moved to the kitchen and requested the room to put through a call to his assistant. He had been tempted to spend the night with Rime Or Reason but had opted to get what meager rest he could before the world went crazy. Anyway, the colt was in good hands; Cole Robertson was the best horseman he knew.

The speaker beeped twice and the operator's ever-cheery voice filled the room.

"Good morning, WorldWideRacing."

"Morning, Mary," L.T. said. "Can you connect me? I think we're on Lot 81 this time."

"Mr. Barnes, hello! Your colt was moved to 80 ... security and all. It'll take a few minutes to find Mr. Robertson ..."

Peck is always up to something, L.T. thought, still irked by the early call. *Yesterday, it was that commercial he wanted my colt to do for WorldWideGaming. Why in the heck would I let my horse appear in a casino ad?*

L.T. grabbed a container of OJ from the refrigerator. His practical side told him he should eat, but the flock of butterflies already astir in his midsection begged to differ. He flipped on WorldWideRacing, retrieved his copy of *The Times* from the printer tray, and then extended his arms overhead.

Forty-seven isn't old, he reassured himself, but his muscles were surely taking a little longer to stretch these days, and if they hadn't recently switched to a smaller font in the newspaper, his eyes were beginning to show their age, as well.

The excited call of a track announcer caught his attention, and he glanced up to see the stretch duel of a claiming race from Tokyo WWR. The total handle figure in the corner of the screen leapt out at him: $131-million wagered around the globe, and that with most of the U.S. bettors still sound asleep.

It's gonna be a big day for the WWR bean counters. And the day of a lifetime for me.

L.T.'s mind flashed back to the '80s, to his youth spent working his father's farm—caring for horses, breaking them, and, most especially, riding to his heart's content. Like every boy reared around horses, he had fantasized about being the next Pincay or Shoemaker, and he smiled as he recalled long winter afternoons spent alone in the frigid barn, astride a bale of hay, pumping furiously as he rode Seattle Slew to yet another daydream victory.

He had made it on-track, even won his share of races, but the needle on the scale had taken to spinning too far to the right, the calendar pages falling away too quickly, and his dreams of riding a champion were dashed by the reality of his flesh. He had continued plugging along, nourished through hard times by the pride in Nicholas's eyes, and he had never really abandoned hope, until ... the night that Fate intervened—in the guise of a drunk driver—and Nicholas was taken from him.

He knew it wasn't his fault, but still his head rang incessantly with the echoes of his wife's melancholy, and the image of his son's mangled body seemed forever burned onto his retinas.

Five hollow years passed—his desire to go on often questioned—but through it all his love for the game had never diminished. And when computers changed the complexion of racing, he realized he was being offered a gift he could never have dared hope for—another chance to fulfill his childhood dreams.

But the game is different now. Maybe too different.

"L.T., good morning. How're the nerves?" his assistant asked, plucking him from his memories.

"No need for coffee this morning, that's for sure," L.T. replied, chuckling. "How's Rimer feeling?"

"He's perfect. I took him for another walk on the new surface; he seems to like the bounce in it."

"Yeah, it seems even more forgiving than the old."

"Ain't technology grand?" Cole kidded.

"I've got the obligatory round table on WWR this morning," L.T. said, "but I should be to you by 1 at the latest."

"If Peck limits the fibernet questions to a mere thousand, you will be."

"Well, I've got my stock answer ready—'Rime Or Reason will do the talking for both of us.' "

The receiver picked up a snort in the background.

"I'd say he agrees with you, boss."

These animals are amazing. In the face of so many changes, we need to remind ourselves that they are still made of horseflesh.

THE net conference went well enough, L.T. thought as he left the set, *though I could have done without the usual rehash of my botching the WorldCup Juvenile.*

He had gotten into traffic trouble several times in the 37-horse field at EuroWestWWR the previous November and they had finished a well-beaten 11th, one of only three defeats handed Rime Or Reason as a two-year-old. At three, the colt had fleshed out and matured, and he came into the Belmont undefeated for the year, winning the Kentucky Derby by two lengths and the Preakness by a widening seven.

WWR was reaping a financial windfall with the potential for the first Triple Crown winner of the 21st century, and they were pushing the PR envelope. L.T. had gone along with most of their machinations, although at times it seemed the show was coming before the race itself.

L.T. spotted Denham Peck from afar, but despite his best efforts to sneak away, the vice president of WWR managed to corner him.

"My man ... big day for you today!" Peck said as he slapped L.T. heartily on the back.

L.T. detested the man's false camaraderie.

"And for you, as well."

"Yes, indeed. We're projecting a ten today!"

L.T. did the mental math. Ten digits: they were expecting a billion dollars to be wagered on the race. The figure boggled his mind; Peck might just as well have been talking about Monopoly money.

"Needless to say," Peck continued, "we're all rooting for you. Would be a hell of a boost for the year's bottom line to have a Triple Crown winner."

"I'll try not to let you down."

Peck was too self-absorbed for the sarcasm to register. "L.T., I need you to do me a little favor," he said as they moved toward the paddock area.

"Denham, I'm a bit busy today," L.T. replied, softening his voice, hoping to unearth some yet-unseen vein of compassion.

"You won't even notice the camera. We're expecting ten-million new viewers today and we want to give them a behind-the-scenes peek at our game. What better way than to docu-vid the 'now' team in racing?"

"Look—I always play ball, always oblige. But not today. This is too important."

Peck leaned toward L.T., his voice dropping to a whisper.

"I hate to bring this up, but ... remember your contract."

L.T. recoiled as though physically struck.

"You wouldn't."

"Hey, bigger fish than Rime Or Reason have come up with an injury prerace."

L.T. choked back the anger bubbling up within. *The contract. 'WWR requires complete cooperation from all horsemen in publicity matters. Infractions will result in suspensions of horseman and horse.'*

Why do we all sign that damn thing?

Peck straightened and resumed matter-of-factly.

"We'll just follow you around and I'll educate the viewers. It'll be like we're not even there."

There had been rumblings among the horsemen about the power that WWR held over them, and a few had gone so far as to suggest some kind of action was warranted.

Maybe they're right, L.T. thought. *But that's for another day and time.*

He took a deep breath and forced a smile.

"Suit yourself," he said and resumed his original course. Despite Peck's assurances, he could readily hear the commentary begin behind him.

"In the paddock area the horses are outfitted and prepared for the race," Peck said, his words instantly translated into a hundred languages and fibernetted around the globe.

L.T.'s nervousness cinched up a notch as he entered the cavernous building. The countdown clock on the vid-screen overhead showed 25 minutes to post, less than a half-hour to what promised to be the crowning moment of his career.

I'm not going to let anything take away from the experience. Or anybody.

He glanced around the room, trying to imagine what a first-time viewer would make of the scene. Apart from the horses walking in an oval in the center of the floor, it looked about as far from a racing venue as was possible. The large bank of vid-screens suspended from the ceiling was all that kept the space from being completely empty, and the room's boundaries all glowed in a weird, monochromatic blue.

L.T. immediately picked Rime Or Reason out of the group, his colt's gray coat glistening like polished steel.

"The king has a court, I see," Cole Robertson kidded as L.T. approached.

"Court jesters, more like," L.T. muttered under his breath, but Cole heard him and laughed aloud.

L.T. ran a hand over his horse's flank. The muscles were like taut bands, their power unmistakable. The colt turned his head toward the sound of L.T.'s voice and L.T. shivered reflexively. Even after five years, he still got an unsettled feeling seeing a horse outfitted in VR-blinkers.

"You and me today, Rimer," L.T. said, and the colt gave one sharp nod as though in understanding. Behind them, the play-by-play droned on.

"... Don't worry that the horses appear blinded; they are all fit with our patented Virtual Reality blinkers. The room you see is actually one giant blue-screen stage. A computer plots the positions of all horses and people in the room, digitally erases what is unnecessary, and then projects the participants into a virtual paddock. ..."

L.T. craned back to look at the screen labeled 'Composite,' and saw himself beside Rime Or Reason in the tree-lined paddock at Belmont Park, ringed by a colorful crowd under a dazzling sky.

“Nineteen minutes,” a voice announced.

L.T. could feel his hand trembling.

I envy Rimer. He doesn’t have to worry, to remember. He just has to run.

“Good luck.”

L.T. turned to the speaker and was met by the outstretched hand of Francisco Rodas, owner of Turn Me Loose. Rodas’s colt had finished second in the Derby but then skipped the second leg of the Triple Crown, instead using a romp in the Kuala Lumpur Derby as a steppingstone to another shot at Rime Or Reason. Francisco’s 17-year-old son, Scotty, stood by his side.

“And to you, Francisco,” L.T. responded. “Should be a hell of a race.” He turned to the boy. “Nice ride in the Novice Derby, Scotty. You’re almost as good a tactician as your old man.”

The boy’s smile threatened to split seams, but Francisco quickly doused the compliment.

“He’s too indecisive, I’m afraid. I don’t think he’ll ever make the grade as a rider.”

Scotty opened his mouth to defend himself but instead turned away, eyes downcast. L.T. had seen Scotty ride in training races; the boy had talent. It seemed the only one who didn’t see it was his own father.

I wish Francisco would realize what he’s doing to the boy before it’s too late. Nicholas was about Scotty’s age when ...

L.T. looked away.

Did I dash his dreams without a second thought, as Francisco does Scotty’s?

Despite his growing nervousness, L.T. found himself deeply moved, as always, by the bond among the horsemen. Several stopped by to wish him a good trip. “I’m gonna try to beat you, but if I can’t, I hope you do it,” one said. Another offered, “If you win, make sure they drape you with carnations you can actually smell!”

These were incredible people, linked by their love for the animals and the competition. That part had never changed, no matter how strange the game had become. And no matter how cold.

He felt a hand on his elbow and found Peck once again at his side.

"Mr. Barnes, tell our viewers how you are feeling right now. Nervous?"

L.T. blinked incredulously.

Even Peck should know better than to interrupt here.

"A little," L.T. said, and then spun abruptly back to his horse.

"Riders up!" a voice called out, and L.T.'s butterflies flew unhindered. Cole Robertson lashed a BugBoy onto the saddle of Rime Or Reason.

"... These weird, spider-like contraptions you see are electronic jockeys," Peck reported. "Each can replicate the actions of a human jockey and each weighs precisely 126 pounds, making the conditions exquisitely fair for all."

The horses circled twice more for the audience and then were led through a set of tall double doors, proceeding down a short corridor that emptied onto another immense set.

As they moved, L.T. studied his colt, absorbing his body language, beginning his immersion into the zone where he and his horse became of one purpose ... and was yanked back into the show by the grating voice of Denham Peck.

"... Here we have another stage, an electronic wonder. Note the row of treadmills facing the far wall, and the elevated platform behind each. The horses are each positioned on a mill, where our computer will measure their running speed and move them on Belmont Park's virtual track accordingly. The VR-blinkers will present to each horse precisely the view that it would see during an actual race. The riders are also fitted with VR helmets and they pilot their mounts from the platforms, using the BugBoys to control their charge's speed, direction, and effort. Each horse's health is constantly monitored, as well. WWR presents the ultimate combination of competition and safety, eliminating the need for the near-empty mausoleums that were real-life racetracks ten years ago."

L.T. waited for the sales pitch to conclude and then nudged Beck toward the exit.

"You'll have to excuse us now," he said.

Peck uttered a quick segue. Once the vid-cam blinked "off-line," he turned to glare icily at L.T.

"You don't run this show," Peck said, his volume rising. "If I want to follow you around with a vid-cam stuck up your butt, I damn well will. I'm in charge."

Several heads turned at the disturbance.

"Once you pass through there you aren't," L.T. responded, angrily nodding toward the entrance.

"Bull! You're too full of yourself, Barnes. You'd better carefully consider your next move. We're back on in 20 seconds, and I damn well am going to ask you more questions."

Peck raised his voice louder still, obviously aiming to ensure his message carried to all ears on the set.

"You work for WWR! Period! And don't think you're going to get any special consideration just because you go around in a damn wheelchair!"

L.T. stared at Peck, trying to smother the blaze flaring in his chest. The nearby horsemen looked on in shock.

As a vid-cam operator counted down from three, L.T. turned his back and wheeled away. Peck's commentary resumed but the man's voice faded and, on glancing at the overhead screen, L.T. saw he had left the set for the control booth.

Cole helped with the straps on the VR-helmet as L.T. took his position behind Rime Or Reason. The colt was walking leisurely on his tread, pricking his ears right and left as his eyes told him he was entering the track surface at Belmont.

"He's all yours," Cole said, flicking the switch that sent images streaming to L.T.'s helmet. "Have a good trip."

L.T. clucked to his colt as they were announced in the post parade, sending Rime Or Reason into a canter, checking his response to voice and reins. The BugBoy seemed to be working perfectly, and the colt was eager to go about his task.

Nicholas used to get so excited when I rode broken-down claimers. Imagine what he would think now.

L.T. glanced left, at the VR-tote. He and Rimer were 5-to-2 favorites in the bulky field, and the weight of all that confidence nestled on L.T.'s shoulders. A sharp edge of terror sliced at his already frayed nerves as the immensity of what he was about to attempt hit him square on.

The Triple Crown. I'll never walk again, and here I am riding Rimer for the Triple Crown.

Rime Or Reason warmed up beautifully, snorting and arching his neck, omnipotent. The periphery of L.T.'s vision faded away as his senses focused.

Forty years of work, 40 years of preparation—of a true love reserved only for his family and for this—had brought him to the threshold.

The VR-view went red, indicating one minute to post, and L.T.'s entire world collapsed into the intervals between ticks of the clock. He soothed his mount, preparing him for the transition to the virtual gate.

He was vaguely aware of a voice announcing, "It is now post time." The VR went blank for three seconds and then all 28 entrants were magically enclosed in their gate stalls. L.T. ran the entire race in his mind in fast-forward—feeling the rush of the break, choreographing every movement in Rime Or Reason's performance, sensing the poles flash by, tasting the final surge to victory.

This is for you, Nicholas.

He could see his colt coiling beneath him, anticipating the bell. Suddenly his helmet echoed with the sound of the vet's buzzer, and the horses were instantly back behind the gate.

He assumed that one of the other riders had sensed a problem and triggered the halt and so was startled to see the vet standing beside Rime Or Reason, eyeing the colt.

"What's up, Cal?" L.T. asked.

"Sorry, L.T.," the vet said, almost in a whisper. "Computer says he doesn't scan sound."

"What?" L.T. was too stunned to argue.

Could that be right? Have I missed something in all the excitement?

"I'm real sorry, but I have to scratch him," Cal said into space, unable to look at L.T.

"But he seems ..." L.T. stopped in midsentence. He yanked off his VR-helmet and turned toward the control room window. "Peck!"

At Peck's command of, "Loop 'em," the composite screen went into a clip of the horses endlessly circling behind the gate.

"You're vetted, Barnes," Peck said. "The med-scanner is picking up a problem in his left hind. Nothing too serious, fortunately."

"You can't do this!" L.T. said. The other riders had removed their helmets and were gathering around, perplexed.

"What's up?" Francisco Rodas asked.

Peck preempted any reply from L.T.

"Rime Or Reason is a vet's scratch. We'll have a five-minute delay for the bettors. Everyone return to your positions."

A murmur went up among the horsemen; the injury would improve all their chances immensely.

"L.T.?" Francisco asked, disregarding the explanation.

"There's nothing wrong with Rimer."

Cal had undone the colt's blinkers and BugBoy, and Rime Or Reason stood quietly on the tread, awaiting direction. The chatter died away, the horsemen unsure of what to do.

"Return to your horses," Peck repeated brusquely, waving them back.

"This ain't right," someone yelled, eliciting nods of agreement. "We've got to *do* something."

"I appreciate that," L.T. said, "but this is between Peck and me."

"Not anymore," Francisco said as he pushed his way through the group, returning to his horse. He began to undo his colt's equipment, and the others followed his lead.

"What the hell are you all doing?" Peck said. "There's $7-million in purse money on the line!"

They ignored him.

"You all know the score," Peck said. "You have nowhere to go. WWR *is* racing."

"My colt has a problem in his left hind. I'm scratching him," Francisco said, and one by one the others echoed the withdrawal.

"No one leaves this set," Peck said, spitting out the words like a spoiled child.

L.T. scanned the room, and his eyes stopped on an emergency exit. He wheeled over to the door, threw the bolt, and pushed it open.

"You're through, Barnes!" Peck screamed over the alarm.

L.T. led Rime Or Reason down the central aisle and out into the afternoon, with the others closing ranks behind him. Soon the horses were idling among the vehicles in the studio parking lot.

L.T. waved to get the attention of the entire group.

"I want to thank you all for supporting me back there."

"It was just a matter of time," one said, to a chorus of endorsements. "They've been stealing our souls bit by bit."

Francisco grinned at L.T.

"Actually, it was a lucky break for you, Barnes."

"Oh, I don't quite see it that way," L.T. said, laughing. He touched his rival lightly on the arm. "Francisco ... thanks."

"Wouldn't have been any satisfaction in winning if you didn't run."

The horsemen's support personnel hurried around the corner of the building, led by Cole and Scotty.

"They've locked the stable building," Cole said. "They're demanding everyone go back in immediately."

"Demanding, huh?" L.T. said. "That sounds about right."

"What now? Where are we going to take the horses?" Francisco asked, eyeing their surroundings.

"Why not keep them outside?" Scotty suggested.

"Don't be dense," Francisco said. "There are no facilities for them other than the indoor stables."

Give the boy a break, L.T. thought. As his eyes flicked from father to son and to the group around them, a crazy, wonderful idea took form in his mind.

"Scotty is right. Let's keep them outside," he said.

The others gaped at him as though he had gone mad.

"Where?" Cole asked.

"It's a beautiful weekend afternoon, the traffic will be light. Let's take them for a walk. We can head across to the park and take the bike path down to the beach. It's only about a mile."

Francisco considered him briefly, and suddenly his eyes brightened.

"The beach," he said. "Of course."

Before they had gone halfway to the main gate, Denham Peck stormed out to confront them.

"Where do you think you're going?" Peck challenged, gesturing wildly.

"Out for a stroll," L.T. replied, as though describing the most ordinary of occurrences.

"Are you nuts?" Peck was literally hopping in agitation. "That's $500-million worth of property."

L.T. fixed him rigid with a stare.

"Peck ... they're *horses*."

RIME OR REASON probed the water with one hoof, in the telltale manner of horses with VR experience. After some initial uncertainty, the colt began to splash in the surf with joy, and L.T. laughed. Around them, the crowd had swelled enormously, now a thousand souls strong. *You forget the thrill, the sheer excitement of people delighting in horses.*

"We've been missing something, huh?" Francisco offered from beside him.

"You read my mind. Yes, we surely have."

Scotty was standing knee-deep in the surf holding Turn Me Loose by his side and using his free hand to detail precisely to another owner how he could have ridden the horse to victory. The animated reaction of the other suggested he believed otherwise. L.T.'s eyes drifted down the shoreline, to an immense American flag snapping in the breeze atop a distant lifeguard station. The horses had seduced all the sun-worshipers; apart from the crowd around them the beach was now pretty much deserted.

"To the flag?" L.T. asked.

Francisco followed the direction of L.T.'s gaze.

"Looks about right," Francisco replied. "You sure your colt is up to it?"

"He could do it even with me in the saddle," L.T. said, grinning, and Francisco laughed heartily.

At the shrill blast of a lifeguard's whistle, 28 Thoroughbreds with human passengers took off down the beach like a cavalry charge. A line of volunteers had strung along the shore, holding back the pockets of spectators and securing a wide strip of sand along the water's edge.

L.T. looked on from a perch atop the wooden station at the finish line, peering through binoculars lent to him by a delighted lifeguard. The preparations had been chaotic, and Rime Or Reason had been confused by the ragged start. He had hesitated but quickly grabbed the bit and pulled his substitute rider forward in the saddle. The colt showed his innate athleticism as they zig-zagged their way through the field until they were splashing just behind a tight pack of six that had separated from the remainder of the horses after a half-mile. The colt's long legs struck out, attacking the sand, and his jockey fell into a smooth rhythm with the strides.

Two of the sextet tired suddenly and quickly fell off the pace. L.T.'s breath caught in his throat as Rime Or Reason appeared trapped behind them, but the rider deftly steered the colt to the right and swooped far around the danger, skimming very near the chain of onlookers.

Rime Or Reason pricked his ears as they raced past the halfway point, speeding by one struggling colt and then another, until only two remained ahead. He pushed forward, reaching the flanks of the leading pair, and the three of them raced as a team for a good 20 seconds until the middle horse wilted under the pressure and gave up the chase.

L.T. could see the pacesetters clearly now, a quarter-mile down the beach. He zoomed in on the leading horse—Turn Me Loose, being ridden with abandon by Francisco Rodas—as they ran on, spraying clumps of wet sand behind them.

Rime Or Reason gained ever so slowly. L.T.'s heart pounded in his chest, the binoculars unsteady in his hands. He lowered them for an instant and shot a glance ahead.

The finish is coming up so quickly! Come on, Rimer, fly!

Neither colt seemed ready to yield, but then the rider tapped Rime Or Reason once, just once, and he pinned his ears and unleashed a move that made the hair on L.T.'s arms stand on end.

In the blink of an eye they had pulled even. L.T. focused on Francisco as the man allowed himself a peek over at his challenger. Even from an eighth of a mile away L.T. could read the astonishment on the man's face when he realized who was riding Rime Or Reason—not Cole Robertson, as expected, but his own son, Scotty.

Rime Or Reason swept into the lead ... a half-length ... a length. L.T. looked back to Francisco, expecting shock and disappointment, but instead was met by a smile so wide it nearly eclipsed the man's face.

L.T.'s attention flashed back to Scotty. He could feel the boy drinking in the sensations, the adrenaline surging through him, the wind rushing by, the power beneath—and L.T. drank from the cup with him.

Emotion crashed over L.T. like a wave as Rime Or Reason flashed by the flag, triumphant. The crowd around him cheered loudly, a long-lost sound from racing's past reaching forward. Scotty pointed to L.T. in tribute and thanksgiving, and L.T. applauded wildly, saluting his colt and his jockey.

Good for you, Scotty. Good for you. ... Rimer, we are all your witnesses. You are the champion.

L.T. laid his head back and closed his eyes, sending tears streaming down his cheeks. He relished the sun warm against his skin, he filled his lungs with the sea-laden air, and his spirit soared truly free for the first time in a long time.

Nicholas ... today was for us both.

It Can Happen Here

by Catherine Dupree

EVERY DAY at dawn, Abby exercises horses. She zips between puddles and mud in Rutland's backstretch on a dirtbike—walking takes too long. A whip sticks out of her back pocket like an antenna. Mornings are her cocktail hour. Among bales of hay and sweating horses, she networks. She chats up trainers and smiles enthusiastically about every creaky horse she's hoisted onto morning after freezing morning. And, when she returns from each workout, sunlight straining through winter-bare branches, her cheeks stinging from the wind, she reports precisely how the horse ran. Everything in the morning is part of the hustle to convince trainers she's strong and smart enough to race their horses.

This November morning, it rains in sheets. By the time Abby had lifted her bike from the bed of her pickup, her ponytail hung in a stringy brown frond down her back, her sweatshirt soaked. Some things you can't control, she thinks, pedaling through the rain. Her face, glistening from rain, glows beneath her helmet like a pale moon. She leans her bike against barn 17 and ducks inside. A mare nickers. Abby pulls off her gloves and presses her cold fingers to the horse's muzzle.

"Hey, sweetie," she whispers, leaning in close. She shuts her eyes, breathing the salty warmth of horses. In their stalls, the dark shapes move about like silent ships. For a moment, Abby slips away from the leaky-roofed barns, and this unlikely sanctuary engulfs her. Surrounded by ordinary horses, Abby feels an invisible sentience: like standing in an empty cathedral, or at the base of an ancient tree. She craves this sensation of nearness to grand things.

"Abby!" Barry yells from the other end of the barn. He's round and spry with crooked teeth like a jack-o'-lantern. He's trained horses at Rutland since 1960, when 30,000 spectators swarmed the grandstand every Saturday. He's lived in the same narrow triple-decker so close to the track that 30 years ago his wife, pregnant with their first child, stood on their sagging deck and waved a red dishtowel to signal that her water had broken. Abby rode her first race on one of his horses—finished eighth—and that evening he had sat in the stewards' room with her, watching the replay video.

"Here's where you should've kept him wide," he had said, touching the dusty screen with his index finger. "And here's where you needed to shake him up a bit. And here's—" he had pointed at the jumble down the backstretch, "where you lost the race." In the dark, they had watched as her horse faded into the pack.

"He gave up on me," Abby had said. "I don't think he felt like running."

Although the race had finished hours ago, she still felt the tremor in her legs. She could still smell the race: the alkaline leather, the dank, alluvial mud.

"That's your job," Barry had said, his voice even and kind. "You've got to find speed in him. It's there, buried like treasure."

THIS MORNING, Barry bustles toward her, leading a chestnut colt with red bandages.

"Another on-time arrival!" he calls, thrusting a thumbs-up.

"Am I ever late?" Abby says. "Whatcha got for me today? And please tell me I'm racing this afternoon. I've got rent, y'know."

"Awww," he says. "The poor apprentice can't get a mount." He taps playfully on Abby's helmet, then nods toward the colt he's leading.

"You're galloping Mayday first. And—so you can't say I do nothing for you—you're on Duplicate today in the second," he says. Abby smiles. She's ridden Duplicate before, finished sixth. He's sluggish and, as she often says, doesn't believe he's a racehorse. "You could fall asleep on him and be safe," she had told Barry once.

"Then shut your eyes and pretend you're on Secretariat," he answered.

"Barry," she said, winking at him, "I always do."

"Thanks," she says this morning. "But when do I get to race him?" She points to Mayday. Barry shakes his head.

"Abby, you know Jeff rides him." He doesn't tell her the colt's owner scoffs at women jockeys. He had pulled Barry into the tack room last month, grumbling through pursed lips: "No girls. They can exercise my horses 'til kingdom come, but I don't want them racing." And what could Barry have said? The owner had brought him two new allowance horses from Delaware—the best Barry has had in his barn in months.

"Listen," he says. "I'm getting a new one in tonight and she's real fiery. I saw her run up at Nonantum last summer. And," Barry holds two fingers up in the air like a Cub Scout, "you have my word you'll get first crack at her." Abby squints at him suspiciously. "What is she? A $5,000 claimer?"

"Sure. But, Miss Abigail, when has that stopped you before?" She shrugs and throws her hands up.

"My life revolves around claimers and longshots."

"Greatness strikes where it pleases," Barry says. He hoists Abby onto Mayday. She's exercised this colt for years: through rain and flurries, under sun and in winter dawns, under moons. But she'll never race him. Eventually, it'll be different, Abby thinks. She daydreams often about racing at exquisite tracks, on horses purchased as yearlings at select Kentucky sales, in nationally televised races that award wide scarves of lush, brilliant flowers. Napping in the jockeys' room, she returns to these beloved scenes of absurd and hyperbolic glory, images blooming with come-from-behind rallies and sweeping stretch runs. Still bleary-eyed from these ecstatic dreams, she tries to ride her races with the same fervor and thrill that had infused them.

IN THE EVENINGS, Abby cooks chicken broth and sips it in front of the television. She crawls into bed early since her alarm rings at 4:30. Sometimes she flips through her wins album—her mother's idea. "Put in all the photos of your winning races," she had said last Christmas after Abby had unwrapped the flowery album and stared at it, thinking, What will I fill this with? "Then, when you're down, you can see how far you've come!" Her mother had clapped her hands. But the album was a fine idea. Looking at the pictures—most with her arms outstretched, mimicking the horse's elongated dive under the wire—she's astonished. If she stares at the photos long enough, context peels away, then vanishes.

Last night, Barry had called her just as she was curling under the blankets. She answered and there was Barry roaring about the filly who had just arrived in the dark and rain. "I had to call you. You understand."

"How does she look?" Abby had asked. She imagined Barry pacing at the pay phone in the tack room, winding the silver snakelike cord around his finger. Alone among shadows of saddles and bridles, the stinging smell of polished leather. Ten thirty and too excited to go home with a new horse in his barn.

"Like she can run through a stone wall," he had said. "Make sure you're ready tomorrow."

BARRY POKES his head from the stall, waving for Abby to hurry. Inside, the filly is the color of wet earth, with a white smudge between her eyes. She's barely 16 hands but radiates a faint, humming presence. Wow, Abby thinks when she peers in, that horse is alive.

"Meet our new baby," Barry says, slapping the filly's neck. "Vesper." Her eyes are wild and black as oil. Abby traces the white whorled hairs on her forehead.

"How'd she do up north?"

"Broke her maiden first time out. But downhill from there," he says. "Too green. Poor girl never had a chance." How strange to think of these horses, shifting in their dusty stalls, as having a chance, Abby thinks. But at first they do. They start stormy-eyed: charged to run. Then some break bones or tear things in their delicate legs. Some win enough for their owners to display, framed in suburban, carpeted dens, the winner's circle pictures. And some ship to better tracks. But most emerge as mediocrity. Performers. Driven by a speck of memory: when as gawky, bristly maned weanlings, they ran headlong across pastures and realized there was something in their tissue and blood that made them very fast. And, in the following months, they tested it, this queer singularity, placed in them before birth. Palpable and marvelous. Like the gifted child who draws unwittingly an extravagant, flawless sketch. Look! He must think ecstatically. Look what I can do!

BARRY FOLLOWS them to the track. Vesper prances, neck arched like a chesspiece, and shies at paper fluttering on the ground. Abby jerks forward, rain spilling off her helmet onto her cheeks.

"Careful," Barry says. "She's got the devil in her." A subway car clangs past, clattering over his words. Barry pulls his cap farther over his eyes and thinks of the trainers who have fled to Florida, escaping winters and shabby Rutland. "Rats deserting a sinking ship," he mutters. But can he blame them? After all, he hates bandaging spindly legs every morning, praying the temperatures won't strain tendons. He hates the paltry purses and career claimers who bounce from owner to owner—each one swearing he'll make this one a winner. He hates the crowded barns and dwindling handles and annual threats from the racing commission to deny the simulcast license. Don't be naive, he thinks, people don't come for the Rutland nags. They come for the rows of television screens flashing nonstop the million-dollar babies at the million-dollar tracks.

But he can't leave. Sixteen years ago, he had sat his wife down after she had threatened to walk out with their daughters. He explained Rutland was improving. New York trainers were sick of sky-high barn costs. Florida owners wanted a new playground. Even California's lovely palm tree-lined tracks were losing luster. He told her every morning he clocked faster horses, and every afternoon, handicappers drove in to throw larger bills on this flashy new blood. He told her an owner from New York had called him at the barn, promising a colt—a two-year-old son of Northern Dancer—he wanted ready by spring.

Barry told her splendid things, things he believed could happen at Rutland, and she, gentle and desperate, shook her head and touched his arm and left. Later, smoking cigarette after cigarette on the porch overlooking the dark track, he struggled to understand why he had done it. Why had he lied—glorious, ridiculous tales—to his wife?

"HUSH," Abby says to Vesper. She watches for the filly's ears to flicker, listening. But they pitch toward the track yawning before her. She wants to run.

"You'll get your chance," Abby says, galloping her on the outside. Horses running faster workouts hug the rail. Abby recognizes some of them: Izzy's Fortune, a chestnut gelding she had galloped until he switched trainers; Kalliope Kat, a sprinter she had raced on grass. They streak like jackrabbits. Riders perch low, motionless above the barreling Thoroughbreds. With each passing horse, Vesper's muscles gather and wind. The reins cut through Abby's gloves as she holds the filly back.

"Hush," she soothes, hearing the cadence rising behind her. As a gray colt sweeps by on the rail, the filly catapults, head lowered, ears pinned. Thrown forward, Abby inhales the must of mane and horsehide. She hears Vesper's breath, fast but steady. The gray colt's rider turns his head, mouth moving quickly, but the words are whipped away by the wind. In an instant, Vesper catches the colt and the two horses lock strides, eight hooves pounding into one deafening rhythm. The colt's rider shouts again, and Abby sees his eyes: flashing and fierce.

"What the hell are you doing?" he yells. "Where the hell are you going?" She gropes for the reins, looping low down Vesper's neck, and stares ahead as wind cuts tears from her eyes. She wants to let Vesper run. How fast, she thinks, could she go? Later, Abby would remember each arcing, beautiful stride. She would distinctly feel as though—in those airborne seconds that seemed to last forever—she is flying. And then, things slide back into place. Raindrops pelt her face and her arms throb. She is aware of speed—rocking, ricocheting—beneath her, and stillness everywhere else. She tightens the reins and slows down so the gray colt passes. But the filly's energy pulses: faint and certain. Abby glances down and realizes her hands are trembling. I've been a jockey for three years, she thinks, but this is the closest I've been to racing.

A WEEK LATER, Barry and Abby sit on wobbly lawn chairs in front of barn 17. In cut-offs, Barry stretches out his chubby legs—the morning is strangely balmy—and sighs. Giddy from sunlight, he had treated himself to a saucer-sized honey bun from the track kitchen, and his chin shines with glaze. He tilts his face to the sky, closes his eyes and listens—smiling—to the clinks and snorts from the barns. This is my world, he thinks. In front of them, a groom hoses Vesper's steaming back and whistles quietly. She nips at the spray, happy too with the morning.

"I entered her for next Friday," Barry says. "An allowance, but the field is steep. Wendall's bringing his latest hotshot from New York."

"Wendall Mathieson?" Abby asks. He had trained at Rutland when she was starting out. Then he had stumbled onto his break: a speedy filly named Problem Solver and her Philadelphia Main Line owner. Five wins later, he had abandoned Rutland and upgraded to New York.

"What brings him back? Is he down on his luck?"

"Nah," Barry says, rubbing his eyes. "His colt, Ragnarok, started here. Then he shipped to New York. He's run solid against a few colts who've gone on to win stakes, so now Wendall thinks his colt's got promise. Just needs some wins under his belt and he'll be ready for takeoff." Abby turns to him.

"I hope—"

"Abby," Barry says, shaking his head. "You never learn. I gave you my word. She's yours." Abby sinks into her chair, rests her feet on the low rail in front of them.

"Wouldn't it be funny if she's good," she says. Barry laughs.

"She'd get scooped from me faster than lightning." Because that's what happens. A horse wins handily, and the owner starts fantasizing. Several wins later, and he saunters into the barn, stepping daintily over manure and damp hay, and declares with practiced regret, "I think we're moving on."

"I don't see how they can do that," Abby says. "If your horse wins, you're doing something right."

"Doesn't matter," Barry says. "Because I wouldn't leave. There's plenty going on here." She looks at him, sprawled on the chair, drumming his fingertips along his leg.

"There's nothing going on," she says. "Who wants to come here? The horses are tired. And if you say anything to the trainers, they don't ride you back. So, thinking about better places helps." Abby lowers her voice, as she does when her mother whispers into the phone, What kind of life do you have?

"Thinking about where I could go, the tracks and horses, everything I dreamed about when I was little," she says. Barry thinks of the elaborate stories he had told his wife: things he believed could happen at Rutland.

"What you dreamed about, that Black Stallion schmaltz, was it specific? Was it set anywhere? Because it wasn't Rutland, but it wasn't anywhere else, either. It was just you, atop a horse, hell-bent-for-leather. The details weren't important." He pauses, watching Vesper. "And they still aren't. They're just trappings."

"I want to be on good horses," she says.

"Neither of us have left," he says.

NEXT FRIDAY, the sky is gray and flat. The wind whips the infield flags, rips through the horses' manes in the paddock. Inside the women jockeys' room, Abby lounges on the worn leather sofa. It's warm and quiet, like the dwindling hours of a slumber party. Shrill hollers from the adjacent men's jockey room puncture the silence.

The riders aren't allowed to leave these quarters—or the smoky kitchen where tiny, muscular men in sleeveless shirts and white britches shoot pool and shout in Spanish—so they spend their days here. They weigh themselves hourly on a giant, cartoon-like scale, and swear softly at an extra pound. They munch on pistachios. They chat about who's moved on to Florida or Delaware. And with 15 minutes to post, they dash out the room and up the short flight of stairs right into daylight. Most jockeys pause at the top of these stairs, kiss their fingers, cross themselves before they mount their horses.

"You up next?" Jane asks Abby. Jane, a tanned and taut veteran rider with murky tattoos covering her arms, has clawed her way to the top. She's sloppy, fearless, and once punched another jockey in the paddock after he had cut her off down the backstretch.

"The four horse." Jane shuffles through the program.

"Uh-oh," Jane says, tapping the page with her fingertip. "Ragnarok is in this? Watch out, baby. He's a live horse if I ever saw one. I rode his first start and he blew out of that gate—blam!" Jane whacks the program against her open palm. "We won by like five lengths, easy. Tore the whole way." Dawn, another apprentice, watches simulcasts. She whistles.

"She's right, Abby. Colt's got speed," she drawls. "I don't know why he's runnin' here. This ain't no stakes."

"My filly's pretty live," Abby mumbles. But she doesn't argue. Jane likes scaring her ("The grass is a freakin' obstacle course!" she had screamed before Abby's first race in a downpour. "If you don't hold your horse up, you're going down!"); and Dawn doesn't care. She'll quit, Abby suspects, after this winter.

"Just don't be surprised when your head's handed to you," Jane says and stomps to the kitchen for a cigarette. Abby stares at Jane's program crumpled on the table. A vast hopelessness envelops her. There will always be horses faster than Ragnarok.

AS THE VALET hands Abby the purple and gold silks, Vesper begins her walk from barn 17 to the paddock. She flashes her dark eyes at the clusters of handicappers along the rail and prances fitfully when Barry saddles her. A wrinkled man gnawing a cigar leans over the chain-link fence, waving his *Racing Form*.

"Superstar!" he yells at Ragnarok. "Superstar!" Vesper causes no stir. Her nostrils flare into saucers. Her teeth clank on the dull, silver bit.

"Just keep the dirt out of her face," Barry says to Abby, who twirls her whip. He hoists her onto Vesper's broad back and she tucks her legs behind the filly's neck. Her owner stands next to Barry, clutching his horse's blanket. He's taken the day off to watch her race. He has even brought a camera.

In the post parade, a strip of foam glistens on Vesper's skin, under the reins. Ragnarok trots by, his skin shining like a penny.

"Tranquilamente," his jockey murmurs in lilting Spanish. "Tranquil-amente." The colt moves serenely, with strides crisp and confident.

At the gate, Vesper balks when the starter grabs her reins and hauls her into the padded stall. Abby grabs a fistful of mane, balances herself on the tiny saddle, and stares through the green metal bars down the track. Seconds later, the doors spring open with a piercing ring and clatter. They launch out among the eight others, into the six-furlong race.

Vesper and Ragnarok break from the gate together and, within strides, leave the rest a tangle of shimmering silks and fragile, frantic legs. By the half-mile pole, Vesper, on the outside, lurks a head behind the colt. Both jockeys sit still. It's up to them to hold fast, to sing and coo and watch for their horses' ears to pitch forward so they're listening, waiting, for their riders to slip the reins a notch. They glide in tandem down the backstretch: Ragnarok and then like his own shadow a split second later, Vesper. Try and catch me, he taunts. Try and outrun me, she whispers back. And so it goes around the far turn, both jockeys crooning and calling, and both horses propelling the other to run faster, to not give up or let the other pass. At the quarter pole, Abby lets the filly free. She pumps her arms along Vesper's neck, releasing rein, as the homestretch spreads like an open sea in front of them. But Ragnarok matches each stride, and she can't pull away. Yet Ragnarok can't shake her, and his jockey slices the air with his whip—fsssssstt crack!—on the colt's haunches. As the pair hurtles under the wire, Abby can't hear the crowing handicappers, and she can't hear the roar of horses finishing behind her. Instead, she hears gentle scrubbing of leather on sweating skin, and sharp exhalations of Vesper's breath. She feels the cool flecks of mud freckling her cheeks, and smells the sour ocean, carried in on the rising east wind that ruffles Vesper's brown mane. Second by a head, she thinks. Second.

"Great race," Ragnarok's jockey calls to her. He's a sensation in New York. Young, cocky, and shiny-faced, he learned racing at 14 on scrappy Venezuelan tracks. Abby's read newspaper articles about him, clippings her mother sends. In one, the reporter asks if he misses Venezuela. "Nope," he replies. "I left and never looked back."

"Wasn't expecting it," he says, pulling his horse next to hers. Both jockeys stand in the stirrups, allowing their horses to settle and slow.

Abby wants to ask him why, but instead she stares at Vesper's heaving neck. Because you can't expect much here, she thinks wickedly.

"Should I leave Rutland?" she blurts, instantly aware of her desperation but too absorbed in this whirlwind to care.

"For where?" he asks, laughing. "How should I know?" His voice, slurred and blasé, hits Abby with a thud. She pictures him leaving Rutland that afternoon, humming to himself while thinking of tomorrow's card. He claps Ragnarok's neck and turns for the winner's circle.

Ten minutes later, standing in the humid jockeys' room, Abby wipes mud from her face. Jane looks up from the sofa. She had watched the race on the closed-circuit TV.

"Not bad," she says. "You almost had it." Outside, Vesper joins the other horses on the walk back to the barns. Beneath the purple blanket that drapes her body and hoods her head, she looks like a weary prizefighter. Soon, the horses in the next race will parade by and the handicappers will scribble numbers and notes on their *Forms*. Then they'll scramble to the betting windows, stepping on hundreds of losing tickets scattered about the concrete floor.

THE FOLLOWING MORNING, Abby walks into barn 17 and says to Barry, "I'm leaving."

"Are you sick?" he asks, cinching the girth around a gray horse who pins his ears and grunts angrily.

"No, I'm leaving Rutland. I'm going to New York." She winces a little because it sounds so dramatic: the harsh consonants of York hanging in the air like a slap. She feels the walls tilt and the whole barn seems to seize up, pull back, and pause, then rush toward her. Barry roots his hands into his hips, a wisp of straw dangling from his elbow.

"You're kidding, right?"

"I know." Her voice rises. "It sounds ridiculous and you think I'm not ready, but I think I am and I don't want to get stuck here." She rattles off the words like a script.

"Well, I do think it's ridiculous. You'll get creamed. And then I think you'll hate riding and quit." The horse tosses his head, nudges Barry's shoulder.

"I won't quit. I'll just go crazy if I stay here." She looks down at the narrow legs bandaged in bright blue cotton.

"Why?"

"Because the racing's terrible. There's no money, there's no—"

"You are not in this for the money."

"Yeah, well, it would be nice to have some extra cash once in a while. It would be nice to ride racehorses once in a while." She spits the words out, hating his contentment here. Doesn't everyone want to be better? Aren't these things we can control? Barry looks at her, astonished.

"These aren't racehorses?" he asks.

"They're claimers and longshots." She knows she's betrayed him. Three years ago, she had surprised him. Not with her drive—all aspiring jockeys have it—but with her reverence. They shared this, whatever it was that he could never name, and he welcomed her.

"Then, you're not doing your job," he says, pulling the horse with him out of the stall so Abby hops aside.

"You know what I mean," she says.

"You don't have a clue what you're doing. I think all these horses," and he spreads his arms in a wide, sweeping swath around him, "are racehorses." He doesn't walk away, though, because she, tiny and earnest and strong, arms hanging at her sides, suddenly makes him sad. She guides horses and tells them when to run, and, in return, lives an isolated, repetitive life of frigid mornings; failed, desperate relationships; and crawling, empty stretches of time. And this sport, full of bloodlines and strategy and complex fractions of speed, remains a madly spinning mystery with an unknowable ending. And we all try to pin it down, he thinks. We breed and ride and train in order to control what overwhelms us. We try to shape it any way we can. But some of us want to be awed again and again. He walks toward her, the gray horse clopping behind.

"But you're here now," he says. "Are you galloping this morning?"

"I guess so." She looks up at him.

"Yeah." He juts his thumb toward the door. "And then get outta here."

"Deal," she says.

"I was going to have you gallop, but I've changed my mind. Blow him out." He helps her up and as they leave the barn, his palm on the horse's haunch, he stops and waves toward the track.

"Y'know what, you go ahead. Let me know what happens," he says. She calls after him as he walks away. It hasn't occurred to her what he had asked. Let me know what happens. So, she gallops the horse to loosen his muscles, stiff as elastics from the cold night. He pulls on the bit, fighting Abby for more rein. When he's ready, when enough horses have blown by on the rail and his body has tensed and coiled at each one, Abby lets him run. He isn't fast—Vesper runs faster—and he's too tall and barrel-chested to make a stakes winner. But this morning, Abby doesn't think about that. She crouches low, flattening her chest to his neck, waiting. And, gradually, she feels the familiar drag and pull through her body, a sensation like diving: that silent, slow, soaring space of time after leaving the ground and before slipping into water. This instant—flooded with expectation and promise, hope and grace—seems to her the gamble of horse racing. Will everything come together? Is there something in this horse that makes him not just fast but grand?

She paces the horse, ticking seconds off in her head, and eases him when they reach the quarter pole. He gallops for another half-mile, and then she turns him around. As they trot back, Abby thinks of what she'll tell Barry. He'll amble out of the barn and wait until she dismounts and hands the horse to a groom. Then he'll ask what happened.

He ran okay, could've gone a little more, she'll say. But this isn't the answer he'll want. He's trained this horse long enough to know what happens in four furlongs.

What else? He'll ask. What happened to you?

I rated him pretty well, but he fights me, she'll say. Or maybe she'll tell him: Everything lifts away and it's just you and the horse and then it's just the horse but you're somehow part of it, too.

Part of what? He'll ask.

Part of the running.

But there's something else she can't name. Haunting, otherworldly. She feels it stirring in the horses: an inexpressible, barely-there presence. And, sometimes it swells and soars, ineradicable and immemorial. Be grand, it whispers.

So, is this what you expect to find in New York? He'll ask.

New York has better horses, Barry, she'll say.

I think you're searching for more than that, he'll say. But she is not like him. So she leaves that morning, waving from her pick-up as she merges with the snarled rush-hour traffic.

Around noon, Barry will walk across the tarmac parking lot to the paddock and saddle the first of three horses that day. He'll chat with other trainers and listen to their stories. But, when the race starts, he'll watch intently and alone. His horses will finish fifth, then eighth, then first. He'll smile for the winner's circle photo and blink stupidly at the flash. He'll shake hands with the owners, but be eager to return to his barn. There, he'll stay late in the tack room, smoking cigarettes and musing about strategies and upcoming races. Hunched over his notebook, he'll write his dreams down furiously. Around 9:30, he'll shut the barn doors. But, before that, he'll turn off the lights and listen to the presence of these massive, mysterious creatures. He knows he won't leave. He'll drive the short route home in his neighborhood of gas stations and video stores. And, at some point, staring through the windshield at the blinding taillights of all the cars heading somewhere, it will occur to him that whatever Abby's searching for exists here, too. Somewhere lurking in this sad, cold, brokedown place is shining glory, as pure here as anywhere, waiting to be found by the most deserving.

The Murderer, the Pony, and Miss Brown to You

by Susan Starr Richards

JOEL CAME around a curve on Sorter Ridge, hauling a mare to the breeding shed, and found the local murderer trying to choke a pony. The pony was lying in the middle of the road, with two ropes in slipknots around its neck. The murderer and one of his sons were laying back on the ropes, and the other two sons were beating the pony with cedar trees.

Joel wasn't really surprised. Today was the vernal equinox, after all, a good old day for strange, primitive rites. And Sorter Ridge was the logical place for such doings. It was the outlaw edge of two counties, home to deer-spotters and chicken-fighters, and people rumored to deal marijuana out of hollow trees.

And the mare in the trailer was his prize broodmare, Soft Spot. That was the real reason he wasn't surprised.

He stopped the truck and opened the trailer door to check on her, and there she was, looking the way she always did in the trailer—bug-eyed, sweating, shaking violently, as if she expected to be at least mutilated. "You'll be all right," Joel told her, patting her. But he wasn't so sure about this pony. "Don't look," he advised her, closing the shutter, so she couldn't.

JOEL HAD never seen the murderer in person—the man was a recluse. But his sons were grown men, though they still lived with their father, and they sometimes came to town. And the murderer's picture had been all over the newspapers a year ago. It wasn't a face you forget—white skin, long black hair, hacked-out features, fanatical eyes. He'd killed a deer hunter who'd ventured onto his farm. The murderer claimed he'd shot in self-defense, after the hunter aimed a rifle at him. But the hunter had been found with his rifle by his right hand, and a cigarette still clutched between the fingers of his left. And his name was Lefty. Still, the hunter had been trespassing, so they'd turned the murderer loose. Now here he was, blocking the road, doing his best to murder this little spotted pony. He had his rope so tight around the pony's neck that blood was coming out of its nose, and you couldn't get your finger between the rope and the neck. Joel knew, because he tried.

First he asked them if the pony was hurt, if that was how it got down.

"Naw, it ain't hurt," the murderer said indignantly. "It's wild. It'd run right off if we didn't have the ropes on it."

Since the pony was lying flat on its side, all broken out in a sweat, with its breath gurgling in and out, Joel wasn't sure that this was true. He went and got his spare halter out of the truck.

Once you own a racehorse, you never know where or when you're going to meet it running loose around the country, with no halter on. Your mind is full of racehorses—running down roads, through woods, across yards—all without halters. You see them coming at you from every direction. So you always keep a spare halter in your truck, in hopes of capturing some loose horse with it. And Joel made doubly sure he had a spare halter when he was hauling Soft Spot.

Soft Spot had a history of escaping from trailers. On her very first trailer ride, she'd thrown a fit, busted her halter, kicked the tailgate till she bent the five-eighths-inch steel latches, and jumped out, just as Joel managed to stop, in the middle of rush hour on Russell Cave Road. Horses have the right of way in this country, so traffic stopped, and people got out of their cars to help Joel catch her and put her back in the trailer and wire the tailgate shut.

After that, he had the latches replaced with two-inch steel. Still, on the way to a race, she kicked down the tailgate again, got loose on the interstate, ran across three lanes of traffic, and started down the median toward home. She was out of sight by the time he got across the three lanes, but he ran after her, yelling desperately and idiotically, "Softy!" Miraculously, her sweet high whinny came in answer. She galloped back to him, got in the trailer, and made it to Churchill Downs in time to run second in a stakes race.

Now she was stamping and sweating in the trailer here on Sorter Ridge Road, while Joel tried to put his spare halter on a murderer's pony. And the murderer was objecting to having his own ropes taken off his own pony by someone he didn't even know, figuring his pony was already long gone, now that it wasn't actually strangling any more.

But it didn't look to Joel as if this pony would go anywhere. It was lying there in perfect dignity, apparently prepared to die on the vernal equinox, a sacrificial victim in the name of warm winters or wet summers perhaps—who knew what the murderer might have in mind?

Or did he have anything in mind at all? Was his presence here just part of the machinations of Soft Spot's mama, that wily old witch-mare, Miss Brown?

JOEL HAD met Miss Brown when he was first learning the horse business, working as a groom on the old Snyder farm. Her full name was Miss Brown to You. She was then 11 years old, and she'd had only one foal in her life. But that foal was a filly who became Broodmare of the

Year, having had nine straight stakes winners of the Kentucky Derby-Belmont Stakes-St. Leger variety.

Miss Brown was a squat, mule-eared, chocolate-colored mare with bulging eyes that were yellow around the outside, accurately representing her jaundiced attitude. When you went to catch her in the field, she'd walk away from you, fast and steady. If you tried to corner her, she'd run over you or through you. When at last she did let you catch her, she'd drag you to the barn, practically knock you down to get into the stall first, then swing her head around and give you a disgusted look, as if that was where she'd wanted to go all the time. It was at this point that you most wanted to kill her.

But once you got her in the stall, it seemed more likely she would kill you. She watched you all the time, her eye turned back in a baleful glare. If you stood on her left side, she'd pick up her left hind foot and hold it cocked. If you moved around to her right, she'd pick up her right hind.

She had everybody on the Snyder farm buffaloed—especially the teaser. Joel had watched many times as the spotted pony stud they used as a teaser was led through the barn to inquire of the mares, bravely and hopefully, whether each one might be "In" (heat, that is) on that particular day. "Some days they like you, and some days they don't," the teaser man would explain to the teaser. "But she ain't never liked you," he'd add, as Miss Brown roared and backed up, kicking the stall door, the walls, and the teaser. Miss Brown, the pony always reported, rolling his eyes, was "Out."

Still, Joel had watched her in the field, and he noticed occasions on which Miss Brown was almost sociable, for her. That is, she didn't threaten the life of every creature that came near her. On those occasions, Joel suspected, the devious Miss Brown was "In." He thought she'd figured out that the pony was there just to tease her into admitting her vulnerable hormonal state. Joel explained this theory to the people in charge at Snyder's. But he was a lowly groom, new to the business, and they weren't about to take Miss Brown to the breeding shed and let her tear up some high-priced stud on his say-so.

At last the Snyders gave up on Miss Brown and sold her. She went for $2,000. By that time, Joel had his own little breeding operation in the Outer Bluegrass. He was the only one who bid on her. A friend agreed to breed her to his so-so stallion without teasing her, on what Joel judged to be one of her mellow days. There in the breeding shed was Miss Brown, looking evil as ever. The horse was brought in. He wasn't a great horse, but he was a Thoroughbred stallion, not a pony teaser. As Joel had suspected, Miss Brown knew the difference. She stood for him.

The day Miss Brown was to be examined for pregnancy, it took 50 minutes—a new track record—to catch her in the field. Joel's friend the veterinarian, who knew Miss Brown well, said as he waited, "If you ever do catch her, and she's not in foal, let's cut her throat."

Miss Brown didn't get her throat cut. It took her 12 months, instead of the usual 11 months plus; still, at the age of 19, she had her second foal, a brown filly built like her, but with little ears and a wide-eyed, innocent face. On his rocky rail-fenced farm, Joel had a filly who was a half sister to a Broodmare of the Year. He was ecstatic.

And Miss Brown loved her baby. The other mares weren't allowed to even look at her foal. If the foal strayed off to play with the other babies, Miss Brown would call her back. She had a deep, husky, authoritative bellow, like a horse blues-singer. Several times a day, Joel would hear that distinctive call, then the foal's sweet, high reply, and see her racing back obediently to her mama's side.

Every morning, Miss Brown took her daughter out and taught her how to run. Joel watched the tiny brown filly shadowing the little brown mare as they turned big counterclockwise circles around the field. Both of them ran like hound-dogs, their heads down low, with a flat, noiseless, stretched-out stride that seemed unlikely on such high-butted sprinter types. Joel named the filly Soft Spot; she was the one soft spot he'd found in Miss Brown's fierce heart.

SOFT SPOT was what people out here called "real pettified," as sweet and friendly as her mother was shrewd and suspicious. Like a lot of overprotected children, she grew up to be sensitive, a worrier, always a little bewildered, as if she were still expecting her mother to tell her what to do.

Joel trained her himself, at the local tracks. She won six races and some decent stakes, and last fall Joel had brought her home to replace her mother in his broodmare band.

Because after Joel solved her teaser problem, Miss Brown managed to develop an exotic infection that kept her from getting pregnant. She was, anyway, 22 years old. So Joel and his wife had officially retired her—trailered her up to their cattle farm and turned her out. They took off her halter and watched as she galloped away, hollering and tossing her head as if she'd been waiting all her life for this moment. Joel's wife got tears in her eyes, and sang "Turn My Horses Free."

After that, nobody tried to catch Miss Brown anymore. She had her own house, an abandoned cabin that she haunted, lurking in its shadows along with owls and bats. But when Joel's wife had gone up to leave feed for her recently, she came back saying she thought Miss Brown was depressed. "She doesn't eat. She hardly even comes out to graze anymore. Maybe she's lonely," she added, giving Joel a significant look.

"Oh no," Joel said. "We're not bringing her back here. No, no, no," he repeated, to himself as much as to his wife. He too was uneasy with the image of Miss Brown alone in her dark house, peering out from under the doorway, her forelock full of cockleburs. And he sort of missed having her drag him to the barn every day, knocking him sideways, giving him sarcastic looks.

Still, there was Soft Spot. Soft Spot didn't have her mother's prejudice against teasers. In fact, she showed "In" enthusiastically, to everyone and everything—the teaser, the other mares, Joel, stray dogs and cats. Joel had every hope of getting lots of foals out of Soft Spot. Miss

Brown had taught her daughter to run, it was true. But he couldn't have her giving Soft Spot advice on her new career, lest she also limit her production to one foal per decade. "I don't want her anywhere near Soft Spot," he said.

But she was near Soft Spot now. Around the next curve, here on Sorter Ridge Road, was Joel's cattle farm—Miss Brown's abode.

HE HADN'T wanted to bring Soft Spot this way. He'd been surprised, in fact, at how much he hadn't wanted to. But a flash flood had blocked the other road. And after all, he'd asked himself, what can Miss Brown do? Lay a hex on her through the trailer window as we drive by? Leap over the fence and throw herself down in front of the truck to stop us?

Now, on her first trip to the breeding shed, with a perfect, large, very soft follicle on her left ovary, Soft Spot had been stopped, in what was undoubtedly Miss Brown's force-field, by this murderer and his pony. Joel nodded grimly, patting the pony as he took off the ropes.

The pony didn't seem to care much. Joel could understand its depression. If it did get up, after all, it had to go home with the murderer—he owned it. "I been hunting it all over," he kept muttering.

At last Joel got the halter on. The ropes were loose, looped around the pony's neck. He patted it till it relaxed—its legs drooped down, instead of sticking straight out like a china pony knocked over on somebody's mantel, and its head sank toward the ground. Joel folded its feet under it, and rolled it up on its sternum. The murderer and his sons glanced at each other warningly; clearly, a sitting-up pony was the next thing to a running-off pony. Joel walked up to the truck to get his whip, which is the other thing horse people carry with them all the time, to load up all the loose horses in their mind, although you have to know which horses to use it on.

Take, for example, Soft Spot. She'd never seemed to mind the whip when she was running, but she'd become very sensitive to it when it was associated with loading into trailers. She was so sensitive by now that if you even touched her with a whip anywhere near a trailer, she'd try to kill you with her hind feet. You whipped, she kicked. Instantly. Every time. A big snapper kick, one of those where you could hear her joints pop.

So this morning Joel had explored alternative horse-loading methods. He'd tried chucking pieces of gravel at her. He'd tried a broom. He'd tried feed, and a blindfold. Nothing worked. What worked, finally, was desperation—he put his arms around her neck and begged her to go in the trailer, telling her sincerely that he loved her, that he'd never asked her to do anything dangerous, and he wasn't this time, either. Of course, he hadn't considered the possibility of murderers and ponies.

"Hold on," he said to Soft Spot now. People are always saying to their horses what they need to hear themselves.

He got his whip out of the truck, a little whip like a spinning rod. He cut the pony with it lightly, and the pony stood up.

And the murderer and his sons laid back on the ropes again, yelling at each other, "Look out! There it goes! It's going!" And the pony fell back down on the road.

JOEL WENT through it all again, got the pony sitting up, got it to relax. "Now don't pull back when it gets up," he told them.

"Oh, it'll be gone," said the murderer. But his sons agreed not to, and this time one of the sons actually helped get the ropes loose. The pony got up again. It stood with its head hanging down, upright but fixed, never going to move again, this pony. Been cast in bronze in the middle of the road—a monument to the inhumanity of man to ponies. They had some corn in a plastic cup they'd used to catch it in the first place, so Joel held the cup out in front of it, to get it to take a step. But it stared at the ground and wouldn't move.

Now, Joel knew this was serious. A pony that won't take a step to get a bite of feed—this is a deeply troubled pony. A pony that won't eat is a pony that has given up and is on its way to the big pony farm in the sky. At last Joel took a handful of the corn and held it right on the pony's nose, where the pony had to smell it. Very delicately, the pony took one grain out of his hand, then two. It didn't take a big sniff and inhale all the corn, like a regular pony would do. Still, this was progress.

He stood away from it and offered it the cup, and the pony took a step. The murderer and his sons were poised, ready to haul back on their ropes and stop the rogue pony from dashing into the bushes. Joel patted it on the withers and the rump, and it began to walk, slowly, beside him. It was six years old, they'd told him, and it had never been broken to lead. It was a mystery what they wanted it for, in that case. But they'd obviously been willing to kill it to get it back.

They had three miles to go to reach home. Joel cut a length of rope for a makeshift lead shank, gave one of the sons his whip and said, "But don't hit it. If it slows down, just shake the whip at it." He could only hope they'd follow instructions better than some jockeys he'd had.

He started out with them, leading the pony over the top of the hill behind the trailer. Then he handed the rope shank to the son that had helped him with the ropes, asking that they put his halter and whip back by his mailbox sometime.

"If it stops, don't haul on it," he said. "It's sulking, so you have to back off. Just pat it here and here," showing them, "and I think it'll go with you all the way."

The murderer said, by way of thanking him, Joel supposed, "I knew a cow would sulk. But I didn't know a horse would."

Joel watched till they got over the top of the next hill—the little spotted pony, the four big men. The pony went along sedately between them. The murderer was now carrying the whip, Joel noted, and they were all watching the pony warily, but they were doing what he'd said. The wife of one of them had been sitting up the road waiting for them, in a vast, ancient Buick. It shook into life, loosing a cloud of exhaust, and chugged off at a stately pace to follow them home. Joel turned and started jogging back to his truck.

When he neared the top of the hill above the trailer, there was a sound like a rifle shot. He froze, feeling sick. Then there was another sound, the same kind, and he realized the sounds weren't coming from behind him, the direction of the pony. They were coming from ahead of him—the direction of Soft Spot.

As he raced over the hill, there was another bang, and he saw the tailgate of his trailer bulge. The bangs came faster and louder, like a frenzied drum solo. At last there was one huge double bang. The tailgate heaved twice, looking oddly fluid, and flopped open, and Soft Spot came slithering backward out of the trailer, squatting down, her busted halter dangling horseless from the tie-strap, and her eyes wild, as if she were being attacked by demons.

Joel moved toward her quickly and quietly. But she started away from him, up the road. On the one hand, she was running the opposite way from the murderer and the pony.

On the other hand, she was running toward his cattle farm—Miss Brown's territory. "Softy!" he yelled, as desperately as he'd done that day on the interstate.

And he heard, in reply, a faint, shrill, mournful whinny. But not from Soft Spot. The sound came from behind him. The pony had answered him.

Soft Spot had heard it, too. She came running back. She'd recovered her sweet-young-thing look, and went bouncing past him with her ears pricked, heading straight for the murderer and the pony.

What would the murderer do, Joel asked himself as he ran after her, at this new threat to his reclaimed pony? Did he have a gun stashed in the Buick that was following them? When Soft Spot came barreling over the hill like the marauding wild horse the murderer obviously thought all horses to be, would he shoot her and claim self-defense of pony?

As Joel got to the top of the next hill, Soft Spot was bearing down on them. There was a great shout in front of him, white faces turning. The sons scattered. The murderer stood his ground and raised the whip. Soft Spot spun. The murderer was down. Joel winced, but he couldn't help thinking of the dead hunter. "Lefty, you may've just got your revenge," he said.

Then Soft Spot was heading back in Joel's direction. And the pony was loose and following her, transfigured—prancing, his neck arched, his eye bright and careless. They disappeared over the next hilltop, running as a team.

At this point, Joel didn't care much about the murderer. It had come to him that his stakes-winning half sister to a Broodmare of the Year, in heat and with a large very soft follicle, was running loose with what they delicately call, out here, a male horse. He'd been carefully calling the pony "it," to stave off his sense of impending doom. But he'd seen right away that it was an entire male horse. True, it was a short male horse, but Soft Spot was a short Thoroughbred mare, and there were plenty of convenient hillsides nearby that would make a Thoroughbred-pony liaison possible.

Joel could see his application for registration of foal next year—"Black, brown, chestnut, and white colt, out of Soft Spot, by Murderer's Pony."

Then he heard a voice—a deep, blues-shouting equine voice—a voice of authority. He heard Soft Spot's sweet, high reply, and a rapid-fire series of squeals, grunts, thuds, and finally the crunch of wood breaking. He put his hand to his head.

And the spotted pony reappeared, running toward Joel, transformed again. Chalk-eyed, his neck and shoulders lathered, he was suddenly the Pony Express coming down the road, and this pony was really hauling the mail.

Still, he was no match for his pursuer, though she was 23 years old. With her long, low, racy style, Miss Brown was literally eating him up, savaging him at every stride. All her old fury at these Pretenders, the spotted ponies of the world, had obviously boiled over onto this one hapless pony that had tried consorting with her daughter.

Then the murderer, who had unfortunately not been killed after all, came running back down the opposite hill, followed by his sons and the backing-up Buick. The pony looked up. Finding himself between the murderer and Miss Brown, he chose the murderer. At least, he went that way. Miss Brown went after him.

And so at last the murderer and his sons made the acquaintance of a truly wild horse. Eyes bulging, mule ears pinned, wicked head snaked out, teeth bared and snapping, Miss Brown slung herself straight at them.

They all propped, looking like they'd swallowed their tongues. Then they ran behind the Buick. So did the pony. Miss Brown started chasing them around the car. The men would all dive for one door, screaming and shoving. The pony would pop up and try to get in the door, too, because Miss Brown was always right on top of him. The first man in would slam the door, and the others would have to run around the car again. The car was shuddering in place, belching smoke, and taking explosive hits from Miss Brown's hooves.

She loaded all three of the sons in the Buick that way, but then they either couldn't or wouldn't open a door for the murderer. Finally he staggered to the trunk of the car, yanked it open, and sat down in it. The engine backfired, the pony out-broke the Buick, and the murderer rode off backward in a puff of black smoke, chasing his pony again.

Soft Spot had come jogging up, looking amazed. She started to follow the pony, but Miss Brown headed her off, kicking her once, emphatically, and herded her back downhill toward Joel and the trailer.

So things were simpler now. No murderer, no pony, just one mare he couldn't catch, and one he couldn't load, both with no halters. And his spare halter, of course, was running off up the road with the pony.

Then Miss Brown charged at Joel. She knocked him aside, galloped straight into the trailer, turned her head around, and gave him one of her "Hello?" looks, as if she'd been waiting all year to get in this trailer. She spoke to Soft Spot. Soft Spot stepped in beside her. Joel grabbed a stray piece of the murderer's rope, tied the tailgate in place, and the three of them went off to the breeding shed.

A YEAR LATER, Joel's wife came dragging in from the barn at dawn. Soft Spot was overdue, and they'd been watching her day and night for a month. "She's running milk," his wife said. "Not dripping it, running it. Her butt looks pointy. She started pacing at one o'clock. By three, she looked real uncomfortable—digging up the stall, stomping her foot. She actually lay down, once, and I thought she was going to do it. At five, she quit pacing and started eating hay. I put her back in the paddock. But you know what? I think she's waiting to get out in the field with the other mares. I don't think she'll do it without Miss Brown."

"Of course," he groaned as he struggled out of bed. "It's all a conspiracy, anyway."

Soft Spot was in the paddock behind the barn, where they could get to her quickly if she needed help foaling. She looked like a child's drawing of a horse—a round circle of a belly on four little stick legs. Joel checked her milk bag and her ligaments behind. "Trust me," he muttered in her ear. "You're ready for this." She gave him a perplexed, appealing glance, still the perfect horse ingenue—12 months pregnant and no idea what to do about it.

Beyond the fence, in the mare's field, stood Miss Brown, looking like a short, fat, vicious mule. After she'd saved her wayward daughter from the pony, Joel had brought her home to stay. For weeks, she'd been hanging on the fence, waiting for Soft Spot to foal, as he was. What now? Should he call the veterinarian and get him to induce labor?

Joel walked up and looked into Miss Brown's ancient eyes. As he stared into that sphinxlike, brooding gaze, he suddenly saw Soft Spot, when she was just a tiny brown spot curled up in the middle of a big green field, her short little squirrel-tail switching up occasionally out of the grass, while the dark, still block of Miss Brown watched over her. And it came to him that Miss Brown knew more than he did about Soft Spot's interminably interesting condition. She also knew more than he did about giving birth.

He went to the gate and opened it. "It'll probably take me two days to catch her," he said to himself. But for the first time in her life, Miss Brown came right to him, practically put her chin in his hand. He led her into the paddock. She and Soft Spot touched noses, greeting each other. Soft Spot dropped her head and started grazing. Miss Brown kept herself between Soft Spot and the other mares, who crowded the fence, watching.

Twenty minutes later, Soft Spot kicked at her belly twice and went down, breaking water. She lay, huge and sweating, helpless on the dewy grass. Miss Brown moved protectively behind her daughter. But when Joel squatted down between them, she did not offer to kick his head off. She only watched closely as he slid his hand inside the protruding white bubble of the birth sack, to make sure the foal was coming right. "Two front feet and a nose, and we're smelling like a rose," he told her. Then he stepped back.

Soft Spot began grunting the foal out, inch by inch—the soft, still jellylike feet, the blind muzzle, the floppy ears, the deep chest. And every time her daughter groaned and pushed, Miss Brown raised one foreleg, high and slow, and dug at the ground, as if she also felt the birth pang. One big push, one big dig—deliberately, painfully, patiently—till a tiny, chocolate-colored, mule-eared filly sat on the grass, checking out the world. Soft Spot reached her head around and sniffed the foal, her nostrils fluttering tenderly. "Huh-huh-huh-huh-huh!" she said, like she'd just figured it all out.

"Huh!" Joel agreed, like he'd figured out some of it, anyway. Because here they were—Soft Spot, with her first foal safely on the ground, and himself and Miss Brown, side by side, watching over them. Miss Brown stood head down, her knobby spine sticking up, showing her age, her whole body looking peaceful and spent, as if she herself had just dug this little creature out of the green earth.

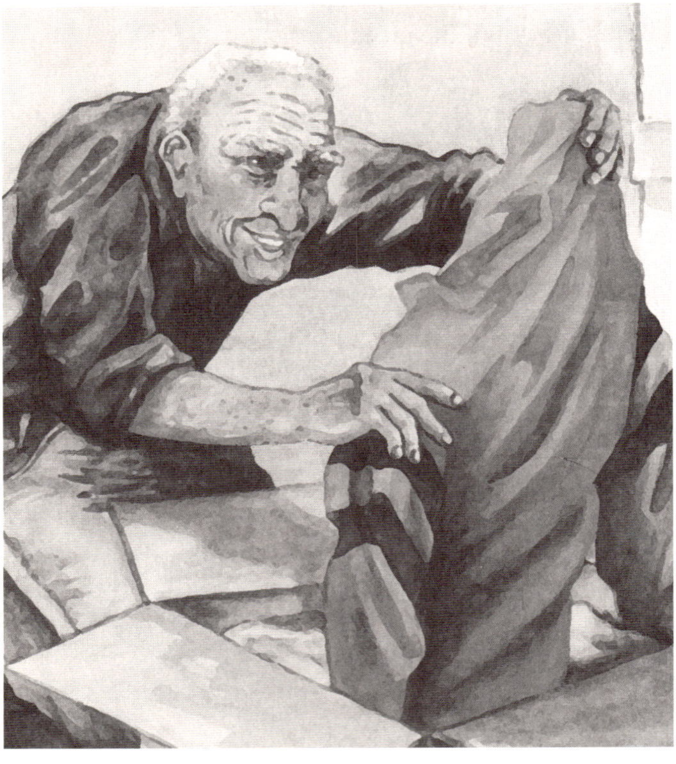

Arlen Gone

by Kevin Harrington

THERE, framed in the center pane, a gibbous moon shone through the lighted window above the landing. Raymond Belanger stopped in the stairwell. He made this trip so often but never found the moon waiting for him; he wondered why. Thinking through the confluence of phases and seasons, allowing for overcast skies, only a few minutes each year would he find it so, waxing nearly full. Preoccupied, Ray got caught by surprise even after he had steeled himself for this time.

Arlen Cawley was dead. The same bold moonlight glinted off one open eye as he lay, the only way he could, on his side. Sinking slowly, back against the door, Ray tried hard to read his expression, seeking answers in his death mask. Nothing beatific, his mouth gaped, lips puckered without his dentures. Did he wake and know it was his time? Ray had pictured himself bedside for the last moments and feared they would be painful for Arlen. He saw no such sign. Arlen stared back, gaze clear; he looked resolute.

A feathery sax solo coasted from the boombox glow on the shelf. Ray resisted the urge to touch, check for temperature or blanching, gently close his eyes. This shouldn't be disturbed. He was gone, but it wasn't over. He should report the death. The other calls—Social Security and the like—could wait until morning. Hell, it could all wait.

Ray recognized the sax player as Johnny Hodges; a piano run then bits of the melody flourished. Oh, God. It was "All of Me." With a stifled chuckle came the first tears. Whatever was still happening, Ray was part of it, in on the joke now. Because Lord knows there wasn't much of Arlen left to take.

The room didn't smell bad yet. There was still the faint sour old-man smell; Ray had battled with lemon cleaners, scented candles, and incense. Arlen favored cinnamon and vanilla over anything coniferous or herbal. "Like laying in a candy store all day," he said. Too, he enjoyed the flickering light up along the stucco and crown moldings.

The drummer kicked up the backbeat accent and Hodges, full-throated now, more robust, put a rouse in the chorus. The band wound out. Done with the shimmy, all shake now, the medley ended with a swank punch, rimshots and a cymbal crash like a lewd wink from a go-go dancer.

Ray rose, opened the kitchen window and scrunched his shoulders as the old sash crackled. The darkness between the street lamps cloaked the neighborhood, casting it vintage rather than shabby. Blue lunar light pooled on the rooftops and allowed the church steeple to throw a night shadow. As always, the distant towers atop the Sears building pulsed a steady red beat. Cardiac, life, man, it was a strange trip. If it hadn't been for horse racing, a sport Ray grew to hate as a boy, Arlen would have been another curious someone in a neighborhood full of curiosities. Now, Ray was the closest thing to next of kin.

HE HOPPED himself up on the counter. So many thoughts ricocheted; still in the back of his mind he kept count of the throbbing lights above the black-aluminum skyscraper, diastolic—systolic. On the boombox, Billie Holiday wondered what a little moonlight could do to her.

Arlen, the old Irishman, would've turned 86 next month. Stooped from birth, he never completely uncurled: a congenital kyphosis, hunchback. Upright, he resembled the knobby end of a gnarled stick; he had a shillelagh toughness to him almost to the end. Arlen embraced his fate, found his trade close to the ground.

Reared in Montana, he apprenticed in the Butte copper mines. A full shift filing then shoeing the mules taxed the burliest farrier. Arlen had just the right posture. "It was the job the Lord suited me for," he said. But they slung the mules to the bottom of the lift cages and brought them up blindfolded against the sunlight. The electric engines went down the shafts for assembly. Arlen hoboed east during the Great Depression to find work at the tracks and breeding farms. He was skilled at the forge and under the animals, and the hardboot trainers liked his way with skittish and mean horses.

Ray grew up in Chicago, the youngest by a stretch, his mother, a nurse; his father was a Cook County prosecutor. At the courthouse there was a longstanding Friday tradition; some assistant prosecutors finagled the calendar, curtailed appointments, and caught an Arlington Park race card. In fourth grade, his mother was diagnosed: cancer. Mildred died surrounded by her family, emaciated, drowning in her favorite robe; their tears soaked the terrycloth. The best death she could have, mercifully fast after the treatments failed. His dad, Leo, found diversion and a focus for his concentration in the *Daily Racing Form*, calculating time and distance over varied tracks.

With Ray's older brother and sister either in college or working to help pay tuition, Ray was too young to be left home. A boy can grow weary even with endless ice cream and hot dogs. Ray came to dread the long Saturdays that started on opening day, Mother's Day. The bitter irony was not lost despite his youth.

Recently, Ray had dropped out of life in a sense. His older brother and sister considered him a fallen man. Oh, he still worked, but as a bartender, honest toil. The slow breakup and weary legal wrangling of divorce had taken an inevitable toll. He'd been the first one to speak up at the hospital so supervisors were waiting to pounce. He had the sense to resign before they nicked him to death. He could still be working in the field. God knows they needed nurses. He wasn't ready to be one of them again, not yet, no matter the pay.

He still parented. Loved his daughter but didn't see her much. He couldn't bring her back to this apartment building.

THE BUCKINGHAM was a pretender. Built in 1927, name wrought in block letters on the glass front door, gray swirls in the carpet, and ornamented architecture, it suggested style back then. Seven floors cased in a basic dark brick. Heavy cooking smells from the old, poor, and foreign-born hung in the hallways. The exterminator visited but never enough. The place really said tenement now. Too far from the light and open grass Ray worked so hard to stake out. His daughter now ran across a lawn that was no longer his.

Ray had seen Arlen before, but they met a couple years ago on the Fourth of July. A few guys, widowed, divorced, or otherwise disenfranchised, felt a patriotic duty to sit on the Buckingham front steps. Just to let the drug dealers and gangbangers know it was their America, too.

There was John, the stubby Aussie manager of the building. Gray hair and whiskered proper, as it was also a holiday from shaving, too, he hawked and spat his way through his own ribald tales of a thousand nights. Brothels and booze, brawling and whoring, his green eyes just emerald crescents when he smiled. Powerful, tattooed forearms reminded Ray of "Popeye" cartoons. Fresh from betrayal and separation, John's bawdy blasts from exotic ports comforted Ray. Maybe he needed a commercial liaison? Ray was lonely but still hurt too raw for anything more sophisticated.

Cab driver and assistant manager of the corner grocery store, Ayman took the day off from both jobs to honor America's birthday. They teased him, called him "The Sheikh." Dark curly hair, long eyelashes, olive skin, and a big, white smile, he had a little desert dash. Women noticed. John's stories intrigued him, but Ayman never betrayed shock. From a strict Muslim family where courting was supervised and marriage arranged, he lived in Spartan celibacy. He worked long hours to earn enough money to bring his fiancée to the States. "They build a fortress of paper, but I will defeat them." Ray helped Ayman deal with the confusing procession of government forms.

Calvin pronounced himself a player. Until the factory closed, he shot craps and pool, hustled card games and women all between swing shifts on the assembly line. But for some years he had been afoot. He claimed to have a job, vaguely suggesting he worked undercover for a government agency. No acronym ever revealed. Ray sometimes saw him clandestinely peeking into trash bins. Lean and lanky, Calvin had a dark vine-toughness to him, but the younger corner boys deemed him a nappy, ashy, old dude. His real gift was playacting. He could mimic almost anyone, play multiple parts. Finished, he would sit back down and mop his face with a hand towel he kept over his shoulder like a pelt.

UNDER THE elm tree, Arlen wasn't with the stoop group. He checked both ways down the street as he rapped a rolled newspaper against his thigh. Ray recognized the distinctive red banner: *Daily Racing Form*. A stocky guy, Mexican or Indian, strode through traffic. Certainly the guy Arlen sought, his agitation increased on approach until it looked like polka steps. Arlen, maybe 5'6" if he could straighten, reached up to threaten the guy with the rolled-up *Form* as his billy club. The guy claimed car trouble kept him from putting the bet down. Yesterday's trifecta would have paid $762 and change. Ray knew this cat was lying. Otherwise, he would have snatched the waving paper away from his face. He was taking his lumps too easy.

While Arlen blustered, Ray faded into the building, scaled down the fire escape, and dropped to the alley in a crouch like he grew up in the neighborhood. He shadowed the clumsy grifter to a rusting Oldsmobile.

Later, Ray knocked. Arlen led him down a narrow pathway between cartons stacked nearly to the ceiling. They talked in the kitchen. Arlen had set up his cot in a niche saved from the boxes. Arlen sounded sad, beyond anger, when he received confirmation of the deception. "How can I trust him? To lie about a bet?" Arlen rubbed his bristle-cut hair behind his ear. Ray leaned against that same Philco fridge as he listened. It seemed wrong now that an old fridge that buzzes and gurgles outlives a friend.

Ricky DeShayes, former Hawthorne hot walker, didn't just place bets for the old smith; the two planned to be business partners. Ricky claimed to have an "in" with a minority business association. "He was supposed to get us into the incubation program."

Arlen pictured a corner store called "The Clubhouse Turn." A place to buy *Forms* and tip sheets, a place to talk horses and be tempted into purchasing a piece of history. "I don't have to make much," Arlen said. "'Cause I don't need much." Arlen meant to stock the yet to be discovered storefront with racing memorabilia. Until then, he lived in a simple maze, kitchen to the bathroom to the door.

RAY OFFERED to put down his bets at an off-track stand near work, then call back to confirm. He didn't want to get too involved. But he cringed at the sight of the old guy walking to the El stop with a pocketful of betting money. He became a soft touch for the occasional ride to the track. "Out in the open air, under the sky God give us. Will do you good." Arlen could spin doctor.

Ray hadn't been to Arlington since they rebuilt the grandstand following the spectacular fire. Clipped grass and blooming flowers still perfumed the summer heat. Ray rediscovered how impressive a Thoroughbred can look springing from the gate. Bright silks blurred past. In full stride they actually flew, his dad told him. All four hooves off the ground for "an almost imperceptible instant. Some people wouldn't believe that, photography settled the argument."

Ray enjoyed these trips to the track. While his dad had kept his face in the *Form*, Arlen rarely had time to sit down. He scrutinized the horses from paddock through the post parade, then rushed to the window last minute. Ray kept up, interested to hear his judgments on horseflesh. Arlen had a code with one teller so that even if he was deep in line, he could signal a bet before the race went off. Between the track and Ray's stops at the OTB, Arlen made a few hundred a month. Good thing, too, as all he had was his government check.

Arlen shunned Ricky. An unrelenting silence coupled with denial of existence in the Gaelic tradition. Once, Ray nodded acknowledgement. A fierce, blue, accusatory glare from under bushy brow, Arlen put the evil eye on Ray. There would be no store. Ray vowed to avoid getting tangled in that mess but got sucked in anyway.

Just after St. Patrick's Day, Arlen nailed a race for a big payoff. He bet the longshot winner across the board. His place and show horse rallied to get second at the wire. He had those two horses in the exacta and keyed the trifecta. Ray stuffed the money in his sock and made sure no one followed him out.

Arlen was matter-of-fact about it all. "A quick favor before you go, Ray," he asked, his brogue in bloom. "Slip that top box down for me, please. The traitor put it up there. Tis light, nothing really." Like a fish hooked at the jaw hinge, Ray never felt the barb sink in.

Arlen let himself down slow. On his knees, Ray thought he took on the shape of the number two. The box open, Ray stared into a jumble of jockey silks.

Arlen looked up at him. "Looks like Walt Disney himself threw up in there." He pulled them out one after another to a litany accompaniment. Ray recognized some names. Sacred farms and families, canonized jockeys: Sagamore, Shoemaker, Claiborne, Johnny "Pumper"

Longden, Conn McCreary, Darby Dan, Ogden Phipps, "Iceman" Woolf, Ted "The Slasher" Atkinson. Last, Arlen held up red silks with dark blue hoops on the sleeves, the great Arcaro. Ray recognized the devil red silks, Calumet Farm. His dad taught him.

One jersey, torn down the back, came with a story. An older jock, in the irons past his prime, rode down the backstretch flanked by a promising apprentice rider "aboard a gray with red blinkers. A hole opened up before the turn. The kid had a lot of horse under a hard hold. This big gelding gets into the bit." As the bug boy went by, the older jock grabbed him. The gelding won. The veteran finished clutching a handful of polka dots. Out of the money.

ARLEN STARTED collecting when he came east: saddle blankets, tack, goggles, whips, and jockey silks; betting stubs, shot glasses, commemorative pins, postcards, win photos, and programs. All things Thoroughbred. For a time he traded from the back of a battered '67 Ford Country Squire station wagon. "I became like a magnet," Arlen remembered. "Some of them gave me stuff just 'cause they knew I was collecting."

Ray knew it would take considerable effort to reverse polarity and empty the apartment. Arlen inventoried each item in a ledger book, fountain pen notations in neat Palmer script. Ray pulled boxes down and held up each item. Arlen operated the Instamatic. It wasn't too bad. Not Ray's thing but clearly special. His dad would have gotten a big kick out of it all.

Ray's dad, Leo, had passed away suddenly: heart attack. Ideally, he wanted to "keel over in line with my two last dollars in my fist. And I hope the guy behind me snatches the money as he steps over and gets to the window before he's shut out." Leo died in his own kitchen.

Arlen liked to indulge his taste for fancy coffee and old jazz. He would go down to the new café in the morning. Bleary-eyed, with bed-head hair, Ray would come down to latte and swing music from a car radio hooked to a DieHard battery. Thoroughbred museums in Kentucky and New York bought small lots. Track gift shops didn't take anything, content to sell the new, cheap, and mass-produced. Together, they worked flea markets like the 7-Mile Fair. Arlen splurged big time. First the boombox and then that cappuccino maker. He gloried in his cleaning ritual. He fed the machine vinegary concoctions and disassembled parts to bottlebrush.

No one wanted the horseshoes, though the race dates and the horses' names had been carefully painted on. Arlen had shod some famous horses. But even the museums feared a hoax. "Like I was selling a splinter from the cross, disgraceful," he said, letting his brogue flare. Disgusted at the price old newspapers fetched, he wished he had saved more. Empty boxes broken down, they ripped up the old carpet and found terrazzo flooring. Arlen bought the used daybed and a new mattress.

Kitchen open. Arlen preferred his main meal, a big breakfast, in the afternoon. Ray, gaunt through the face and hollow about the eyes, filled out on fried potatoes with chopped bacon and melted cheese. An expert at eggs over easy, Arlen claimed a one-time string of 194 unbroken yolks. "Close to 200, I got too tense," he said. Both found a bit of home around the gray Formica square. Somebody had to cook and somebody else set the table. The meals relieved Ray from frozen dinners alone in the schizo-blue television glow.

Ray liked that he could tell emergency room stories at the table. Never could have done that with his wife. Ray needed to talk loud; not that Arlen was going deaf but to be heard over the flatware clatter and grunts of satisfaction. Arlen consumed his meals with noisy relish while sharing veterinary treatments. "Leave a pail of buttermilk out," he said waving his knife, barely looking up from his plate. "Feed it to a horse with a twisted stomach."

One afternoon Ray had been lost in thoughts of his ex-wife during the meal. How could he still be so angry and miss her at the same time? None of it made sense.

"Calf brains, boy," Arlen's accent clear even while chewing a yolk-drenched toast crust.

"What?" Ray struggled to recall their conversation prior to his painful reverie.

"Calf brains and Doan's pills mashed with warm oats before a race prevents bleeding, don't you know." They had been discussing heart and lung treatments. Ray had blathered on about adrenaline, epinephrine, and atropine, administered intravenously. So "calf brains, boy" was not a non sequitur.

"Are you all right over there, Raymond?" Arlen asked. "You look like a man thrown from his mount."

"Do you think it would work for a broken heart?"

"Calf brains and Doan's. Sure you're daft." Arlen pushed his chair back from the table and crossed one leg over. "You're missing the missus and the little one now, aren't you?"

Ray gulped and nodded. "I'd eat calf brains. Hell, I'd swallow ground glass to stop missing them."

"Well, the Mother, God rest her ..." Arlen sipped his coffee then set the mug down on the table. The soft click sounded loud in the small kitchen. "... She said time is the only cure for conditions of the heart."

"Really. Do you think she coined that phrase?" Ray said, surprised at his bitter sarcasm.

"She was right."

"How would you know?" Ray immediately wished he kept his mouth shut and began to apologize. Arlen rose and left. The tenor of Ray's regrets intensified the further Arlen went from the table.

But Arlen returned with an old black-and-white photo. Seated on a top fence rail, the posture disguised his physical anomaly. Much younger, maybe in his 30s, his dark sweptback hair gave him a rakish look. Oblivious Thoroughbreds grazed in the pasture behind him. Alongside stood a beautiful woman; her curly hair pulled back, her face resting against his hip.

"Your wife?"

"Not mine," Arlen said, voice low. "She was married to an adulterer, a wealthy man. He beat her."

"What happened?"

"She wouldn't leave him. And I couldn't bear to stay. Years later, I learned of her death. She drove off from one of those fancy parties to get away from his mean tongue. The roads were icy. The car crashed."

"I'm sorry." Ray hoped his words encompassed both the loss and his own behavior. "Do you wish you would've stayed?"

"No. I probably would have killed her husband. Sometimes the curse is a blessing in disguise."

"Did your mother say that, as well?"

"She did. But you can call the wisdom your own when you pass it along."

SINCE THE Fourth of July, the disenfranchised continued to meet on the steps, weather and work permitting. Ray had to coax Arlen down, but only once. The old smith soon held forth from his lawn chair in turn. Ayman's discourse on unrest in the Middle East inspired John. "We're starting a new PLO: The Power Loungers Organization." They'd hassle Ray as he walked off to "short-pour honest Americans."

At the bar, the dot.commers encroached on more empty stools. Ray served more imported beer and fewer boilermakers. He preferred the crusty blue-collar dwellers, a better tipping lot. But he listened. They met people and even shopped for mates on the computer. Maybe he could help ease himself back into dating? He still hadn't successfully negotiated with a hooker. Ray plunged into the 21st century. With free expert advice he mastered the rudiments. He went to chat rooms and posted on message boards. He sent e-mail to women he would never see. Ray also discovered he could hear races live.

On April Fools' Day, John snuck around to unscrew hall bulbs and wipe doorknobs with a greasy sack. Power Loungers coming home cursed their defiled hands in the dark. John's obnoxious laugh, the machine gun from Down Under, echoed up the stairwell. Arlen was understandably wary when Ray invited him up the next day for a surprise.

Ray clicked the link. The track announcer fired his lingo-laden bulletin.

"They're coming down the stretch in the West Lawn Stakes. C'mon In is full out. Regretful Blues is at his throatlatch and Pat Day goes to work on him. But C'mon In is game today. Playground Billy moves along the rail in the final furlong. C'mon In. Regretful Blues. It's a ding-dong finish. C'mon In looked to get his nose down at the wire from Regretful Blues by a bob and a length further back to Playground Billy. Hooold all tickets. Photo finish."

Arlen later said he felt like Alexander Graham Bell and called it "the cat's ass." Together, they figured out the computer could deliver *Forms*, results, programs, and pictures. A good day at a flea market followed another decent payoff at the track. The sleek, black tower and 20-inch monitor moved in; Arlen went about "breaking it in properly." Better with horses, he sputtered frustration over his screen before rising from his chair.

About the same time, Ricky started to shine around again. At the edge of the PLO, tentative, his weight shifted from leg to leg. Maybe because enough memorabilia sold, or because Easter loomed in the waning days of Lent, Arlen softened. He started to greet Ricky, invited him to sit; they even talked horses. Ray tried to ask Arlen about his change of heart.

"You know, Ray. I've never been able to look back very easy. I gotta turn all the way around to see clear behind me. The Almighty wants me to keep looking ahead. What DeShayes did is forgiven, not forgotten."

Ray remained suspicious. Ricky hovered. Gut instinct told Ray he wanted something. Arlen didn't need to trust Ricky or depend on Ray to get his bets down. He just clicked and listened. Turned out,

Ricky had a knack for computers, too. He taught Arlen about eBay. The old smith could slurp latte and auction memorabilia from his own apartment. After a lifetime waking early, he loved this night owl revelry.

A CONTAGION swept through the PLO first week of May: Derby fever. Ricky, sure this year would yield a Triple Crown winner, touted the powerful chestnut Point Given, nicknamed “The Big Red Train.” Ayman agreed. He liked that the owner was a fellow Arab. Arlen acknowledged Point Given’s prowess but picked a long-striding gray, Monarchos, based on the Florida Derby. “Did ya see him uncork on the far turn and gobble up the ground? That’s what ya need at Churchill Downs with that long homestretch.”

For the Triple Crown races, John ran a hundred-foot extension cord down the hall and out the doors, foiled the rabbit ears, and under elm shade caught a fair picture. Monarchos, six wide in the turn, passed The Big Red Train and others down the stretch to win the Derby. Point Given took the Preakness to set up a grudge match in New York.

On Belmont day, during a commercial, a corner homeboy and his guys approached. Spread-legged, the leader pulled up his T-shirt to reveal his gun handle, an automatic. From under his bib overalls, Arlen had already eased out this old hogleg revolver and leveled it steady over the set. The leader’s jaw slacked. Everyone else froze. Ray clattered out of his lawn chair. Arlen cocked the hammer. Ray winced until he shuddered.

“Your funeral will be the surprise, young man,” Arlen explained. “I’m gonna die soon anyway. We can live and let live. Or you can join me? There’s no glory getting shot by an old man, though.”

The leader flailed and swore but stomped off. Arlen waved off the backslaps and killed the chatter so they didn’t miss the race. Point Given won the Belmont, easy. Monarchos got up for third.

The race and attempted robbery sparked everyone else. Calvin quelled the worry over gang reprisal. He made good on his cop connections. The operation could only be called slick. He worked the street with a walkie-talkie. Ayman trolled in his cab with a government agent. John fixed up the spotter and his equipment in a vacant unit. Before Ray left for work, the undercover cops swooped down on a curbside street deal. In the wee hours, uniforms served search warrants on all the right cribs.

AYMAN SUBLET his cab to start police classes at the technical college. Wet curl to his hair and new black slacks, Calvin was a player again. A cab driver who could find hookers for conventioneers, reefer for the tourists, and tip cops to the real bad guys. On stage for open mike at the comedy club, he softly ridiculed his fares, finding fun in their desperation.

The realty company admired John's work, relative peace, and units mostly full. They asked him to manage a second building. Ricky found work at the casino dealing in a blackjack pit and hoped to bankroll enough to claim his own horse. Arlen helped him study for his trainer's test.

The old smith was right. He didn't have long. Didn't even see the Travers. Started with a cold, always dangerous due to his age and misshapen chest; pneumonia developed. Arlen treated himself with sharp-smelling poultices and painted liniments, literally horse doctoring. He steamed himself in the shower until near fainting.

Ray brought the pressure of the entire PLO to bear. Arlen consented. He visited the doctor. Ray, still licensed, administered the prescribed shots at home.

The westerly moon lingered. To Ray, it seemed stubborn, stalled in the blue-black sky over the city; he wanted to get outside under its cool light. The bureaucracy of death proved too slow. An hour until a Division Street sector car arrived. Two uniform cops with no reason to hurry.

The guy is already dead. They had questions. A single detective responded to briefly worry if the former nurse had gone Kevorkian, and more questions. A photo tech followed an investigator from the Cook County medical examiner; she had questions, too. Arlen's eyes clouded. The transport attendants, in their charcoal jumpsuits and baseball caps, appeared in the hall. The moon set.

After some discussion, they used a larger body bag. Ray wished he had waited until dawn to call. Just zipped shut and strapped up sideways onto the gurney.

Ricky huffed up the stairs, a leather satchel with embroidered beadwork over his shoulder.

HE DIDN'T ASK. He demanded they open the body bag, on religious grounds. After a solid half-hour wrangling about rights, they consented, unbuckled one strap and unzipped him to the shoulder. Arlen stared fog-eyed from the double-layer vinyl cocoon. Ricky knelt. With slow reverence he unwrapped a deer hide. That brought a sigh from a uniform cop. A smudge of tobacco, cedar, and sage in the shallow of a rock, Ricky fanned the smoke over Arlen with an eagle feather. Ray saw all hats had been removed. This was not going down unmarked. Even though they would attend hundreds of deaths, Arlen's would be recalled. Ray liked that.

Ricky rose. They again secured Arlen. Hiccup-quick, they snapped the gurney upright and wheeled him to the elevator. Ricky drew back the gated door. Ray grit his teeth as the gurney bounced to the stoop. Under the elm, John, unsteady from drink, pushed himself up. The empties under his lawn chair indicated he might have been there since the cops arrived.

"We—Power Loungers—we're pleasantly miserable." John swayed on his sea legs and raised his bottle to the brassy light. "Miserable at your departure. Pleased by the assurance of your imminent arrival. Put in a good word Up There for all of us."

It kept Ray smiling until the gurney folded into the van and the investigator padlocked the doors. They guided John to his couch and cleaned up his bottles.

Back in Arlen's flat, a heavy morose scent outlasted the smoke. Nervous that Ricky might vulture, Ray felt guilty for being nervous. Over his shoulder, he could see him in front of the computer looking up at the horseshoe collection.

Ray reached over the bed to yank open the reluctant window. He drew the shade down just to the sash. The low morning light scooted in on the breeze with traffic racket. Ricky reached to take down a squat cinnamon candle.

"Until he's buried, you should keep a candle burning to light the way as his spirit journeys across. Keep a glass of water out, too, for thirst," Ricky said.

A VIGIL, good idea. Ray slowly pulled the bedsheet tight, erasing Arlen's last crumple. Tucked and hospital-cornered at the foot, he tugged the spread. Paper rustled. Amused, Ray picked up the pillow and found the *Form*. Ray recognized the marks and notations. In the kitchenette, the water tap coughed on; glassware clinked in the cupboard.

"Ricky, I got Arlen's picks for today at Arlington." Ray, up all night, didn't want to drive. So he asked Ricky, "Your car running?" He suffered quick regret. He saw the question cut Ricky.

"No, Ray. That's why it took me so long to get here. My heap is down. Needs parts."

"Well, not to worry," Ray said, hoping to smooth it over. "We can take mine, if you'll drive."

"You know I never stole the old man's money. I just figured there was no way those horses were gonna fill out that ticket. So I laid it down on a horse to win. I was flat broke before they even came to the gate. I couldn't put any bet down. And I did run out of gas on the way home."

"You were his friend before I knew him," Ray said. "You sent him off the right way. He would have liked that."

They decided to offer the others a chance to come along. What if Arlen had received divine inspiration as he contemplated his last *Form*? Everyone deserved a chance to cash in. The PLO started the wake at the track. The candle stayed lit. Some water must have evaporated while they were gone.

Ice Storm

by Danny L. Talbot

THE DOOR at Billy's Fuel & Food was heavy with ice and age. I pushed hard on the cold, rusty bar that served as a doorknob and let an old man in a black-and-red flannel coat go in front of Susan and me. Shivers rippled over my body as his ice-covered boots scraped across the oak plank floor. His pants cuffs, frozen hard as fence boards, made a harsh, metallic sound as he gathered a few groceries.

We bought 30 gallons of number two diesel fuel for the horse van and a quart of coffee for us. It had been a slow, cold drive from the city racetrack with seven of Susan's horses in the borrowed van. I waited impatiently to pay for our fuel and coffee while Susan looked around the little store. The clerk behind the well-worn glass and wood counter told the flannel-coated old man about how the clerk's dog, a blue heeler, had fallen off a truck and broken its hind right leg.

"Darn thing won't hold still back there, Samuel," the clerk said. "He runs all over the bed and the cab. I say put him down, but the kids and the wife won't hear of it. So now I got a dog with three good legs. Whoever heard of a dog with a cast on his leg? I say put him down, and put him out of my misery, at least."

The old man spoke softly, but everyone in the store listened. "Sounds like a little goat I have over at the farm, Billy. Broke its leg jumping off the haystack. Had to go in for a checkup that day, so I stole two tongue depressors from Doc Healey's office. I came home and fiddled with that goat's leg until it felt like everything matched up, then I taped her leg between those two sticks. She walked around kind of like a pirate with a wooden leg for six weeks. When I took them sticks off, she was a little stiff in that hind leg, but, tell you what, the little nanny did fine.

"While she was healing up, she started following my big, red colt around the farm, maybe for protection or maybe just for some company. Pretty soon that red horse wouldn't go to the races, to the vet, or anywhere else without her in the trailer. We call that goat 'Peggy.' Still have her. Must be five or six years since she broke that leg."

Little torrents of ice water ran down my back as snow melted off my collar. I shook badly from the cold and spilled hot coffee over my frozen hands.

"Damn it!" I half shouted. Heads jerked toward me from the three booths along the streetside wall. There, six or seven people sat drinking coffee and looking over the *Daily Racing Form*. A couple of handmade wooden racks by the tables held several old copies. Everyone at the tables turned toward me. Embarrassed, I said in a voice louder than I wanted, "Does it ever get warm enough around here to melt the ice?"

Susan looked at me over the top of her glasses and said apologetically to no one particular, "My city-bred husband does not appreciate the weather. Please excuse him."

The old man shifted toward the door, and I paid for our fuel and coffee. Billy, the counter man, dropped change into my shaking hand, a few coins at a time. "Wait 'til it gets to be winter," Billy said slowly, with a glance to the other customers. "Things can get dicey when it gets a little icy."

"Dicey enough for me right now," I said, staring down the people watching us.

"What, it don't get ice and snow in the city?" asked a tall boy about 16 with a wad of what could have been gum in his jaw. "My mother didn't have no power for 14 days straight last year during the big ice storm. And she lives just down the street here. Right here."

"Oh, yes," I said deliberately, "it snows in the city, but in the form of flakes, not ice cubes. And the ice hangs sort of down off things, not sideways like out there."

Susan ushered me out the door to outright laughter from the people inside. "That's a good idea," she said as we climbed in the truck. "Let's try to alienate everybody around here before we even move in." I slid in the truck and turned on the glow plugs to warm the diesel fuel before starting up. A voice came through the snow and into the truck. "Enjoy your ride and be careful." It was the old man in the flannel coat. "The ice is treacherous, but it can also be beautiful at sunset. Looks like a million prisms painting the light as the sun dies away."

"Will do," I said, hitting the starter. "Wouldn't miss it for the world." I couldn't see him in the rearview mirror or beside the truck as I eased out onto the road. He must have gone back up through the snowbound fields behind the store.

"Why can't you at least give this place a try?" Susan said tersely as we drove away from the little store. "I need a place to race these horses from. It is beautiful here most of the time and only an hour back to the university. You can do a lot of your work at home, anyway."

"Look,' I said, "you're the horsewoman. I'm glad you're going to try training on your own, but I don't like the country. There aren't any sidewalks. The post office is five miles from our house, and people hang out at a gas station, for goodness sake. This may work for you, but I may be someone else." Susan answered my restrained tirade with silence. The horses rocked slightly in the van as the lane wove itself around the ice-covered trees and up the hill, toward our new home. The light played across the truck hood and through the trees and fences. The old man in the store was right. It did look like a thousand prisms painting the light.

At mile marker 102, I turned the van onto the long gravel drive, past the house, and directly into the barn. The horses were stamping their feet, sensing they were about to be unloaded. Erica, a hot walker from the track who had agreed to work for Susan, came out of the barn office. "How was the ride from the city?" she asked as I pulled down the side ramp and began setting up the rails that ran down each side of it. "These ponies will be glad to be away from the track for a while. Seems like they can't wait to get away from town and can't wait to get back." We took each horse into its newly bedded stall. The barn was cold, but dry. The horses looked glad to be there.

"Sounds like someone else I know," Susan said quietly. "Just can't be sure where home is." She was waiting by the door as we finished stabling the horses. I watched as she turned and walked briskly away. Erica looked busy and acted as though she hadn't heard Susan's comment.

"You go on in, Dr. B.," she said. "You've had a big drive. I'll look after things here."

"Thanks, it has been a long day," I answered. We lifted the big ramp back onto the van. "I think I'll call it a night," I said, and walked slowly up to the house.

THE NEXT MORNING, I woke early and looked out our second-story bedroom window. The neatly kept pastures around the house looked different from those I had seen in the fall when we first visited the farm. Then the paddocks were lush, flowing seas of green bounded by sturdy black oak fences. But now, the wind and ice had sculpted a different landscape. Everywhere, a frozen shroud enveloped the fields. Fence posts appeared ethereal, like translucent tree trunks in a van Gogh painting. The ice weighed down power lines, making them look like sagging strings of cold spaghetti, strung haphazardly between their poles.

Looking across the trailer turnaround behind the house, the horses and an old dog we had inherited with the farm appeared to be getting along well despite the weather. Some of the horses were eating hay in a paddock where Erica had turned them out early that morning. The dog, a black and white midsized spaniel called Elmo, seemed to love the weather. As I watched, she ran from the barn to the house, sliding the last ten feet or so on the slick ground. Her antics seemed bent on making us feel welcome.

Susan was already out in the barn, wrapping and unwrapping horses' legs and doing whatever Thoroughbred trainers do. She had gone out before dawn, probably to avoid another chapter in our all-too-familiar argument about buying the farm. We both knew the story well. She wanted to try training on her own and wanted a farm from which she could base her operation. The trainer she had worked for since she was a teenager encouraged her to strike out on her own. He and many of our friends frequently told her she had a gift with horses and should pursue it. She could tell if they were sick before they even looked ill. She could lead them around the shedrows at the track with no halter, just her hand under their jaw. This made people a little nervous, so she tended to do those kinds of things only when no one else was around.

I was a city boy with a nice job at the university teaching chemistry and saw no sense in moving 50 miles from my job and away from the comforts of town. We had argued constantly about the pending move. And for the past several months, there had been a new level of strain between Susan and me. Neither of us had spoken the words, but we knew our lives were growing apart. I was a scientist. I wanted concrete things that could be seen and touched and proven with theorems. Susan seemed sometimes to live in another dimension, where things were felt and known without the benefit of reality. I resented her long hours at the track and the frequent travel to other tracks. If we tried to spend time at the track together, it only made things worse.

A month earlier, our last time at the track together, was typical. She stood entranced by each race in which she had a horse, watching the field of jockeys and horses make their way up the stretch. She was seemingly transported to a different dimension from the one I occupied, often brushing hidden tears of joy quickly away from her eyes as she plunged onto the track to pick up her horse, who had no doubt finished fourth. Trying to be part of the scene, I bet on a few of her horses. If I bet one to show, he ran fourth. A win ticket purchased by me ensured a sturdy run into second place. "But he didn't win," I pointed out. "Would it have killed him to put his neck out a little farther?" I asked. She looked at me with a face that was both disgusted and unbelieving.

"Didn't you see his move?" she said, softly rubbing the horse's neck when we were back at the barn. "He ran like a hero. Next time. He'll be ready, next time. He was just a little nervous at the crowd today. He says he will be ready next time." "He says?" I thought to myself. Then there were hours of walking and rubbing and wrapping, Susan in a state of horse heaven and me somewhere else.

As we argued more and more often, Susan sometimes pointed out that she had spent many years working long hours at tracks while putting me through school. Now that I had a professorship and a steady job, she felt it was her turn to pursue her dream of being a trainer. Most of our friends agreed with her. She had a gift, they reminded me, and I should support it. Only partly in jest, I had once said that it seemed to me a "gift" for horses was something in which children enthralled with ponies were likely to believe, right after reading *The Black Stallion*. Our friends, and Susan, were not amused.

I WORKED away that first morning at the farm by reading student papers and wrote a few letters into the early afternoon. Finally, it was obvious Susan was not coming back anytime soon. I started out to the barn several times but stopped. I wasn't about to go out there and rub horses' legs with Susan and Erica while they talked endlessly about heat and tendons and vitamin B-12. I bundled up in all the Orvis and Eddie Bauer I could wear and stepped outside into the icy air. Elmo was immediately bouncing at my feet.

"How about a walk, old girl?" I said into the wind. "Since the mall is 20 miles away, let's take the lane. It looks like it's been cleared a little." I slid my way to the road that runs along the paddocks by our house. Elmo, ears flopping as she bounded along the icy path, looked like a dolphin playing in the waves as she ducked in and out of frozen shrubs.

The narrow road, bounded on each side with black four-plank fence, wandered west, through groves of naked oak trees, painted white on the windward side, where dusty ice lay caked, frozen like frosting layers on bizarre angular pastries. As we reached the first turn in the lane, I glanced quickly back at the house. I could see Susan standing just inside the opened barn, watching us. I almost called out, but at the last moment pretended not to see her. We walked on. The wind calmed to a satiny calm. Ghostly wisps of blue light danced across the hoary horizon.

The sun shone shadowy through the saberlike limbs of the tall oaks. "Where's the bus stop?" I asked Elmo, mostly to hear my own voice, "I'm getting a little tired." She insolently ignored me and bounded on. In fields to our left, two men led several mares, heavy with foal, back through their paddock to their barn.

For a few miles, the lane wound silently through the trees, went up a small hill, and passed a slight depression that was not quite a valley. A once-cultivated circle of junipers surrounded the vale. Rising from within the circle of odd green trees were crumbling buildings that long ago housed others who had chosen this life. Whether these people vacated this frozen desolation of their own volition or were driven to less-hostile places, I could only guess. Smart folks, either way.

IT WAS getting late, and both the dog and I were tired and cold. We left the road to seek a rest among the ruins. The abandoned farm held the remains of a two-story house and a large barn. The house was one room wide. It had small windows front and back and part of a handmade shake roof still intact. A tilting stone fireplace, 15 feet tall, stretched its bony column upward from the center, like a monument to this vain agrarian effort.

The base of the towering chimney loomed over a fireplace large enough to stand in. Heating this house must have been a high priority for its long-ago inhabitants. Judging by my numbed feet and hands, I could see why a fireplace would have been the center of this homestead. Behind the house stood the massive old barn made of rough-sawn timbers and planks. The venerable but battered building was mostly whole and laid resting from many years of hard use. Elmo and I walked around the house and up to the barn. The main door hung by one rusted hinge and was tilted slightly open, frozen in place.

Without disturbing its angle of repose, we slipped quietly inside. I was tired, cold, and glad to be out of the frigid air. My eyes adjusted slowly to the yellow light filtering through small holes in the barn roof. I looked around. Rusting farm implements lay quietly where they'd been left years before. As I surveyed the expanse of the barn, a large shadow moved behind me. Startled, I whirled around to see the long head of a horse peering at me from over an old, but sturdy-looking stall. I walked closer. The head held a set of huge brown eyes, soft and clear, that never let me from their gaze. I rubbed the horse's nose and forehead, and she murmured deeply.

The horse looked as though she received great care and regular attention—unlike the rest of the place. Her coat was clean and shiny.

Her stall was bedded deeply with straw. Somebody loved this old girl. Bits of gray were showing in her flanks and around her nose and eyes. She was a big mare, maybe 17 hands, Susan would probably say. Leaning over the stall front, I saw that her left knee was about twice the size of her right one. One bad step on the clubhouse turn, perhaps. It looked like this lady had rolled down the lane many times in her career.

I looked around the barn. To the side of her stall, a rickety ladder led to a loft above. The loft, still full of ancient hay and straw, covered the back half of the barn. Putting the old dog under one arm, I gingerly climbed a slivery ladder and peered over the rail.

The loft was larger than it appeared from below. The wood floor was steel gray with age but looked sturdy. Elmo scrambled out of my arms and began sniffing every inch of the loft. Exercising much more adventure than usual, I took the last few steps up the creaking ladder and stood looking down over the expanse of the barn. From this height, the farm equipment and the old mare looked toylike, as if they belonged in one of those little farm sets people buy their grandkids. Turning carefully around, feeling that the next step might send me rocketing to the floor, I made my way to the back wall and sat in the deep, musty straw. A stairway led up the back of the barn to the other side of the loft. It looked infinitely safer than the ladder. I quickly resolved to use those stairs if I ever came here again. I nestled back against the rough-sawn timbers and rested my head against the wall. Tiny dry-ice crystals drifted softly through cracks in the ancient wooden roof.

The old dog laid contentedly on my boots as if she knew the warmth from her furry coat was welcome, indeed, to my city feet that were unused to hiking on other than shoveled sidewalks and shopping mall floors. The icy flakes came lighter and softer. We rested there in the growing silence of the receding wind. Elmo's eyes were heavy. Her eyelids dropped closed and then opened quickly again as she struggled to stay awake, wanting to see every important event.

The musty smell of straw rose warmly into my nostrils. Only an occasional snowlike crystal now glided down through the warm, yellow light. Through holes in the loft floor, I could see the old mare go back to eating and murmuring softly. High in the rafters of the barn, a large white owl made muffled hooting sounds. I wished Susan was here to see him. She loved animals in the wild. I was quite sure she had never seen a white owl. The bird's huge amber eyes peered down and scrutinized us, as if deciding whether to let us stay.

The owl's soft, rounded sounds blended into the ancient wood and disappeared, then were again in my ears as the barn-watcher continued his soothing song. Elmo was almost asleep. Her rhythmic breathing kept time with the soft creaking sounds of the slightly swaying primitive barn timbers.

I lay back on the warm straw. My eyes, too, were getting heavy. Drifting into sleep, I closed my eyes and saw the long arms of the oak trees arching skyward. In a half-dream, I saw Susan walking under the oaks. I called to her, but she could not hear me. I walked toward her, but the snow was too deep, the ice too slick. My legs were leaden. Struggling like an ancient mammoth in the tar, I called to her again. No answer. I struggled, trying to run toward her as she grew fainter in the swirling storm.

FROM THE stairway on the back wall, a gravelly voice spoke. I stirred, then lurched to full attention as I realized this voice was not from my dream.

"Kind of nice in here, isn't it?" the voice said quietly.

Jumping up, wide awake now, I saw a large man with a walking stick standing in the shadows of the far wall near the staircase. He wore a heavy flannel coat with a bright red shirt underneath. On his head was a wool hat, like trainmen sometimes wear in the winter. It was the old man from the store.

"Who are you?" I asked. "Is this your barn? I hope I'm not trespassing," I said, startled, conditioned by too many years in the city where signs and fences and locks told one where you could go and where you were not welcome.

"I'm Sam," he said. "Live across the field. I don't own this place, though I keep Yelda here in the winter. No one seems to mind, and outside the cold bothers her joints, especially her knees. She went out 71 times when she was racing, you know. Won 29 of them. She was an iron lady, but you get old and the bones tell you to slow down. You probably saw her on your way in. She has a bad knee. They were going to send her to the canners. I had watched her fly over that track so many times and talked to her so much from the rail, I felt like she was partly mine. I couldn't let her go to the killers, so I bought her and took her home. Best move I ever made with a horse. She has the magic, you know."

"Yes, I saw her on the way in. Definitely a nice horse," I said. Did he say "magic"? I asked myself. "By the way, I'm Derrick Brown. I teach at the university in the city. The woman in the store with me last night is Susan, my wife. She trains horses."

"Ah, yes, you two were at Billy's. I think you spilled coffee on your hands. Let's see now, I thought I recognized your wife. Suzie Brown. Right? Good trainer. I've watched her a lot over the years. The horses communicate with her. She listens. She has a gift."

"So I've been told," I said. "Yes, well, we finished moving in last night. Just before the storm got really bad."

"Good house you bought, good barn," he said. "Got steep, good roofs. Smart to put a steep roof on the place. It can snow here, now can't it," he said more as a statement than a question. "Gets a little icy, too."

"Yes, it does. They said it snowed here, and they said it gets icy, and they were right," I said, gaining a little more control of my startled voice.

Elmo woke up. She jumped around the loft in joyous greeting of our visitor. No watchdog, this one, I silently observed. The old man bent slowly down on one knee and whistled staccato notes to her. She bounced instantly to his side.

"Nice dog," Sam said. "Cocker spaniel?"

"No guess," I said. "She came with the house."

Sam tipped his head up and peered at me through the corners of his eyes.

"What brings you to the barn?" he asked.

"Nothing, really," I answered. "Just out for a walk in the pristine countryside."

"Not everyone likes to be out in this weather," he said. "Too bad. They miss a lot."

I had a feeling that Sam expected me to know what it was people missed by not walking in weather like this.

"True. They do miss a lot," I said, thinking to myself that cold feet might be one thing. "There aren't many places like this anymore."

"Ah," he said again. "I disagree. There are plenty of places like this, and times. Only, people don't see them. No time for magic any more. No time for enchantment. They don't take time. The problem is Descartes."

"Day who?" I asked, not sure that I had heard him correctly.

"Descartes, the philosopher. Started the 'Age of Reason.' Said people's minds are filled with reality. No room for magic. No room for enchantment. Everything has a cause and an effect. Science. Linear logic. What nonsense. The crazy part is how we all just took to it."

I wasn't sure what kind of conversation this was. I was not used to discussing Descartes in barns with strangers who carried walking clubs. "I agree," I said, inching toward the stairway. "Not much room in the world today for enchantment. I'd like to talk to you about it sometime."

"And how about that idiot Rousseau," he continued. "Two peas in a pod, and the whole Western world went along with them. You believe in magic, sir?" he asked wryly. Still a little groggy, I looked around the barn. Standing there in the fading light of the afternoon, as tiny rays of glistening light filtered through the roof and softly warmed the floor below, the ancient barn appeared almost as though it could be magical, or at least enchanted. I was no longer in a hurry to leave, and thought I might bring Susan here tomorrow. She would think it was magical, I was sure.

I paused, thinking over the past several months. "I'd like to believe in magic," I said, finally, more to myself, than to Sam. "This place makes me want to believe in ... something."

"That's why I keep old Yelda. She reminds me of what magic is," he said, looking down gently upon Yelda. He appeared to be thinking of another time and another place.

"When she ran years ago," he said dreamily, "she seemed to fly on top of the track, never touching its surface. On the day of the race, she glowed from within, like she was carrying some galactic package on a mission of speed to somewhere special. Then, on the track, she glowed with joy of her movement, with the sheer joy of her speed." He paused and looked directly at me. "You can still see that glow in her eyes some mornings," he said. "It was magic then, and it is magic now. No reason. No cause and effect. No logic. Just magic. I'll bet your wife sees magic in the horses. It's why she's so good." He smiled. "You should ask her about it sometime.

"But now I've got to be going," he said. "I have someone waiting for tea and cards. Every day at 4:30. Tea and gin rummy. Wonderful game. We don't keep score. You and your wife should join us one day. We'll talk about magical horses!"

I nodded and mumbled something affirmative sounding. Sam leaned down once more and rubbed Elmo between the ears. She lapped him with her tongue and then turned and sat quietly looking at me.

SAM AND I walked down the stairs without speaking again. Elmo followed happily. Sam stopped to rub Yelda's ears as he left. She watched him intently as he slid through the opening in the doorway. The old man walked down the lane toward his house, his heavy cane moving lightly through the snow, his feet steady on the ice. Occasionally, he stopped to view the expanse around him. Apparently in no hurry, he knew how long it would take him to make his tea and cards. I felt a brush of air across my back. Turning, I saw the huge white owl swoop from the barn rafters and glide silently out the loft window. His wingspan was greater than a man's outstretched arms. The long curved feathers barely moved as he made one circle, then banked and followed the old man across the fields toward the glowing lights of Sam's house.

I smoothed Elmo's coat with my gloved hand and looked once more around the now almost lightless barn. Yelda was dozing standing up. As I passed her, she opened her dark, warm eyes and looked directly into mine. Standing there, I remember the dream and losing Susan in the storm. I realized that we were making our own endless tempest, and I didn't want to lose either of us in it. Tomorrow I would bring Susan here. I would tell her that I, too, had seen something in Yelda's eyes. She would be able to explain to me what it was.

"Perhaps the owl will return tomorrow," I whispered, not wanting to disturb the magic of the place.

"Come on, old dog," I said. "Let's go home."

Root Doctor

by Scott Travis Hutchison

WHEN THE farm boss determined I was old enough to move up from grass-cutter to work with the Thoroughbreds, he put me with Lucas Jefferson. The boss just grabbed me up one day when I was stowing my mower, took me to the layup barn, stood me in front of Lucas and, hand on my shoulder, said, "Listen to Lucas. Damn near everything you need to know about horses you can learn from this man, and then some." Then he walked away, leaving me there with that crazy old coot.

Lucas was an ancient, light-skinned black man with freckles. He had shaky, palsied hands, and a bad leg that he tended to pull along with him rather than walk with. Lucas was thin, wiry, a whisper inside his clothes—he was scraggly bearded, bad-toothed, and, truth to tell, he scared the hell out of a kid like me.

"How old are you, boy?" Lucas's voice was soft and deep. I already didn't like this new job.

"Thirteen."

"Thirteen. That's how old I was when I got this leg thinned by the polio. You know what polio is, boy?" He gestured for me to sit down, just as he was doing, against the concrete wall shaded by the shedrow roof. The shade lent some cool to my typical day. Horses pawed in their stalls or picked at their hay—the only other sounds besides the old man they'd tied me to.

"No, sir, I don't." I was expecting Lucas to go ahead and start teaching me whatever it was everybody said he knew about horses, and here he was talking about his bad skinny leg. For the first time in my young life, I had a pang of longing for my weeder and the scorch of the Kentucky summer sun.

"Polio is a disease. Kills quite a few, lames up the rest. Maybe that's why I work with the broke-down horses—we've got something in common. Anyway, this bad leg of mine I drag around with me, the only reason I've still got it is my mama poulticed it night and day—poultice is a hot, moist mush you put on hurts, I'll be teaching you 'bout it soon enough with these here horses we've got to nurse back to health—my mama poulticed this leg with white vinegar, mustard, creosote, and the pistils of water lilies all mixed up in bran. That's the only reason I've still got my leg, only reason I ain't crutching my life around using a Y-shaped stick."

Lucas Jefferson looked me straight on. His voice dropped an octave. "You ain't got no need to be scared of me, boy."

He put his age-pocked hand on top of mine for a second, then lifted it, shooed away a buzzing fly, and smiled. And from that moment on—I could hardly tell you why—I don't think I've ever been afraid of much of anything.

"HORSES HAVE wild blood in 'em, same as most people," Lucas said one day when we were on our rounds in the layup barn, going from one sick or injured horse to the next. Lucas took the time to explain every little thing to me, which was good—I was full of questions, and not that many adults had the patience to listen to everything spinning around in my head. "They also have great hearts, righteous needs, which actually makes horses better than most people."

Lucas was continuing with my newest lesson: how to hold horses. I was fine for mucking stalls, scrubbing water buckets, haying and feeding all the sick and injured horses in our care, but holding horses—taking care of the horse as well as whomever might be working with them, be it groom, vet, or blacksmith—and administering to a "noble Thoroughbred's" various medical needs was something he told me I'd have to grow into, and grow into right, because there was more to it than just hanging onto the end of a shank. "You respect a horse proper, you listen to him and find out what those needs are, then you'll be all right standing there with him."

We were working on a two-year-old colt who recently had been pin-fired. Seemed like some medieval torture to me, but Lucas assured me that brought along correctly, the colt's legs and muscle tissues would be better for it in the long run. Still, when I looked at the pattern of burns in the colt's shins generated by metal and electricity and someone's need to get their money's worth out of this horse, I couldn't help but think that if it had been done to me, the pain would be insufferable, and I'd probably be thrashing around, throwing a fit. You could tell the colt was thinking along similar lines.

"Now I ain't partial to this method of getting legs right," Lucas said as he patted the young chestnut's neck with one hand while pulling me into place beside him. "Can't rightly say if the vets like this neither, but it's what the owner wanted. There's only one problem in this whole business of Thoroughbreds. And it ain't all the owners, 'cause there are some fine, compassionate owners, but it's the impatient types, the ones who think about racing before they think about the horse himself. Sometimes the folks with the money don't always want to hear what's best for a horse—sometimes they just want to hear what they call the 'most expedient' method of getting a Thoroughbred running again."

Lucas studied the pin-firing pattern on the colt's shins. "Maybe we have to clean this up since somebody else is writing the paychecks, but me, I ain't gonna teach you the fast way." Lucas continued patting the colt, and his voice lowered, his eyes narrowing. "So, what do you think this horse needs, boy?"

I thought that was pretty obvious. "He needs some medicine on those shins, probably needs some painkiller."

Lucas turned and looked at me, frowning. "We already have our share of dumbasses working this farm. If the boss man wanted another one of them, he'd have put you with somebody else to learn horses. Now, slow your hot brain down for a second—and if you're angry about me calling you a dumbass, then get over it—and pat this horse. Slowly, sleek and slow, with a little love of who and what he is mixed in—look him in the eye, and tell me what this horse needs."

Lucas backed away from me and the colt, moving toward the stall door.

First, I decided to cool out and stop being mad that some rickety, old, half-crippled, uneducated man had called me stupid, since when it came to horses I was, admittedly, pretty stupid, and so far Lucas Jefferson seemed worthy of the trust so many people put in him. I patted the colt's strong neck around his mane line, and I did what I was told: I looked him in the eye as best I could, even though the colt was jerking his head up and down and his eyes were rolling to whites.

"This horse is scared." I kept my chin up, kept eye contact, kept patting.

I heard the voice behind me. "Good. Good. So what's he need?" Lucas had a way with his teaching. He tended to ask me questions, and he gently demanded me to reach inside myself for the common-sense answers. The colt hesitated in his head tosses.

I thought about that colt before I spoke. "He needs to not be scared. He needs to know we want to help him."

I didn't even hear Lucas move up beside me. "This horse is gonna be all right. Know why?" I shook my head. "He's got me, and now he's got you. We know what that wild blood—that strong racing heart—needs. He's gonna be all right, and you're gonna be all right, too, boy. Now, how do we tell him that?"

Lucas's old fragile hands seemed to steady as he took to patting the horse once again, slowly, slowly, on the other side of the colt's strong, young neck. He winked at me, and then I watched him. I slowed my hand down to Lucas slow. He took his time. Whatever time it might take, I reckoned. I watched him as he tilted his face up and looked the colt straight in the face, and his face said worlds. His face said, "Trust me, I won't let you down." I was unsure.

"Tell me how, Lucas."

"I'm telling you."

BILLY BRADLEY, 12 years old, was my successor on grass cutting. And when his mower went over the top of a yellow jacket nest hidden in the ground in the boss's yard in early July, Lucas and I were the first ones to hear and answer his howlings. I sped ahead, Lucas was no match for my speed, and I rolled the kid on the ground away from the hole, away from the now-dead mower that was getting stung just like Billy himself. I pulled my T-shirt off and slapped at the remaining yellow jackets that the rolling hadn't crushed.

The kid was hysterical. There wasn't much meat on Billy, so the stings were prominent. He looked to have about 20 of them on his arms and face where his clothing hadn't covered skin, and even though the sting spots were welting, he didn't look like he was puffing up with any big allergic reaction—just pain and panic and an uncontrolled wildness coursing through his bloodstream. Lucas finally arrived, but instead of coming over to me and Billy, he bustled as best he could to the boss's wife's flower bed and started picking leaves off of some plant. Meanwhile, Billy was doing some serious tossing back and forth and crying.

I straddled over the top of the kid, putting my knees on either of his arms to keep him from any more swatting and scratching. I took Billy's face in both my hands and looked him in the eyes.

"Billy! Listen to me! Listen!" He was cursing and whining, and it took a bit for him to focus on me. I dropped my voice. "Billy, it's all right. Hey, you want that pain to go away?" His face nodded quickly in my hands. Lucas finally leg-dragged his way to us with a handful of leaves. Lucas winked at me, and I patted Billy's head. "Then you got to trust us. We're gonna help." I climbed off Billy and looked to Lucas.

I had no idea how we were going to help. Lucas handed me a leaf. He stroked one of the leaves in his hands with a long, yellowed fingernail. "See how I'm scratching just the barest little bit of skin off this leaf? Getting to the moist inside? You do that, too, then put it on the stings."

I did what I was told, and together we worked on Billy, even as some of the other farmhands finally made the scene. Lucas smiled at Billy and said, "These leaves, they're cooling off those stings, ain't they?" Billy nodded and actually smiled back. Lucas and I kept scratching the leaves and putting them in place. "My mama taught me 'bout these leaves. But she also taught me you can't hold nothing against them yellow jackets. They're just doing what they're supposed to be doing: Living the best way they know how, doing what instinct tells 'em."

By the time the boss and Doc Hardacre—the farm's veterinarian—arrived, Billy was sitting up and laughing. Doc Hardacre practically elbowed me out of the way to take charge of Billy. He looked at the leaves, looked at Lucas, then pulled out some packaged pills.

"Here," he said, tearing a package open, "here's some quick-dissolve Benadryl. This is what you need right now."

Doc had Billy stick his tongue out and he placed the pills there, then he started picking the leaves off the kid before turning to Lucas, who continued kneeling beside them both.

Satisfied with Billy, Doc's voice went cold as he addressed Lucas. "So, the old Root Doctor is up to his tricks once again, eh?" I saw an uncomfortable look come into some of the farm workers' eyes.

The boss must have seen it, too, because he started yelling for everybody to get back to what they were doing. Everyone shuffled away except for me and Lucas and the Doc. The boss helped Billy up, took him by the arm, and escorted him off, saying he was going to drive Billy home where he could rest for the remainder of the day. Billy called back, "Thanks, Lucas!" and that's when the Doc unleashed.

"I've warned you before, Lucas Jefferson—you need to leave off with these old, quack, folk medicines. First the horses, now this boy. I'm going to say it again: You are not a vet, you are not a doctor, and when you go putting your root and herb concoctions on wounds, you are in violation of medical standards—and the law."

Doc Hardacre was usually a pretty decent man—he had all the dedication you could ever ask of a vet. From what I'd seen and heard around the farm, he would come at any hour, he would spend any amount of time doing whatever was required to help an ailing horse. He and Lucas, and now me, went through the layup barn together on a daily basis, and even though it was hard, intensive work there was something about it that you could tell meant more than money to both the Doc and to Lucas. And now me, too.

But on this point, Doc was not playing around. He was a fairly tall, stout man, and he was using that height and heft advantage to tower over Lucas and wag a finger in the old man's face. "You could go to jail for practicing ... well, I don't want to even call it medicine, so let me just say it again, Lucas: You leave off. You hear me? If not jail, at the least I can get you canned from working here with the horses. Which would be a damned shame, 'cause you know there isn't anyone else I trust like you for holding horses when I'm working on them."

He cast a quick glance my way, then returned his focus to Lucas. "So this is the last time we're ever going to talk about this, right, Lucas?"

Lucas was calm and even, as usual. "Yes, sir." He smiled, crinkled up his freckles. Lucas was typically deadpan dry with his delivery in any kind conversation, so watching his smile while getting reamed out seemed sort of off his character. "No more root-doctoring from me. If I'd known you were around when that boy got stung, I'd have called you first. Absolutely."

Lucas smiled wider, and put his hand out to the Doc. Doc Hardacre backed up a step, looked down at the hand, then back at Lucas without taking the hand. He obviously had one more point he wanted to make.

"This is like the summer sores. You and that goldenseal. How long has it taken me to get you to stop that nonsense? That stuff's no good on a summer sore, Lucas. In your heart of hearts, you know that. It's just some of that old hoodoo voodoo learning you got from your mama. That's not what these horses need, not what this boy you're teaching needs. You just keep putting that salve on the sores like I told you. And leave the doctoring up to the professionals."

Doc's eyes had gotten big and round, a strange alarm somewhere in the back of them. Lucas continued to stand in place, hand extended. Doc cocked his head to the side, sighed, then shook Lucas's hand. He put his arm around Lucas's shoulder, and the two of them began slowly walking back toward the layup barn, Doc yammering on about the benefits of modern medicine, Lucas smiling and nodding his head.

AT THE END of every workday, Lucas would pull out from inside his shirt a little cloth pouch that was attached to a leather thong hung around his neck. The two of us would go through the shedrow, tending to the horses who had cuts or scrapes or procedures that had developed into summer sores, putting goldenseal from the pouch on each of the open wounds that the flies tried to pick at or lay eggs in.

What I liked best about the goldenseal was that it had a drying effect on the sores. If any of the horses in the training barn or the mare barn or the stallion barn got a summer sore, the grooms of those respective barns dutifully used the pharmaceuticals that Doc Hardacre prescribed. But I never really saw where those salves helped a single bit.

"Only thing closing up those summer sores at the other barns is autumn," Lucas would say. That was a kind of patience that Lucas did not advocate. The horses in our charge would have a sore maybe two, three weeks tops. We put goldenseal on in the evening, and first thing each morning we would wipe the yellow coloring away with a damp sponge. Then we'd take out a bottle of the goop Doc had left us, and we'd paint it on, just to keep up appearances.

And the world was none the wiser for it. I guess I finally came to understand what that old saying really meant.

THAT FIRST summer, I did a lot of things some people would call silly or backward or wrong, and I did a lot of things that if they could talk, the horses would probably tell you were right.

I think it was something of a testament to Lucas Jefferson when the workers from the mare barn would turn to him when they had a sick foal. Sure, Doc Hardacre would give the baby a shot of something, and they'd rub yet another kind of pharmaceutical goop in its nostrils. But when Doc would finish up his rounds in the midafternoon, they'd call on Lucas, with me in tow, to do a little secret root-doctoring. He'd bring in all sorts of flower petals and roots he'd collected, have me get a towel and a bucket of boiling hot water, then he'd crush his mixture up and stir it into the water. I'd hold the mare, and I'd watch as Lucas whispered in the ear of the foal, who would ultimately let Lucas drape the towel over his head, coaxing the steam up for the foal to breathe in deep. He'd do this for 40, 50 minutes at a time for three consecutive days.

When the foal would spring back, all cleared up, Doc would take the credit for his shots and salves, and he'd charge the big dollar that owners willingly would pay for their investment's health. Meanwhile the workers in the mare and foal barn would buy Lucas a bottle of Old Mr. Mack, a potent, sweet wine that Lucas held a special penchant for at the end of the day.

The exercise riders were different, though. Lucas would put a hand on my shoulder and hold me back from returning fire when one of the riders who worked in the training barn talked trash our way. The lane to the training track ran right between the layup barn and the training barn, and when the riders were walking their horses to or from the track and they happened to see us, they always thought it great sport to call out to Lucas Jefferson.

"Hey, Root Doctor. How 'bout you put a spell on J. C.'s mount today?" Angel taunted. "J. C. keeps saying he can't get no speed out of that plug he's riding. You could maybe spark some lightning into that horse's rear end, maybe throw a few bolts into J. C.'s butt while you're at it!"

Lucas would just smile and wave slowly as the riders ambled by on top of their mounts, laughing and cocky and sure of themselves. Lucas always seemed calm in the face of Doc's warnings, wild crazy horses, and other animals like these that didn't fully understand the wisdoms he gladly would share if asked. On that day that Angel was making fun of J. C.'s horse, J. C., as well as Lucas, Lucas explained why he didn't want me reacting to their taunts.

"It's like this: Now Doc, he's a good man. He's scared of licensing boards and losing his connections with the big drug companies. Still, his first values are to the horses. Me and Doc respect each other, and sometimes when you don't dab the yellow off the sores quite good enough, Doc gives me a look when he sees it. But he doesn't say nothin'." My face must have registered my quick fear. Lucas waved it off. "You didn't know that, did you? Yeah, sometimes he gets all fired up, like that day with Billy and the stings, but Doc, he sees what's good for a horse is what matters most. His heart is all about these animals we're privileged enough to work with. Me, I've got nothing against Doc, no."

Lucas looked across the paddocks to the various horses grazing in the summer sunlight, squinting his eyes as he took in their calm munching while swatting flies with their tails. His voice was smooth like the bluegrass fields themselves, quiet as the air with little more than the occasional snort from a horse dismissing dust.

Then he motioned for me to follow him, and we took our time walking toward the training barn where the riders were hosing off their mounts. "But those rider boys, they ain't like Doc, ain't like you and me. They don't all have the same respect. They're all the time thinking speed, they think crop-popping, they think beating the other man around the curve and through the straightaways. Not all of 'em, but Angel and J. C., they're just speed freaks, they're into dogging every ounce out of a horse they can for their own needs, never thinking 'bout the horse. They're all about the race."

Lucas Jefferson and I stood off a ways, observing the wash racks, watching how fast Angel and J. C. worked on their horses with hoses followed by scraper blades. Angel and J. C. were my size, but they were men—hard-muscled, young men—and they both had dreams of getting skills on the farm circuit before moving on to racetracks and big money. They finished up in the wash racks and whisked the horses off to the electric walker.

Lucas motioned for me to follow him once again, and we moved on to where the whirlpools were located on the other side of the wash racks. The two whirlpools smelled strongly of chemicals and chlorine. A horse was tethered and unattended in one of them, cold-water jets bubbling at his legs. The horse looked uncomfortable.

"Back in my day—back when I was a younger man—we didn't have any electric walkers. Even me with my bad leg, I hot-walked Thoroughbreds when they came off the track. I'd spend 20, 30 minutes with a horse, walking, grazing, communicating—man and a horse, in close together, sharing a part of the day."

Lucas looked at the whirlpools, frowning and pointing. "And we sure didn't have nothin' like that."

Angel popped by on his way to somewhere with a bridle and spied the two of us. "Hey, Lucas, we got an open bay for you there," he laughed, though there was something hard in his face and voice in spite of his mirth. "How about we put you in there, fix up that bad leg, then you and me can have a race?"

Lucas flagged for me to follow him, and we started walking back to the layup barn. Angel's voice chortled emptily behind us. "How about it, Root Doctor? I know the ways to get you right!"

THAT AFTERNOON, Lucas introduced me to what quickly became my favorite part of working with horses who needed a little help with sore legs. The Newfound River, which in truth wasn't long enough nor wide enough to have the designation of "river," ambled down behind the paddocks of the layup barn, and Lucas and I each led a horse through the lower paddocks, out of a back gate, where we coaxed them into the shallows of the Newfound. We'd rolled up our pants legs, and we led the horses in shin-deep where the cool, swirling waters could embrace us all.

"Don't know why men bet on Thoroughbreds," Lucas said, handing me one of two small branches of sassafras he'd plucked off the bank. I followed suit, peeling the bark off like he did, before sticking it in my mouth for a sweet little chew. "Thoroughbred legs, now that's a risky bet. These horses, they're born to run—it's as fine a sight as anyone could hope to see. I love it, I do, but those legs, oh, they create mighty problems sometimes. But you and me, we've got ways of helping the horses. Don't know how to help the men with the bets, but we can at least help the horses run the way they're meant to, the way they love to run with each other across the fields and around the curves."

Some of the guys around the barns laughed about how Lucas talked, about the way he was "old school." But I was okay with that. I was growing stronger from the good, hard work of that summer. I was growing in other ways, as well. What Lucas knew and understood he shared freely, and I listened to every word he said. He talked about how when he looked at J. C.'s horse, there was fatigue not just in the legs, but inside as well, though J. C. couldn't see it. Lucas wished the young animal were in his charge; he could help him.

And Lucas talked about the beech trees and the dogwood lining the banks of the Newfound, about the powers—good and bad—of the mistletoe growing up in the top of one of the nearby oaks. He could tell you about the sap running in the veins of the trees, about the sparkle of each grain of sand between our toes, about the small, silver fish that didn't spook at the four slow giants in their world.

The horses seemed to grow especially calm in the river—horses that still had vitamin cocktails in their bloodstreams from their time at the track and still had the heart and desire to bolt if given a chance. But when they were in the river, and Lucas Jefferson whispered in their ears, time slowed down, and they would sip at the surface, or nuzzle the two caretakers holding them, or they'd stand and listen when Lucas started soft-clapping time as he crooned the blues into the green canopy above us, into the blue sky beyond.

EVEN WITH my young age compared to so many of the other farm workers, Doc Hardacre didn't want anyone else but me holding horses for him after Lucas passed. He said I was the only one he'd trust wholeheartedly, the only one who truly understood. Lucas Jefferson died the winter after my first summer working with the horses. But at 86 years old, he was allowed to, I suppose.

I've never smelled the perfume lilt of a flower without thinking of the Root Doctor. And when summer in Kentucky warms the air, I still hear his old voice in summer buzzings. And when I think back to how the horses high-stepped out of the Newfound River, I'd swear on a crossvine that Lucas Jefferson danced out lightly, too, his pants legs rolled up, his skinny leg no burden.

My four-year-old son's name is Luke. And when I tend to his childhood nighttime fevers, I look at the measuring spoons and bottles and I want something more. My boy tosses, and his eyes speak to me, I sense his needs. And I touch his hand, lean close, and whisper softly to him not to be scared—I will be there, I will stay by him, do right by him, do the best I know how. We will get him right. That's something I know.

And in the dark hours of the night, I look at that sweet boy, and I think about it this way: Occasionally, I go dancing with my wife, and when my life—my good life—fills, with a sense, with a soft, flowing rhythm, I'm in the current once again—with horses, and song, while the earth flowers, while everything heals.

Huggable Tom

by Howard P. Giordano

PACO VELASQUEZ was raised on a small farm so he took it for granted. "Getting up at 4:30 every morning," he would always tell people, "is the price to do something I love and get paid, too." Some outside his world thought he was crazy. Even some inside it thought that, but for an entirely different reason.

The early-morning hour was still pitched in blackness, and the mired horse path circling the barn was the only sign of the recent downpour that soaked Belmont Park a few hours earlier. The wind had died down, leaving the air sticky and reminiscent of August, upstate at the Saratoga track.

Paco crossed the muddy path between the paved roadway and the barn door. He could feel each step sinking into the muck, producing a suction that tried vainly to possess his worn, scruffy riding boots. Several exposed low-wattage bulbs dotted the barn's wooden ceiling outside the long row of stalls. They splashed their illumination at intervals on the dirt floor. The pool of light collecting midway down, opposite

Huggable Tom's stall, was like a homing beacon for Paco. His steps crunched as he made his way across the gritty surface, past the series of half-doors and quiet stirrings from within.

Approaching Tom's stall, he heard the four-year-old roan colt mutter, "Jeez, that time already? Seems like I just went to sleep."

"Morning, you old plug," Paco said. He swung open the low door and entered the straw-strewn cubicle. The groom grabbed the feed tub and water bucket, and hauled them to the outside. He noticed Tom had emptied both containers.

"Thirsty last night, huh?" Paco said. He tied the horse to the wall while fighting off his resistant head.

"Aw, is that necessary? I ain't goin' nowhere."

"Listen, Huggable, you know the routine." He reached for the water bucket. "Sorry. Nothing I can do to change it. Stay cool, man. Be right back with a refill. Okay?"

"*Hola, que tal*?" The voice came from the semi-darkened end of the barn.

"Lopez, *amigo. Como esta*?" Paco replied. He moved in the direction of the voice and the location of the water spigot. When he reached the water source, he turned on the valve, full force, and filled the bucket.

"Hey, Paco, missed you last night at Esposito's. *Que paso*?"

Enrique Lopez, a groom with more than ten years' experience on the backstretch, was inside the end stall removing the standing bandages from the legs of a chestnut filly. His head of curly black hair and angular, pocked-marked face sat atop a lean, sinewy body with the muscular compactness that came with a decade of hard, sweaty work on a racetrack. Lopez knew his business, but he was also considered one bad dude. You called him either Enrique or Lopez, but never Henry. The scars from knife slashes, decorating his arms like Olympic medals, signaled everyone in Barn 26 that Lopez was not a person to be taken lightly. Paco had been warned a few times to keep his distance.

"Ahh, man, I was too tired for any more boozing. My head still hurts from the other night," Paco answered. Then dropping his voice to a whisper, he added, "Gotta get going. Tom's in the fifth today, a six-furlong claimer."

"Waddya you whispering for, man? 'Fraid the horse'll hear?"

"Yeah, that's right. He always gets sweaty, you know, like uptight on a race day."

"Hey, Paco, you loco! You know that? You talk like the colt understands everything, then talks back to you. Very weird, man. Everybody thinks you lost it. Know what I mean?"

"Dammit, Lopez! Horses do understand. You been on the backstretch long enough. They're not *estupido* like everyone thinks."

"Yeah, but they don't talk. *Comprende*?"

Paco picked up the full water bucket and started back toward Tom's stall. He knew further conversation with Lopez would only escalate into an explosion of tempers.

Five years ago, Paco arrived from Panama at the age of 17 and sought out employment on the backstretch of Belmont Park. The trainer Johnny Camposino promptly hired him for his small public stable. He started in the usual way, by mucking out stalls and walking hots, and finally moving up to groom, impressing Johnny with his reliability and talent for controlling the huge beasts in his charge. From the outset, it was clear the roly-poly trainer had developed a fatherly attitude toward the young groom.

Paco went to work removing the horse's standing bandages. Each time he reached the end of a roll, freeing the fetlock, he could hear Tom expel a noise that sounded like "Aaah."

Within the next quarter-hour, the barn buzzed with hot walkers, grooms, and assistant trainers. Paco's tasks during this early period were unvarying, tending the needs of Tom and the three other Thoroughbreds assigned to him.

After brushing down each one, he sponged the animals, taking care not to expose them to an early-morning chill. The morning sunlight was beginning to show through the dirty barn windows as the track veterinarian arrived for his scheduled examinations. The medical man attended several mares in the front end of the barn before moving on to Tom.

"How you this morning, Paco?" the veterinarian inquired. "Huggable Tom ready for his checkup?"

"*Si*, Doc. The horse is in great shape. But, *por favor*, don't say anything to him about going to the races today. Okay? He don't know anything yet, and no reason to get him upset too soon. You know?"

"Paco, you really do believe your colt understands words, don't you?"

"Hey, Doc, he really does. *Absolutamente*! See it all the time."

"Okay, Paco, won't breathe a word. Bring him out and let's have a look."

The vet completed his examination with routine professionalism, pronounced the horse sound for his race, but waited until the groom returned Tom to his stall before speaking the words. A smile danced across his face as he prepared to depart.

"*Oye*, Paco. Want to grab some breakfast after Eddie takes the colt?" The invitation came from Lopez as he worked the tack on his chestnut filly, getting her ready for a morning workout on the training track.

"Okay, *amigo*, but Eddie ain't here yet."

At that moment the exercise rider appeared at the front of the barn, stopping to talk with an assistant trainer.

"Hey, Eddie, come on, man," Paco called to the tiny rider. "Tom's waiting for you, all tacked and ready to go." As Eddie approached, Paco met him half way. "Remember, man, a slow jog today. He's in the fifth."

"What are you, the trainer now? Where's Johnny?"

"He's at the gap on the training track, by the clocker's stand. Said he'll see you there with the horse." There was envy in his voice.

When Paco first showed up on the racetrack's backstretch, he was a short, slightly bowlegged teenager. While his bowlegged condition remained, during the next five years the young groom grew six inches and gained 20 pounds, forever destroying his hopes of making it as a jockey.

CATEY'S Backstretch Kitchen reverberated with noise; the shouts and loud, hurried conversations filled the eatery in both English and Spanish. Grooms and hot walkers occupied the linoleum-top tables, gulping black coffee and munching buttered rolls. Lopez sat across from Paco at a table in one corner of the cafeteria. He had Paco's *Racing Form* spread out, studying the past performances of the fifth race.

"*Amigo*," Lopez said, without looking up, "the morning line on your horse is 12-to-1. He's better than that, no?"

"Don't know, man. Had some pretty good workouts this past week, but you know, he gets so uptight sometimes. If only his jock knew how to relax him better. Really likes to run but ..."

"How you know that, Paco? He tell you?" Lopez was laughing.

Paco felt his pulse quicken. "Yeah, man, he did."

"Well, he tell you he gonna win?"

"He don't even know he's gonna race yet." Instantly, he realized Lopez was playing with him.

"Well, man, when you gonna tell him?" Lopez teased.

Paco took another swallow of coffee and stood up. "You think a horse doesn't know when he's gonna race? Minute that muzzle goes on, he knows. First change in routine, he knows. Lopez, sometimes you so dense, you ... "

"*Cuidado, chico*. You getting nasty. Don't like that, you know."

Paco reached across the table, gathered in the *Form*, folded it into a semi-roll, and tucked it into his back pocket. "Gotta go."

"Wait," Lopez said, getting to his feet and following him toward the entrance. "I ain't making fun of you, man. Really."

"You fooled me," Paco said without breaking stride.

"No, man, honest. Just find it hard to believe, that's all. I mean, like, if you say the horse talks to you, okay. I buy that. I'm your *amigo*, right? But you should be more secret around the other guys. Know what I'm saying, man?"

Paco didn't answer. The two grooms walked in silence along the paved road, toward Barn 26.

When they arrived at the barn's front door, Lopez stopped and took hold of Paco's arm. "*Momentito*, Paco. I wanna ask you something."

Pulling free, Paco looked directly at Lopez, into his dark, menacing eyes. "What? Make it quick."

"Look, maybe you can ask the horse how he's gonna do today? I mean, after he finds out he's running, of course."

"Come on, Lopez, lay off, will you?"

"No, no, *amigo*, I mean it. I really wanna know."

"What for?"

"Well, if he thinks he's got a shot, maybe we can get a few bucks down on him. Know what I mean? Hey, man, no sense not to make use of a little inside dope. Right?"

Paco spotted Johnny coming toward them from the training track. Huggable Tom was right behind with Eddie aboard. Paco was certain the trainer had seen him talking with Lopez.

"The horse is here. See you later."

"Wadda you say, Paco? Will you ask him or not?"

"What?"

"The horse ... the race. Ask him, *amigo*. Okay?"

"Let me think about it," Paco said, retreating into the building.

Paco removed the tack from the horse and led the roan outside into the warm sunshine where Tom's hot walker waited on the small patch of grass that somehow survived the tread of horses' hooves. After turning the rein over to the youngster, Paco coupled the brass connector of the hose and slowly ran a soft stream over the length of the horse.

Tom remained perfectly still, enjoying the second bath of the morning, and occasionally flinching whenever the water flow washed over a sensitive area. Even when Paco placed the nozzle between the horse's ears, letting a gentle river cascade down his head and face, the colt seemed to luxuriate in his groom's attention.

Paco tossed a plain mesh blanket over Tom's back after disconnecting the hose, and released the animal to his hot walker for a 24-minute circuit around the barn to cool him down further. The path was still muddy from the early morning rain.

When the animal was returned to Paco, he brushed him and carefully cleaned his hooves. As he began to wrap Tom's fetlocks again, he heard the colt caution: "Not too tight, eh."

"You know, if you didn't kick yourself so much, we might not need them all the time."

"Ah, don't do it any more than these other nags."

Paco completed the bandaging. "Hold still a moment while I slip this on."

"Wadda you doing with that muzzle?"

The quick, jerking motion of the horse's head was making it difficult for Paco to secure it in place. "Damn! Stay still."

"What's goin' on? I gotta race today? Why didn't you tell me?"

"Figured you'd find out soon enough. Stop pulling away, will you, and stop worrying."

"Wadda you mean, stop worrying? My last time out I made a fool of myself, didn't I?"

"This one's six furlongs. Last time Johnny was only trying you out at a mile and an eighth. Too long for you."

"Tell me about it. I needed a taxi at the top of the stretch to get home. Thought my lungs would bust."

"Six furlong's well within your range, and besides, you're up against nothing special. You faced most of them before."

"Yeah? Like who? Let's see the *Form*."

Paco unrolled the paper and turned to the page with the fifth-race past performances.

Huggable Tom snorted as he tried his hay bale. "Hell, with this muzzle on, I can't even nibble."

"Smart fella. That's the idea. Okay, let's see who you're facing," Paco said, looking down the list of entries. "Band-Aid, 14-to-1."

"Finished ahead of him three weeks ago, didn't I?"

"That's right. Next, Mogambo's Child. He's 6-to-1. Finished fourth to him back in May, at six furlongs."

"Oh, yeah. I remember. His jock claimed foul on the winner for interference at the top of the stretch, but it didn't stand up."

"Right," Paco said. "Next, Twelfth Night. He's the favorite, 4-to-1. Got beat by him in your maiden race last year at 5½ furlongs. He won by a length."

"It was close. Haven't seen him since. How's he done?

"Hasn't won another. What does that tell you?"

"Lucky the first time, I'd say. Okay, who's next?"

While Paco reviewed the eight competitors, one by one, the colt began to sweat, breaking out in gobs of white, frothy moisture, collecting on his neck and running down to his shoulders.

"Look at you," Paco said, when he finally glanced up from the *Form*. "You're all wet. Why do you get yourself so worked up?"

"Don't know. Hyper, I guess."

"By the way, morning line's got you 12-to-1."

"Sssush! I deserve better odds than that. So I don't win in my last six starts. Been in the money a couple of times, ain't I?

"Well, what about today's race? Think you got a shot?"

"A bunch of crows! Of course I do ... I think."

"Well, do you or don't you?"

"Jeez, don't get pushy. Let's see. I'm usually the early speed, right? So if I hold back a little longer going down the backside, until I hit the final turn into the stretch, bet I have enough left to ... "

"Bet? Did you say bet?"

"Naah, you know what I mean."

"Oh, for a moment I thought you meant you were a mortal lock, that I should get a bet down on you."

"Thought you didn't bet?"

"Usually don't."

"So don't start now or you'll really give me something to sweat over."

"Well, you gonna win or not?" Paco asked again. "Don't matter much to me, to tell the truth, but Lopez wants to know. Gonna bet you, I think."

"Yeah, no kidding? Ain't exactly flattered by his interest, you know. Let's just say, I got a good shot. Leave it at that. Okay?"

"All right, sport. Time to get some rest." Paco picked up the excess rolls of bandage, moved out the door of the stall, and closed it behind him. "I'll be back in a couple of hours with a half ration of oats for you."

"Big deal!"

"That's all you ever get on a race day."

THE LATE-AFTERNOON fiery yellow ball was eclipsed at this time of day by the overhang of the grandstand. The roof line, traveling unbroken nearly the entire length of the homestretch, cast a wide shadow diagonally across the track surface, starting at the eighth pole and carrying beyond the finish line another 20 yards.

Paco and Lopez had positioned themselves within the darkened area, at the gap in the railing where the horses had been led out onto the track for the post parade. The two grooms had the perfect spot to watch the finish of the race, but their low viewing angle prevented them seeing across the wide grassy infield of the racing oval, to where the horses were being loaded into the starting gate. The large, green tote board on the front edge of the infield loomed up, obstructing their view.

"Your horse looked a little sweaty in the paddock," Lopez said, waiting for the track announcer to begin his call of the race. "He okay?"

"Yeah, sure," Paco answered. "He settled down on the walk over from the barn."

"Hope so, man. Went down big, you know. Fifty big ones … to win. Especially since he got the inside post position. He's only 8-to-1 now. They must be betting him a little. You get down?"

"Naah, didn't have time after I got him to the paddock."

"Want a piece of my action?" Lopez asked.

"No, thanks, that's okay. Don't like to bet on my own horses."

Lopez looked at him suspiciously. "He gonna win, right? He told you he would, no?"

"Yeah, course he did. Said so, didn't I?"

"One more to load," the track announcer's voice informed them over the public address system.

"Okay, man, here we go," Lopez said.

There was a long pause before they finally heard the race caller say, "Aaannnd they're off!"

"He get out of the gate okay?" Lopez asked, eyeing the tote board. He was waiting for the initial posting of numbers, signifying the early running order of the first four horses.

"Yeah, yeah, there he is," Paco shouted. "One ... six ... three ... eight. Went to the lead like I knew."

"Good," said Lopez. "Hope he stays there."

By the time the field cleared the tote board sightlines, the horses were in full gallop halfway down the backstretch. The two grooms listened intently to the race caller.

"Down the backstretch, heading toward the first turn, it's Huggable Tom in front, Twelfth Night a close second, Mogambo's Child back a length in third, and Hagley fourth by a half." The drone continued. "Four lengths back to Campfire and Star Pilot, followed by Dance Ace, Sweet Revenge, with Band-Aid the trailer. The time for the first quarter, twenty-three and three."

The pace was not a particularly fast, Paco thought, but that was in Tom's favor. His jock finally had him relaxed.

The nine Thoroughbreds, lungs bursting for air and under the occasional urging by the whip of their riders, were approaching the long curve of the racing oval. Lopez stared at the tote board. When the horses started into the turn, a new sequence was posted.

"One . . three ... six ... eight," cried Lopez. "We still up there."

Paco could see the field lengthening out as they reached the flatter section of the curve. He listened to the announcer go through the call of each entry again, the last time he would hear it clearly.

Behind him, from the clubhouse and grandstand seats, and along the rail at trackside, Paco heard crowd murmurs, low at first, but growing louder, in sync with each stage of the race. As the horses completed the final section of the curve, coming to the top of the stretch, the murmur began to swell. The announcer's call became gradually submerged beneath the mounting wave of sound.

Sixteen-thousand heads strained toward the top of the stretch, eyes fixed on the rainbow of colorful silks blossoming on top of massive forms as they moved into the straightaway. A tingling sensation electrified Paco's body like he was wired directly into the amplifier modulating the rising sound level.

No matter how many times he watched a race—any race—the crowd reaction always produced this phenomenon. As the noise slowly increased, so did the tingling, until both hit their absolute maximum levels as the horses came into unobstructed view exactly 1,097 feet away.

The head-on perspective made the field appear spread out across the sun-drenched track. Paco could see the leading horses driving for the inside rail position. He thought he could make out Huggable Tom's red-and-white colors glittering off the cap of the lead jockey. The time for the half was posted. Forty-six seconds flat.

"Damn, that's faster than I thought," shouted Paco. "Hope he got something left."

For a third time, the numbers changed on the board and Lopez screamed his reaction. "One ... six ... seven ... three. Goddamn, he gonna go wire-to-wire. C'mon you son of a bitch, stay up there."

Now Paco could clearly see the colors of Tom's silks in front. He felt his heart pumping as he furiously banged the heels of his hands on the track railing, keeping tempo with each stride of the horse.

"Go! Go! Go! Go! Go!" The crescendo of screaming horseplayers assaulted his ears, and the tingling sensation was almost painful.

Nearing the eighth pole, Huggable Tom and his nemesis, Twelfth Night, were in lockstep, flying down the soft track surface with hooves that never seem to touch down. The rest of the field appeared to have backed up. The contest was between the two leaders.

The Johnny Camposino-trained roan colt had a full head in front, running, as he always did, with his tongue dangling out one side and his long tail swishing with each step. Muscles and veins stood out on his extended body, accented by the shiny sweat that coated the animal.

It happened so fast, Paco could have easily missed it. At the demarcation across the track, where bright sunlight ended and dark shadow began, Huggable Tom leaped, trying to avoid some perceived danger. It was over in a blink of an eye. Only the switched position of the combatants was proof it happened at all. That, and the fact Twelfth Night hit the wire first.

At once the din went silent as though some mythical symphony conductor had slashed the air with his baton to signal the conclusion of the concert. Paco's tingling had also disappeared.

PACO KNOCKED on the screen door. Dried paint flaked under his knuckles.

"Get the hell in here, kid!"

Paco never heard Johnny call him that before. He sounded angry. Pulling open the door, he stepped into the official headquarters of J.C. Stables.

It was a 12-by-12 windowless room at the far end of Barn 26. A metal desk from the early 1940s, a slat-back, wooden swivel chair, abused for many years by Johnny's wide frame, two wobbly side chairs badly in need of glue, and a small cot pushed against one wall were the total furnishings.

Johnny pointed to one of the chairs. "Sit down, Paco." He was angry.

The groom obeyed and sat silently while the trainer continued talking on the phone.

Paco gazed around the room, taking in the spartan appointments. His focus settled on the ornate coat stand behind Johnny's desk. It accommodated mostly tack, giving the appearance of free-form modern sculpture. A saddlecloth, cap and goggles, shadow roll, and several pairs of blinkers dangled freely from its curving arms.

Pictures of famous stakes winners had been thumbtacked to the wall opposite. They were color plates, torn from the pages of the Richard Stone Reeves book, *Decade of Champions*. Johnny had given Paco his own copy of this collection of equine portraits for Christmas last year.

The trainer hung up the phone. "Paco, what the hell's going on?" His voice boomed across the desk like a shotgun.

Paco suddenly flashed to the stories he'd heard about Johnny's youth, growing up on the streets of East New York, kicking ass. He considered bolting for the door.

"Wadda you mean, John? About the race today?"

"No, goddamn it, not the race. Yeah, it's about the race, too, but right now I'm talking about you and Lopez."

Paco looked puzzled.

"How many times I tell you, stay away from him outside the barn?"

Paco remembered this morning when Johnny spotted him with Lopez. "Christ, I was just talking to him."

"Talking, my ass. You tell him the horse gonna win, that you get it from Tom himself? That's what he says you did. Came in here after the race screaming you were a certifiable nut case. That you hear the horse talking to you, and it cost him 50 bucks."

Paco was beginning to perspire, feeling the sweat trickle from his armpit area, down the inside of both arms. The T-shirt he wore provided no help at all.

"I didn't tell him."

"Don't lie to me, Paco. I hear the rumblings around here, that you have conversations with the horse."

Paco looked toward the door again.

"Listen to me, dammit. I don't want you going around telling anybody you hear Tom talking. You understand? 'Specially that loony, Lopez. You ever see him explode after a few shots of rum in his snoot? At Esposito's? You messing with the wrong guy. I'm telling you."

"John, I just handicapped the race myself. Honest. Told Lopez I thought the horse had a good shot. That's all."

"Cut the crap. I know what's going on." The trainer had lowered his voice. "Happened to me once when I was a kid, breaking my hump for that public riding academy in Central Park."

"Wadda you mean?" Paco asked.

"What do I mean? I mean, the only voice you hear is the one you invent in your own head. Right?"

Paco sat up straight in the chair.

"I mean, you got so tight with the horse you think you hear him speaking to you. Right? Am I right?" A knowing smile formed on the trainer's face.

"Yeah, I guess," Paco said.

"Damn straight, I am. Hey, Paco, don't make me have to break up your love affair by taking Tom from you. Don't want to have to do that, understand? No more goddamn conversations. Okay?"

"Okay, no more."

"And Lopez. Stay away. Please?"

"Sure, and I'll keep Tom away, too. The horse ain't crazy about him, either."

Johnny sat motionless. He appeared deep in thought, staring at the gallery of champions tacked to his wall. When Paco got to his feet, the trainer looked back.

"He run a goddamn good race today, didn't he?"

"Yeah, his best one yet," Paco said.

Johnny slowly shook his head. "Damn! Still can't believe the horse jumped that shadow out there today. Never got spooked like that before, even when he was a two-year-old. Shadows never bothered him. Beats the heck out of me, I'll tell you. Got any ideas?"

"Well, I got one," Paco said, heading toward the door.

"What's that, because I need something to tell his connections?"

"Like I said before, Huggable Tom ain't crazy about Lopez."

"Get the hell outta here!" Johnny shouted.

THE NEXT morning, Paco found Lopez sitting outside of Tom's stall, astride an overturned water bucket. Lopez was facing the colt's protruding head, studying his drowsy eyes when Paco called to the groom from the barn's entrance.

"*Oye*, Lopez, *que paso*?"

"Nothin', man, just waiting for you. Wanted to ask the horse—I mean you—something."

Paco approached cautiously as Lopez got to his feet. "What? Waddya wanna ask?"

"I heard Johnny say yesterday he gonna run the colt in the Sword Dancer in a couple of weeks."

"Yeah, what about it?"

"So, you get any good dope on the race, you know, maybe you let me know straight away. Right, *amigo*?"

"I don't know, man," Paco replied. "Johnny don't like me talking about the colt's races with anybody anymore." He watched the man's expression as he continued. "But, if I hear anything ... " Paco was grinning as he let his voice trail off.

"Great, man. Then, see you later at Cathy's for breakfast. Okay?" Lopez didn't wait for an answer but strode toward the rear of the barn and disappeared into the bulb-cast shadows.

"Maybe," Paco said softly, "if I have time." He heard the smugness in his own voice and smiled again. When he looked over at Tom, the colt's head was bobbing up and down at a furious pace.

Author Biographies

Catherine Dupree was born in Cambridge, Massachusetts, and lives in Los Angeles. She graduated from Williams College in 1995 and received a master's degree in journalism from Boston University in 2002. She was a 2006 Mid-Atlantic Arts Foundation Creative Fellow, in partnership with the National Endowment for the Arts. Her short stories and nonfiction have appeared in *Zoetrope: All-Story, The Connecticut Review, Boston Magazine, Hemispheres, Harvard Magazine, National Geographic Traveler, Gastronomica,* and *Nylon,* and they have been featured on Chicago Public Radio.
"It Can Happen Here", page 181
(Originally published March 16, 2002, THOROUGHBRED TIMES)

Howard P. Giordano, a native of New York City, received a B.A. in English from Hofstra University. After a successful 18-year career managing a variety of advertising accounts with major advertising agencies on Madison Avenue, he joined the New York Racing Association in 1979 as director of marketing. He was later promoted to executive director of broadcast programming. In 1987, he was appointed president of the New York City Off-Track Betting Corp. by Mayor Ed Koch and served in that capacity until 1990. Following a five-year period of consulting work, he retired to Naples, Florida. He has been writing short stories for 17 years, and his fiction has appeared in 15 small literary magazines. His racetrack stories have been published in THOROUGHBRED TIMES, *The Texas Thoroughbred,* and *The Stable Companion*. He just completed his first novel, a thriller, and has begun work on a sequel.
"Huggable Tom", page 261
(Originally published May 14, 1993, THOROUGHBRED TIMES)

Kevin Harrington lives where he was born, in Milwaukee, Wisconsin, a city too far from the nearest racetrack. He and his wife, Kathy, are still raising the youngest of three sons. He graduated from Marquette University and worked at the Milwaukee *Journal* as a police reporter. For the last 13 years, he has worked as a victim-witness specialist with the Milwaukee County District Attorney's Office in the Crisis Response Unit, providing services to crime victims, witnesses, and next-of-kin families. He is the eldest of six, and his father, uncles, and paternal grandfather all worked in the copper mines in Butte, Montana. Harrington first started to become interested in horse racing as a child. At ten, he picked his first and only Derby winner when Dancer's Image was disqualified and Forward Pass placed first in 1968. Besides picking a second Derby winner in 40 years, he hopes to work in the Thoroughbred industry after his children have flown the coop. Between working, handicapping, and writing, he and his sons play hurling, a traditional Irish sport.
"Arlen Gone", page 213
(Originally published March 13, 2004, THOROUGHBRED TIMES)

Alan P. Henry has had a distinguished 28-year newspaper career with the Chicago *Sun-Times*, Boston *Herald American*, *Middlesex News*, Boston *Globe*, and Pioneer Press Newspapers, during which time he has won numerous state and national awards for news, investigative, feature, and column writing. He co-authored, with David P. Schippers, *Sellout: The Inside Story of President Clinton's Impeachment*, which was on the New York *Times* bestseller list for 12 weeks in 2000. He has competed in five of the seven THOROUGHBRED TIMES fiction contests, placing third or better in each of them. He is currently working in Illinois state government as a communications director. He has owned shares in 18 racehorses through Dogwood Stable and Eclipse Partners, which he co-founded in 1989. He is married, has two grown children, and lives in Deerfield, Illinois.
"The Legacy", page 15
(Originally published March 26, 1993, THOROUGHBRED TIMES)
"Mr. Bo's Last Dance", page 71
(Originally published March 16, 1996, THOROUGHBRED TIMES)
"The Painting", page 121
(Originally published March 18, 2000, THOROUGHBRED TIMES)

A racing fan since Secretariat's Triple Crown in 1973, **Avalyn Hunter** began studying pedigrees at age 15, beginning with Sir Charles Leicester's classic work *Bloodstock Breeding*, which detailed the pedigrees of winners of the Epsom Derby during the first half of the 20th century. Twenty-five years later, Sir Charles's book served as a model and inspiration for Hunter's first book, *American Classic Pedigrees 1914-2002*. Covering the race records, antecedents, and descendants of the winners of the American Triple Crown races plus the Kentucky Oaks and Coaching Club American Oaks, the massive work took some two years to write and was released in May 2003. Since its release, she has continued to write extensively about Thoroughbred pedigrees and racing history in trade publications. Her second book, a biography of the great sire Northern Dancer, is titled *The Kingmaker: How Northern Dancer Founded a Racing Dynasty* and was released in April 2006, while her biography of Mr. Prospector (tentatively titled *The Gold Rush*) is slated for release in fall 2007. She also has hopes of eventually writing a novel. A former Air Force officer, she is a graduate of Vanderbilt University (B.A, psychology) and Southern Illinois University at Edwardsville (M.A., clinical psychology) and has worked as a mental-health professional since 1993. She lives in Florida with her husband and two children.

"The Passing of the Torch", page 55
(Originally published March 2, 1996, THOROUGHBRED TIMES)
"The Foundation", page 151
(Originally published April 1, 2000, THOROUGHBRED TIMES)

Scott Travis Hutchison grew up on his parents' small Thoroughbred farm in Virginia and, beginning at age 13, worked for Ed Stevens at Rocketts Mill Farm either full or part time for 16 years. His works have appeared in more than 70 publications, and he was honored as New England Poet of the Year in 2001 by the New England Association of Teachers of English. His book of poetry entitled *Reining In* was published in 2003 by Black Bird Press. He is state director of the New Hampshire Young Writers' Conference and on its faculty. He and his wife, Gail, and their daughter, Caitlin, live in the Belknap Mountains of New Hampshire.

"Teaser", page 85
(Originally published March 7, 1998, THOROUGHBRED TIMES)
"Root Doctor", page 247
(Originally published March 18, 2006, THOROUGHBRED TIMES)

K. M. Jones became interested in Thoroughbred racing when she bought an old stallion register in a used-book store in Portland, Oregon. Fascination with the bloodlines in the sire book led the then 21-year-old to visit now-defunct Playfair Racecourse in Spokane, Washington, where she developed a love of racing that eventually led her to the Bluegrass. After running the foreign research department of Bloodstock Research Information Services for six years, she managed the Kentucky headquarters of Team Valor racing stables, for which she traveled to South Africa, Hong Kong, and Dubai in addition to England, France, and Germany. Her interests aside from horse racing research include foreign languages, library sciences, genealogy, and metaphysical studies. Now married to Barry Irwin, she resides in Lexington, Kentucky.

"The Saratoga Derby", page 29
(Originally published April 9, 1993, THOROUGHBRED TIMES)
"Time Exposure", page 111
(Originally published April 13, 1996, THOROUGHBRED TIMES)

Bill Melzer is an optometrist in private practice in Culver City, California. He has been a Thoroughbred fan and avid handicapper for more than 30 years and considers the highlights of his experience so far to be seeing in person the greatest displays of Thoroughbred brilliance (Secretariat's triumph in the Belmont Stakes in 1973) and Thoroughbred heart (Seattle Slew's nose loss in the 1978 Jockey Club Gold Cup after vying for the lead—at a blistering pace—for the entirety of the grueling 1½ miles and, once passed, still almost fighting back to win). In his spare time, he enjoys writing, computers, and attending the movies.

"Third Jewel", page 163
(Originally published April 15, 2000, THOROUGHBRED TIMES)

Caroline Nesbitt became hooked on racing and Thoroughbred pedigrees at the tender age of ten, when her godparents began passing along back issues of *The Thoroughbred Record* to her. Now the artistic director of Advice To The Players, a small not-for-profit Shakespeare theater with a strong teen mentoring program, she also breeds, rides, and drives Connemara ponies. She is the author of *The Pony Breeders' Companion* (Howell Book House, 1995) and numerous essays on both horses and theater. While life as an actress and writer precludes the ownership of a racehorse, she still dreams of owning a mare by Alphabet Soup or Pleasant Tap. In the meantime, she makes annual pilgrimages to Saratoga Race Course and lives happily in New Hampshire with her family.

"Phoenix", page 97

(Originally published March 21, 1998, THOROUGHBRED TIMES)

Dennis M. Patterson was born and raised in Southern California, where at age 11 he got his first horse, a bay filly he named Venus. Despite never having ridden a horse before, he took up the challenge of breaking Venus himself. He spent the rest of his boyhood years riding Venus in the hills of Topanga Canyon near his home. While still in high school, he got his first job, working at Amarillo Ranch in the San Fernando Valley. He began working at Hollywood Park as a groom the day after graduating from Notre Dame High School in 1953. Four years later, at age 21, he obtained his first trainer's license at Caliente Racetrack in Mexico. Later that year, he married his high school sweetheart, Theresa. The couple started a family, three sons and a daughter, before relocating in 1965 to the San Francisco suburb of San Mateo. He currently conditions a 15-horse string at nearby Bay Meadows Race Course.

"Tack Talk", page 139

(Originally published April 18, 1998, THOROUGHBRED TIMES)

Susan Starr Richards was born and raised in Winter Park, Florida, and schooled at the University of Florida and the University of Washington. She and her husband moved to the Bluegrass when she obtained a teaching position at the University of Kentucky, and in short order found themselves in the horse business. They began as market breeders in Fayette County, raising yearlings to sell in both the summer and fall Keeneland sales. They subsequently moved their operation to Harrison County, Kentucky, and raced all the horses that came off their farm. When they retired after 30 years in the business, they also retired their broodmares and racehorses, including stakes winners Raw Power Patty, Mahalia, and Pattypower, and track-record setter Wolfgang Grr.

She has published *The Life Horse*, a book of poems (Larkspur Press, 2005), and *The Hanging in the Foaling Barn*, a collection of her short stories that was chosen as the third volume in the Woodford Reserve Series in Kentucky Literature (Sarabande Books, 2006).

"The Hanging in the Foaling Barn", page 1

(Originally published March 19, 1993, THOROUGHBRED TIMES)

"The Murderer, the Pony, and Miss Brown to You", page 197

(Originally published March 30, 2002, THOROUGHBRED TIMES)

Danny Talbot and his wife, Rebecca, raise Thoroughbreds on their Sunrise Farm high in the Wasatch Mountains of Utah. The Talbots breed, race, and market their Thoroughbred stock with the help of their grown children Jacob, Olivia, Monica, and Michael. He and his family have raised horses for more than 30 years, and the horse business became a full-time operation for the Talbots in 2002. They now travel between Utah, Kentucky, and California to attend the sales and races when not tending to the farm. He has written several articles for horse industry magazines, along with professional pieces related to his previous work as a public school principal, superintendent, and adjunct professor at the University of Utah.

"Ice Storm", page 231

(Originally published March 27, 2004, THOROUGHBRED TIMES)